HONOLULU RED

HONOLULU RED

Lue Zimmelman

St. Martin's Press
New York

 For information, address St. Martin's Press, 175 Fifth Avenue, New York, N.Y. 10010.

Design by Glen M. Edelstein

Library of Congress Cataloging-in-Publication Data

Zimmelman, Lue.
Honolulu red / Lue Zimmelman.
p. cm.
ISBN 0-312-03735-X
I. Title.
PS3576.I465H66 1990
813'.54—dc20

89-27137

First Edition
10 9 8 7 6 5 4 3 2 1

This is for Herb and Elaine Costello, Laureen Kwock, Chassie West, Linda Hayes, and, always, Joseph.

HONOLULU RED

ONE

ALL DAY A LIGHT rain had fallen, but when evening came the rain turned hard and cold, and the thunder and lightning started. Sammy Tabor was glad to be indoors even if it meant putting up with his mother, who was still hoping he'd get a regular job like the one at his Uncle Mickey's used car lot out in the Valley and marry some nice girl and give her a handful of grandchildren. He'd let her go on and on about it, all through dinner and afterward during the commercials in the football game. She'd even stood in the doorway of the bathroom yakking at him while he was brushing his teeth. He didn't care. Her nagging didn't get to him anymore. It was like the music they played in supermarkets: it was there or it wasn't, depending on whether you tuned in or not.

Anyway, on a night like this, he could put up with a lot to be inside with good food in his stomach and a clean bed to lie in. Plus tomorrow he was getting paid. Ten thousand bucks, which he was thinking hard and long about taking to Vegas. Lately he'd been feeling lucky.

He lit a cigarette, found an ashtray on the nightstand, and centered it on his stomach. If he didn't go crazy at the crap tables, if he stayed away from the women, he could make the ten thousand last three, possibly four weeks in Vegas. Unless he hit, and then who knew how long it could go? Maybe he'd use half of it in Vegas and half in Reno. He'd never been to Reno and, from what he'd heard, there were good times to be had there. It was something to think about.

When the cigarette was burned almost to the filter, he crushed it out, set the ashtray on the floor, and pulled the covers over his shoulders. He was drifting off to sleep, thinking, Shit, how the hell can I stay away from the women?, when he heard the front door open and his mother scream. Something fell, he could hear glass crashing, then heavy footsteps thudded down the hall. He was hunting for the gun he'd left under the bed when the door flew back.

Two Chinese men were aiming shotguns at him.

In disbelief, Sammy Tabor pushed into the headboard, shaking his head, holding up a hand as if to stop them. "I gave you the cop!" he cried. "What are you doing? I gave you the cop!"

The shorter of the two men stepped forward, smiled, and pulled the trigger.

They were sitting in a black Chevrolet parked in Chinatown, waiting for the rain to ease up. It was one in the morning. The street was deserted and dark except for one streetlamp that cast a blurred yellow light across the front of a Chinese restaurant, then spilled weakly into an adjacent stairwell.

Rachel Starr eased her window down a couple of inches, enough to let in air but keep out the flood. She was a big woman with dark red hair, pale skin, and deep green almond-shaped eyes. Her mouth was soft, but there was something stubborn about it. Her cheekbones were strong and high. She was very beautiful, but it didn't matter much to her. Through the rain she made out a row of windows above the restaurant with a narrow landing in front of the last. From the landing a fire escape snaked down the side of the building, stopping eight or nine feet above the ground. She was scared of heights, but if she had to, she could make that jump. It was an old habit, finding an escape route. One she'd learned from the man beside her.

When Johnny Haid called, she'd been in bed listening to the rain and John Coltrane, halfway through her third shot of scotch. She'd wanted to say no, she couldn't help, but they'd been partners once. Everything she knew about being a cop he'd taught her. They'd been through good times together and helped each other over some tough ones. They were still friends and she owed him. More than that she felt guilty because the word going around the station was Johnny Haid had slipped over the edge, that the death of his wife six months ago had knocked him down and now he was sliding in a free fall to nowhere.

The reason she felt guilty was sometimes she believed it.

She'd seen him stumbling around drunk, seen him acting up, acting crazy. A couple of times in Blackie's Bar she'd had to pull him out of fights. Then, three weeks ago in the middle of the station, he'd punched the assistant chief of police hard enough to put stitches in the man's face and get himself suspended.

She wasn't sure if it was smart right now to get involved with Haid. At the same time, she felt lousy thinking that way.

Tonight he seemed okay. A little tired maybe and maybe he'd lost some weight. But he was sober and his hands were steady and he had that old intensity he used to have when they rode together.

She must have been staring hard because he looked over and said, "So what do you think? I pass or not?"

She glanced away. "What I like about you, Johnny, is you've never cared what people think of you one way or the other."

"You're right, I don't. But for the hell of it, tell me anyway."

"You pass, Johnny. In my book, you always pass."

He gave a nod, then reached into the glove compartment for his gun and a knitted black cap. "Put this on. Cover up that hair."

"You're sure the papers are up there?"

"Yeah. Tai keeps them in the safe."

"And you know the combination?"

"I caught it yesterday when he opened it. You'll see when we get up there how easy it was."

"What's in these papers besides names?" Rachel said.

"Dates, transactions, cash involved. The whole operation."

"A stolen jewelry ring?"

"Maybe more than that. Tai claims a cop's involved. A high-ranking L.A.P.D. cop."

"He say who it was?"

"No. It could be anybody. That's why I came to you, you're the only one I trust."

Rachel began pulling on leather gloves, working them over her fingers. "How'd you get in with Tai?"

"Remember Teddy Duroy? Burglar working the Venice area? He shaves his head and wears a goatee? Real ugly son-of-a-gun."

"I remember him."

"A few weeks ago I caught him coming out of a jewelry store on Wilshire, this was around midnight, with fifty thousand worth of loose diamonds rattling around in his pocket. He was looking at ten to twenty, so he made a deal. Said he knew these Chinese running a jewelry ring out of Chinatown. Said it was a big-time operation. He hooked me up with a guy named Sammy Tabor who'd been doing some freelance stealing for them. You ever heard of him?"

"Tabor?" She shook her head.

"He's got a record and wanted to stay on friendly terms with the police, so he took me to meet Danny Tai. Introduced me as Johnny Hoyle, small-time thief looking for the big league. Guess Tai liked me because I got hired. But according to Tabor, Tai's strictly a middleman. Somebody else heads the whole set-up. I think his name and the cop's name are in the papers in the safe. If they are, I've got a shot at nailing a big case."

He wrapped his hands around the steering wheel and she saw that they were trembling slightly. "You're suspended, Johnny. You take the case to the D.A., they'll flush it down the toilet."

"That's why you're here," he said quietly. "I'm giving this to you. From now on we work it together, and you can take the credit. All I want is your help at the suspension hearing. Just tell them what I've done."

"Jesus, Johnny, is that what this is about?"

"Yeah." He gave a soft, ironic laugh. "That's what this is about. Being a cop is all I've got left. I want to do something that'll get me my badge back."

She rubbed the steam off the window and looked down the street. It was still empty and almost beautiful the way the rain was hitting it. "If we're going to do it," she said, "let's do it and get the hell out. I don't like it around here." Without looking at Haid, she opened the door and was about to slide out when he caught her arm.

"Hey, Starr."

"What?"

"Thanks."

She went first, her shoes slapping through the water, her feet going numb, her face aching from the icy wind. Haid followed a few seconds behind her. Reaching the other side of the street, they ducked under the awning fronting Tai's restaurant, then ran for the stairwell. In the cramped, dimly lit space they shook off the rain and listened. The building was quiet.

"Let's go," Haid said, and started up the stairs. At the top he stopped her. "You wait here. Watch for visitors."

"Just make it fast."

"Right," he said, and moved into the dark.

Wind howled up the passageway. Lightning streaked the peeling walls, then thunder rumbled. Rachel kept her eyes on the square of roadway framed by the entrance. She was suddenly nervous, suddenly wishing she hadn't come. She didn't like storms or lightning or the dark. She didn't like Chinatown. There were too many shops and narrow alleys. Too many traps and dead ends.

A silver car turned the corner and rolled by, headlights reaching through the rain like glowing arms. She pressed flat against the wall. It was too shadowy to make out passengers.

"Got it," Haid called. At the same moment the car swung onto the cross street and she let out a tight breath.

"Good." Keeping her hand to the wall, she made her way toward his voice.

The room was larger than she expected, furnished, she saw as Haid swept the flashlight back and forth, with Chinese hutches, tables, chairs. Behind a carved desk sat an enameled safe buckled shut by an oversized gold lock. Haid walked over to it and gave it a slap.

"Can you believe this thing?" he said. "I watched Tai open it yesterday. I was sitting over there and I could read the combination, the goddamn numbers are so big."

Rachel jerked as another crash of thunder shook the windows. "Can we hurry it up?"

"What's going on? Got a hot date waiting?"

"The only date I want tonight is another shot of scotch and my warm bed."

He laughed and handed her the light. Then he started on the lock. Three turns and the door popped open. He grabbed a sheaf of papers and spread them quickly across the desk.

Rachel lowered the flashlight. "Christ, Johnny, they're in Chinese."

"So we'll get them translated." He tossed her a small camera. "Start taking pictures. I want to get home, too."

The silver Mercedes circled the block and doused its headlights as it slid to a stop in front of the Kowloon Canton Restaurant. The back doors opened and two men in black overcoats stepped out. Both yanked their jackets shut against the downpour, then took the shotguns the driver handed them through the half-opened window and waited.

A minute later a short, fat man pulled himself out from behind the steering wheel. Reaching into the car, he picked a derby hat off the dashboard and put it on, straightening the brim so water wouldn't collect. Then he glanced at the windows above the restaurant and said something sharply in Chinese. The other men nodded. Couching the guns against their sides they hurried through the watery gleam of the streetlamp to the narrow sidewalk fronting the restaurant.

Then they started for the stairs.

* * *

"Okay, that's it." Rachel shoved the pages toward Haid and dropped the camera in her bag. "I hope to God we got something."

"We got something," he assured her. "Believe me." He evened up the pages, placed them in the safe, and spun the lock. Then he said, "Just in case," and pulled out a yellow handkerchief and began rubbing the dial. When he was done, he pitched it to her. "Catch the door while I get the desk." He moved the ashtray, the pencil holder, the calendar, the photograph of a thin, tense woman and two shy girls back into place. Then he clapped his hands silently, trying to warm them. "Jesus, it's so cold, my bones think I died."

"Yeah? So do mine. They think we're all in Kleinman's morgue. You touch the jamb?"

"Probably," he said, fooling around with the top drawer, trying to open it.

"What about the inside handle?"

"I think so. Come over here. Take a look at this."

"Hold on." Deciding to be safe, she went around the door and buffed the inside knob.

She heard the footsteps when they were halfway down the hall. Two, maybe three people moving fast, caring less and less about the noise they made the closer they got. She thought, Christ, we've got trouble, and was spinning to warn Haid when the door crashed open.

Two Chinese stormed in, one tall, one short. She knew at once they didn't see her. They saw only what she saw: Johnny Haid looking up from the drawer, the flashlight on the desk throwing an eerie glow over his face as he reached into his jacket for his .38.

Both men raised the shotguns even with their waists and fired. Haid's arms flew up and out as he was blown back into the safe. The impact made a cracking sound; then he buckled forward, spilling blood across the photograph, the calendar, the cherrywood desk, and the green satin chair, before sagging to the floor.

"Check him," the taller man said.

The other rushed forward, gave Haid's chest a hard kick, then crouched to look into his eyes. "He's dead." He was smiling as he eased around. Suddenly the smile died. "Behind you!" he shouted.

His partner twisted sideways and fired wildly. Shotgun pellets splattered the wall, missing Rachel by a foot. In the second it took him to pump the gun, she jumped through the doorway and raced along the corridor, fumbling for her gun, finally getting a grip on it as she reached the stairs. Another man, fat and out of breath, was lumbering up them, blocking her way. She darted past the opening and ran for the last door, slamming it shut behind her.

Boxes and bags were strewn across the floor. She stumbled through them and grabbed at the window, pounding and banging and cursing it when it wouldn't lift. Then she caught herself and looked around.

Gallon cans were stacked against the nearest wall. She had two in her arms when the door moved slowly inward like someone had given it a cautious push. A gun appeared, then the man holding it. She saw him aim and she knew she was dead. Only she didn't want to die, Rachel thought, not yet, not like this. Hurling herself forward, she drove the cans into the glass, then dove through the jagged hole and leaped over a railing onto the fire escape.

She was in the car when the gunman reached the bottom of the ladder. He fired one shot, then another. Buckshot ripped into the roof. Jumping onto the road, he pumped the gun and aimed again. She gunned the engine and the car swung wildly sideways, churning up a wall of water, skidded, then lunged at the man. He tripped backward, pulled himself up, and fired.

Across the street the window of a dry cleaner's shop exploded. While the glass flew into the rain, she floored the gas and roared off.

The next morning Rachel went looking for Teddy Duroy. All she knew was that he sometimes hung around the beach in Venice, so she spent a few hours walking that stretch of sand, talking to lifeguards and surfers and drug pushers, trying to get a lead on the man. No one had seen him in days. No one knew where he lived or where he hung out when he wasn't at the beach or who his friends were, if he had any.

She also asked about Sammy Tabor, but nobody knew anybody by that name.

At three o'clock Saturday afternoon, with the rain still pouring down, John Edward Haid was buried beside his wife and daughter. A priest stood over his grave reading from the Bible, but Rachel wasn't listening. Johnny had never had much use for priests, wouldn't want this one mumbling over him. Haid's religion was simple. Keep your eyes open and your back against a wall. Enjoy life but don't trust it. Expect shit with the roses. Never let them see you cry.

She bit her lip and held in the tears.

The cemetery followed the slope of a hill in Santa Monica. Rachel was standing on a grassy rise along with the few other cops who'd showed and a handful of friends not in the department. The family was farther down the hill, gathered under black umbrellas around the grave. There weren't many of them, a dozen or so adults and a couple of children. Some of the women were crying.

The priest closed his book and stepped back. A woman and a girl came forward dressed in black, with black veils over their faces, and dropped flowers into the hole. When they were done, the group started down a muddy path to their cars.

Two men, their white dress shirts plastered to their backs, began shoveling in dirt.

Rachel walked down to the grave. She'd bought a bunch of tiny yellow roses tied together with a white ribbon. She thought about throwing them into the hole, then changed her mind and put them with the other bouquets.

Jesus, Johnny, she thought, and tears filled her eyes.

"You all right?"

She felt a hand on her shoulder and turned slightly to see Capt. James Towers standing behind her, holding a wide umbrella at an angle to keep it from knocking hers. She was surprised to see him. The brass ordinarily wouldn't attend the funeral of a suspended cop, especially when that cop had split the lip and eye of an assistant chief.

"I'm okay."

"It's tough losing a friend."

She nodded.

"He was a good man," Towers said. "A good cop."

"I never met a better one." She started down the hill, and he came with her.

"You have any idea what happened to him?"

She shook her head, keeping her eyes on the lawn in front of her. Whatever she knew she wasn't giving to the department. "I hadn't seen him much since his suspension."

"You two were partners once. I heard you still hung around together at Blackie's Bar. He didn't tell you if anything was up?"

"Nothing."

"He wasn't working a case? On his own time?"

"If he was, he didn't tell me, and I didn't want to know. The truth is, Captain, he was going down and I didn't want to tag along. I was making a point of staying away from him. Maybe if I hadn't done that, he might still be alive."

"If somebody wanted him dead, he'd be dead. Nothing would've changed that."

"Maybe not."

"Look, don't take this on yourself, Detective."

"A couple of times at Blackie's he looked like he needed to talk. I didn't sit with him. I didn't have time to hear it, and I didn't want to hear it."

They had reached his car, a sleek gray Continental with leather upholstery. The rain had become a light mist and they closed their umbrellas.

Towers said, "You due any vacation time?"

"A couple of weeks."

"Take it now."

"I don't need . . ."

"Take it. You lost a friend. You need some personal time."

She stared at the water beading off the car's chrome bumper and dripping onto the newly mowed grass. Two weeks could be time enough to find out what Johnny was really on to and who had killed him and why. She said quietly, "I'll put my name on the schedule."

"You got anybody you can visit?"

Rachel thought a moment. "A friend in Oregon has this cabin by a trout stream."

"Then get a fishing pole, get out of town, and get some rest."

"You know what, Captain? That actually sounds good."

"Bring me the paperwork. I'll sign it and you can leave next week."

"All right. Thanks."

He gave a nod and looked back at the grave, where the men in white shirts were almost done. "We'll catch his killer. Johnny Haid's a murdered cop. We take care of our own."

After leaving the funeral, Towers called his office, canceled his afternoon appointments, and drove over to the Marina. He spent a few minutes on the pier watching the wind rock the sailboats.

He'd always wanted a boat, even knew which one he was going to get when he finally put out the money: that sixty-foot number there on the first jetty with the blue-and-white railing and the varnished hull. When the deal came down, he'd make the offer, buy some sailing clothes, send the wife to her mother's in New Jersey, and take Cilla down to Acupulco or Mazatlan. Someplace warm. Someplace it didn't rain.

He crossed the road. Cilla's town house faced the water. She'd bought it six years ago, before the prices went crazy. It was worth plenty now. He liked the way she kept the stairs, with the plants and Mexican pottery hanging from the beams. He liked the red mat on the porch with the orange letters that spelled PRISCILLA and the smile face underneath. Cheerful, the way she was.

He needed cheerfulness in his life.

Even though he had his own keys, he rang the bell and heard her call his name, sounding thrilled that he was here five hours before he was supposed to be. Maybe she was. Maybe she wasn't. He wondered sometimes if it even mattered. Maybe all he really needed was someone who acted thrilled.

She was wearing black tights, her long blond hair piled on her head. Her skin was shiny with sweat and she was breathing hard. "I'm almost done," she said, giving him a kiss. "You hungry? There's stuff in the fridge. I'll be right back."

She jogged into the living room and turned up the VCR. A woman's voice counted off numbers. Towers leaned against the door jamb and watched her stretch, left, then right, breasts lifting and falling. All morning he'd thought about taking her to bed and now that he was here all at once he didn't feel like it.

He went into the kitchen and stood by the window. The ocean was gray and choppy. He thought again about the men shoveling mud into Haid's grave. Mud covered things up. Mud kept you quiet. He reached for Cilla's phone and punched in a number. When it was answered on the other end he said, "Okay, I talked to her. She doesn't know anything. We're clean."

TWO

FRANKIE LIGHT WORKED OUT of a small room above a used-book store in Venice. When Rachel got there Sunday morning, the store was closed. She went around back and took the wooden steps up to Light's place two at a time. At the top, she rang the bell.

She'd known Light about three years. He called himself a photographic artist, which was a classy way of saying he took nude shots—boudoir photos he called them—that he sold to four or five porno shops up around Hollywood Boulevard. On the side he did some film developing and, when business was slow, played snitch for her and a couple of other detectives.

Rachel rang the bell again, then leaned on it, remembering Frankie liked to sleep in and enjoying the idea of waking him up. A minute later, she heard an inside door slam, somebody shuffle across the room, swearing, then the door was yanked back and a bleary-eyed Frankie Light said, "What the hell do you—" He stopped when he recognized her and looked vaguely guilty. "Hey, Detective. Long time no see. What's up?"

"How you doing, Frankie?" She glanced past him, seeing if anyone else was around, but the place appeared empty.

"Not bad, not bad. No complaints. What can I do for you?" He was dressed in shorts, a wrinkled T-shirt with a pit bull on it, and rubber slippers over red socks.

"I need some film developed, Frankie. Right away."

"How right away?"

"Now."

"Jesus," he said, tucking his hands under his armpits, "I'd like to help you out, but I'm kinda busy right now."

She pulled one of his hands free and put the film in it. "Sure you are, but take care of this first."

"But I . . ." Reading the look on her face, he sighed. "Yeah, okay. Come in."

Frankie crossed the room ahead of her, kicking aside newspapers, magazines, beer cans, making a path. A green-and-yellow parrot was sitting on a lamp and, as he passed it, he took a swipe at its rump and the bird screeched to the sink, wings flapping wildly. Frankie gave it a malicious smile, then he threw a pile of dirty laundry off the couch and motioned Rachel to sit. "I'll need about thirty minutes," he said. "Ignore the goddamn bird."

A half hour later he came out of the darkroom carrying the prints.

"How'd they come out?" Rachel said.

"They came out fine except for one thing. They're in Chinese or Japanese or something." He dropped the photos on the coffee table in front of her.

"Chinese," she said and flipped through them. They were still slightly damp and gave off a pungent chemical smell.

"You read that stuff?" Frankie asked, collapsing on the other end of the couch as though worn out.

"No. But I figured you'd know somebody who does."

All at once his eyes turned alert. "I might. It depends."

"On what?"

"C'mon, Detective. Don't embarrass me. It depends on how much you can pay."

"This one's for free, Frankie. You owe me."

"I owe you? For what?"

"For not busting you."

"What're you talking about?" he said, beginning to look guilty again. "Not busting me for what?"

"This." She lifted the top of a ceramic bowl that was sitting on the coffee table. Stuffed in it were cigarettes, rolling papers, and loose stalks of grass worth roughly, Rachel figured, a grand.

"Hey, c'mon." Protectively he put the cover back on. "This stuff's strictly recreational."

"Not in L.A. County."

"Shit."

"Give me a name, Frankie."

"Man, this isn't fair," he whined. "Information's my living. You know that."

"Right now I'm short of funds."

"Man," he said, putting on an injured look. "You can't trust nobody these days. Nobody."

"That's the truth, Frankie."

For a moment they measured each other, then seeing she wasn't going to budge, Frankie blew out a long breath and said, "Okay. What do you want? Somebody discreet?"

"Exactly."

"Then talk to Joe DeLonzo. His mouth's so tight he could starve to death."

"Where do I find him?"

"He's got a bookshop in the Village. A place called Rarities on Westwood. Tell him I sent you."

Rachel gathered the photos. "Thanks."

"Hey, anytime. I love giving out freebies."

"I'll make it up to you, Frankie."

"Yeah?" He pointed his hand at the parrot perched on the faucet and pretended to shoot. "That's what they all say."

Climbing the stairs to Danny Tai's office, Towers wondered if the rain was ever going to stop. The air had a chill in it that felt like winter in Brooklyn. It made him remember being a boy and buying booze and running bets for his old man. Snow, rain, sleet, wind so cold it could freeze your ass off, it never mattered. The old man needed a drink, the old man had a sure pick, and out of the apartment little Jimmy would go, down to Benny's

Liquors, then on to the betting parlor. Trudging through the cold, buying whiskey on his old man's bad credit, placing bets that never won, Towers had sworn one day he'd live somewhere hot.

He'd thought L.A. was the place. All those travel brochures he'd collected with the bright-eyed blondes playing volleyball on the beach, and the blue sky, and palm trees, and air that felt warm even in a picture.

What a joke, he thought, and the joke was on him.

He moved down the hall and stopped at the third door, gave it one hard knock, and went in without waiting. Tai was standing at the window, coatless, in a shirt that looked a couple of days old. When he turned, Towers felt some satisfaction. The man's usual arrogant expression was gone. He looked tired and scared, which was how he should look. Tai had screwed up good.

"You got anything yet?" Towers said.

"My men are asking questions," Tai said coolly. "It's only a matter of time—"

"So you got nothing?" Towers cut him off, not liking the Asian's tone. He walked behind the desk and looked over the floor and safe. "You took care of the blood?"

"Yes."

"Now all we need is the witness who saw a cop get blown away here." Enjoying himself, he glanced around at the other man. He liked seeing Tai's jittery eyes. "You made a bad mistake, Danny."

"I didn't know he would bring someone."

"It was a dumb idea setting him up. What'd you tell him was in the safe anyway?"

"Some names of people involved. Some dates. Some numbers."

Idly Towers picked up the photo of Tai's wife and children and said, "You actually have a list like that?"

"Yes. One list, that's all. To keep track of transactions."

"And you keep it here?" he said, replacing the photo.

"In the safe."

"He get to it?"

"No. He was killed first."

"Let me see what you got."

Tai came over from the window, the expression on his face half furious, half humiliated. It was an interesting combination of emotions, Towers thought as the Asian worked the combination and then pulled out the papers.

"They're in Chinese," Tai said, giving over the stack.

Taking his time, Towers thumbed through the sheets, shaking his head like he knew what he was looking at, like it was bad news. Finally he said, "I'm going to give you some advice, Danny. First, you don't hire people without checking with me. I check them out, make sure they're clean, then give you the go-ahead. You got that? If you'd told me about Haid, none of this would've happened."

The other man gave a tight-lipped nod.

"Second," Towers said, throwing the papers down, "you don't keep shit like this around. I don't care if it's in Swahili. Third, you don't kill a goddamn cop in your own office. You take him to the dessert or the canyons and do it there. That way when the body's found nothing points to you. Haid was picked up six blocks from here. That's too close, Danny. Fourth, you don't assume things. Like Haid would come alone. You plan for contingencies. And fifth, and this one's the big one, you don't let goddamn witnesses get away."

"I'll find the witness."

"It's been three days," Towers shot back. "Trails get cold fast."

"I'll find him."

"Make it soon. Our mutual friend is not happy. Not with this. Not with the take you've been skimming off the top."

Tai's head snapped up and the fear was back in his eyes.

"Yeah," Towers said. "He knows."

"What are you talking about?"

"Don't insult me, Tai. And don't waste my time. You've been taking one percent, two percent of the profit, thinking we wouldn't find out. How long did you figure to get away with it?"

"I never took—"

"Shut up." Now bored with the conversation, Towers walked

back to the door. "You have twenty-four hours to find the man who came in with Haid."

"Then what?"

"Then we'll see."

The bookshop stood between an all-night drugstore and a lingerie boutique specializing in leather and black lace. A bell rang as the door closed behind Rachel. She crossed to the long glass counter against the back wall, where a man was flipping through a magazine.

"Joe DeLonzo?" At his nod Rachel said, "Frankie Light sent me. He said you could read Chinese."

DeLonzo took off his glasses and leaned back in the swivel chair. "Some of it."

"What about this?" She handed him the photographs and let him look at them awhile before she said, "You know it?"

"Yes."

"Good. I need them translated as soon as possible."

"You're talking eight, nine pages. It'll take time."

"How much time?"

The man gave her the briefest smile. "That depends."

"Right," she said, catching on. "What's it going to cost me?"

"How soon do you want the work done?"

"Tonight."

"Tonight? For all this?" He fingered the papers, calculating. "I need to get two hundred dollars."

She looked at him as if he was crazy. "For nine pages? No way."

"That's the price," DeLonzo said and folded his hands firmly on the counter.

"Christ." The way his hands were, she knew he knew he had her. She gave it another few seconds, then nodded. "When can I get the translations?"

"Come back at ten."

"Ten o'clock sharp I'll be here."

"I need half the money up front."

"Half the . . . Jesus." She found two fifties under the flap in her wallet where she kept an emergency stash and threw them on the counter. "I'll tell you something. Frankie Light could take lessons from you."

DeLonzo grinned benignly.

"Have it done by ten."

He was still grinning as she moved back through the rows of books. When the front door tinkled shut, he dialed a number. "Frankie? It's DeLonzo. Okay, she showed. Yeah, I charged her a hundred. No, she wouldn't go higher. Yeah, you're not kidding. A real stubborn broad. So anyway, thanks for the business. Come by tomorrow and pick up your half."

At ten o'clock Rachel handed Joe DeLonzo two more fifties and he gave her six pages of neatly printed handwritten notes. She glanced over them as she walked back to her car.

She took Westwood to Wilshire and followed it down to the beach. A few blocks before her apartment she stopped at Charlene's, the all-night diner where she ate three or four nights a week. The food was good, the decor strictly functional, which she liked. Formica-topped tables, brown vinyl chairs, booths in the back. A chalkboard near the door scrawled with the evening's specials.

The place was busy when Rachel walked in. She ordered coffee and the stroganoff from the waitress who usually waited on her, then crossed to the back booth where she usually sat, hung her coat on the peg, and spread the translations across the table. She was pretty sure that what she had in front of her was a two-hundred-dollar long shot, maybe worse than that, but at the moment, it was the best shot she had. She nodded thanks as the waitress gave her a mug of coffee and a plate of stroganoff; then she kicked off her shoes and began going carefully over each sheet.

Forty-five minutes later, feeling the low-burning excitement of maybe having something, she called Molly Stokowski, who worked in the department's records section. The phone rang ten times before Molly's boyfriend finally answered it.

"Bert, it's Rachel. Sorry to call so late, but I need to talk to Molly."

"Hold on."

She waited ten seconds, then Molly came on and said, "What's up?"

"I need to see you."

"When?"

"Right now."

"You gotta be kidding."

"It's important."

"Bert's here. Sunday's our one night a week."

"Yeah, I know, but Bert'll have to understand. I have something I want to show you." Rachel heard a groan, then Bert Weiss's muffled grumbling in the background.

Molly said, "How important is this?"

"Very. I wouldn't break up your Sunday if it wasn't."

"Okay. Where are you?"

"Charlene's."

"Give me twenty minutes."

"Thanks, Stokowski."

"Thanks doesn't cut it. You owe me, Starr."

Exactly twenty mintes later, Molly Stokowski slid into the booth, ordered coffee and a slice of apple pie, and gave Rachel a dry look. "This better be good," she said. She was a tiny, delicate-looking woman with direct blue eyes and short wheat-colored hair.

"It is."

"So tell me."

"I was with Johnny Haid when he got killed."

"What?" Molly said it so loudly, nearby customers turned to look at them.

Rachel motioned her to keep it down. "I was with him. I saw it happen."

"His body was found in a dumpster in Chinatown."

"Just listen, okay? I'll tell you what I know."

"I'm listening. Talk."

"Johnny was working on a case. One involving a jewelry ring stealing major pieces of jewelry."

"What do you mean working on a case? He got suspended three weeks ago."

"He was working this on his own."

"And you were working it with him?"

"No. He called me the night he got shot and said he needed my help. Told me to meet him at his place. When I got there, I found he'd rented a car. We used it to drive to this restaurant in Chinatown."

"Why?"

"There were papers in a safe there that he wanted. They were supposed to be a record of the jewelry ring's transactions, naming names, dates, what was stolen, where it went."

"Are those the papers?"

"Yes."

"Do they name names?"

"Names, dates, everything."

"Jesus."

"Hold on. It gets better. One of the names supposedly belonged to a high-ranking cop."

"L.A.P.D.?"

Rachel nodded and Molly let out a low whistle. "No wonder he was killed," she said. "Tell me how it happened."

"We were in a guy named Danny Tai's office. He owns the restaurant. The safe was his. We'd taken pictures of the papers and relocked the combination when two Asians came in with shotguns."

"Christ," Molly said.

"I was against a wall. The only light was a small flashlight and they didn't see me until after they shot Johnny. They tried to get me, too, but I ran. I don't know how, but I got away." Seeing the moment over again in her mind, her face hardened. "He didn't have a chance, Molly. It happened so fast. One second Johnny was standing, the next he was on the floor." She dropped her gaze, folded both hands into fists, and let the guilt engulf her. "And I keep thinking that I could've saved him."

"From shotguns? Forget it."

"There was a moment. A split second when I could've gotten my gun out. . . ."

"Hey, Rachel." Molly reached across the table and gave her hand a hard squeeze to stop her. "You would've saved him if you could. What counts now is you. You're a witness. They've got to be looking for you.

"I know."

"Did they see your face?"

"I don't know."

"What about the car? Do you think they caught the license?"

"I don't think so. I was doing my damnedest to run down the guy who came after me, so I don't think he had the time."

"Then the next question is, what are you going to do? Take it to the department?"

"How can I? The department might be involved."

"What then?"

"I've got some ideas, but I need your help."

"What do you want me to do?"

Rachel shoved the translations over. "Take these. Pull out all the names and run them through the computer. See if any of them work for the department. After you do that, run them through again for background. I want to know who they are, what they do, if they have priors."

"That's easy enough. What else?"

"These dates over here." Rachel pointed to a column of numbers. "All are days when jewels were stolen. Run a check to see if the cases were reported and, if so, what their status is."

Molly nodded.

"One other thing. One of the names on the list is Victor Chang. About eight months ago, I was watching the man. I had a tip that Chang was brokering stolen gems and art. The piece I thought I'd get him on was a diamond Cartier necklace, but before I could move, Chang was found dead in his room at the Beverly Hills Hotel. No trace of the necklace. Except here." She flipped back a few pages. "There's a Cartier necklace on the list."

"Think it's the same one?"

"The stones are the same weight and the setting matches."

"So maybe whoever killed Chang might have killed Johnny?"

"It's possible."

"What about this Danny Tai? He seems the mostly likely suspect. It was his office, his safe, his papers."

"He's in on it, but he's not the head man. Johnny said Tai worked for someone else. Someone who gives the orders. That's the person I want. Johnny thought these papers might tell us who he was."

"Do they?"

"Maybe. Somewhere in these names, one name might stick out. That's why I'd like to get the info as soon as possible."

"Bert'll kill me, but I'll go in early and get on it."

For the first time in days, Rachel smiled. "Thanks, Molly." She motioned to the waitress for the check. "And tell Bert thanks, too."

Molly said, "In the meantime, what are you going to do?"

"Keep looking for Johnny's killer."

"On your own?"

"Yes."

Molly leaned forward as if to emphasize her point. "Will you do me a favor, Rachel?"

"What?"

"Remind yourself now and then it wasn't your fault Johnny Haid died."

"Yeah," Rachel said softly. "I'll keep it in mind."

At midnight, in an office four blocks west of Danny Tai's Kowloon Canton Restaurant, Robert Moon was playing poker with three other men when his phone rang. He picked up the receiver and said, "Jacob?"

"Hello, Robert."

"How is our deal progressing?"

"Smoothly. The ship carrying the container of drugs from Lee Chan will reach Honolulu in three days."

"Chan's drugs are mixed in with Kincaid Inc.'s sugar containers?"

"Yes. The customs check should be perfunctory."

"Kincaid knows another drug shipment is arriving?" Moon asked.

"Yes, but he doesn't know we have a new Asian source. And he doesn't know we're storing the drug container in his warehouse. He won't like it when he finds out."

"How long do we have to store it there?"

"Until Lee Chan arrives from Hong Kong and we pay him."

"Chan is a trusting man to make the delivery before getting paid."

"Not necessarily trusting, Robert. Lee Chan knows his prices are the best available. He has many clients, more than he can accommodate. He knows that we understand it is our good fortune that he has finally agreed to do business with us. He also knows we would not jeopardize the relationship by stealing from him now, when it is far more profitable to nurture a long-term friendship. Especially since he is willing to take full payment in gemstones."

"So we no longer need Towers or his Mexican drug connection?"

"Not anymore. But don't cut the captain off yet. To be safe, let him think we still want the Mexican shipment until the deal with Lee Chan is completed. Then get rid of him."

"All right."

"We are cleaning house, Robert. No outsiders from now on. Only our own people. Only Chinese in the inner circle. It is better that way."

At eleven the following morning Molly rang Rachel's extension and said, "Meet me at Nate's in fifteen minutes."

Rachel could hear the tension in her voice. "You got something?"

"Just be there," Molly said and hung up.

Nate's was a delicatessen five blocks from the station and a favorite hangout for cops going on or coming off shifts. At any time of the day or night, two or three tables had police officers sitting around them.

Molly met Rachel at the door and, without saying anything, led her all the way to the back, where they could talk without being overheard.

"Was a cop on the list?" Rachel said as soon as they sat down.

"No. And I cross-checked the names for every station in the L.A. area. Nothing."

"Then what've you got?"

"A name. One name that sticks out like you said it might. Maybe the head guy's name. Jacob Tong. You ever heard of him?"

"I don't remember. Was he on the list?"

"No. Not in black and white, but take a look at this." Molly placed a printout in front of her. About a dozen names were listed, each one followed by several paragraphs of background material. "I pulled these names from the papers you gave me. Every one of these men is an immigrant from Asia. Every one has a green card, which means that a company filed with Immigration to employ each of them. What's interesting is they all work for one company, an outfit called White Ginger. White Ginger supposedly imports perfumes and bath oils from the Far East. I did some digging and found that White Ginger is a subsidiary of Golden Lotus. Golden Lotus is a subsidiary of Red Dragon. Red Dragon is part of a company called Eastern Enterprises and Eastern Enterprises is owned by an outfit called Asia One. And Asia One belongs to Jacob Tong." Molly sat back. "Asia One also owns Danny Tai's restaurant, which means Tai works for Tong."

"What did you find out about this Jacob Tong?"

"Some interesting stuff. Tong's a jewelry broker. Buys and sells high-priced gems. Works out of Honolulu but has shops in New York, Hong Kong, and Tokyo. He's a very wealthy fellow who moves strictly in high-class circles. Has a respected personal collection of art and jewels. Respectable enough to loan pieces to museums."

"You think he could have a scam going with the jewelry?"

The other woman nodded. "I think it's a damn good possibility. A couple of these men," she said, tapping the printout, "were arrested for burglarizing homes in Brentwood. White Ginger posted bail for both of them. What could be happening is jewelry pieces get stolen, then maybe they're taken apart and reset or redesigned so they can't be traced. And the new pieces are sold through Jacob Tong's high-class retail operation. It would be a neat little setup."

"Any idea where Tong is now?"
"I checked. He's in Honolulu. Why? What have you got in mind?"
"I've got two weeks' vacation. The department thinks I'm going fishing in Oregon."
"But you're not?"
"No." Rachel took a breath and looked the other woman full in the face. "You remember how tight Johnny and I used to be?"
Molly nodded.
"I owe him a lot, Molly. A whole lot. I want whoever was responsible for his death."
"You're going to Honolulu."
"Yes."
"And you don't want anyone to know."
"No. I'll need my cover tight on this one."
"Tell me what you need."
"The usual. Photo I.D., a couple of credit cards, a driver's license."
"Under what name?"
"Make it Caitlin West. Since Tong's interested in art, I'll be a freelance writer specializing in the subject. It'll give us something to talk about."
"How soon do you need this stuff?"
"Can you do it by this afternoon?"
"Do I have a choice?"
Rachel smiled. "And I'll need some money."
"Under-the-table money? That one's a little harder. Let me call accounting and see what I can swing." She signaled the waitress for a refill, then said, "I've got to say this, Rachel. I don't like what you're doing. I don't like you going someplace you've never been, without backup, to track down someone who might be a killer."
"I won't be alone. Pono Smith lives over there. He and Johnny were friends. I'm giving him a call. I think he'll help."
"I remember Smith. He quit L.A.P.D., what—four, five years ago?"
"About five."

"What's he doing now? Working for the Honolulu Police?"

"He runs the family farm."

The coffee cup stopped halfway to Molly's mouth. "Jesus, you're going to have a farmer as a backup?"

"He was a cop for ten years," Rachel reminded her.

"Yeah, but five years of not being a cop is a long time."

"He'll do okay. And I might be taking someone else along. Someone who could have a stake in bringing in whoever murdered Johnny Haid."

"Who?"

"A man I was watching the same time I was watching Victor Chang. His name's Nicholas Snow. He's a professor of art history at UCLA. He writes books. Lectures. Edits catalogues for museums. He's a top authority on Impressionism. He could also be a jewel thief." She paused, remembering how close she'd been to catching him that last time and how he'd slipped away. "I was pretty sure Snow stole the Cartier necklace, and that Chang was trying to sell it for him. Which means when Chang was killed and the necklace disappeared, Snow lost a few hundred thousand dollars and a broker for his stolen goods. He might be interested in knowing who got the Cartier and who had Chang killed."

"What are you thinking?"

"I'm thinking if Tong is the man we want, and if Snow finds out about him, maybe Professor Snow would like to even the score."

THREE

AT EXACTLY 11:23 P.M. the museum guard would turn the corner of the Impressionists Gallery, stroll past six Renoirs, two Monets, three Pissarros, and without a glance at any of them, enter the short corridor leading to the Special Exhibition Hall. The corridor would take eight seconds to cross, Snow noted, which meant that he had precisely seventy-six seconds until the guard showed up.

In the unlit room, only the faint glow of the moon coming out from behind the rain clouds fell over Snow as he crouched and pressed his fingers along the back panel of the display case. He was a brown-haired, plain-featured man except for the eyes. Under a wide forehead and straight, fierce brows, the eyes were deep gray, intensely intelligent, and saved his face from homeliness. Hearing a soft click, Snow began loosening the back panel, his motions precise and casual, as if what he was doing he'd done a hundred times.

Which he had. And more.

When the panel was off, he reached a gloved hand into the velvet-lined case, lifted the pink diamond from its pedestal, and deposited it in the side pocket of his coat. From his other pocket he drew out a shiny object, gave it a polish with his cuff, set it in the diamond's place, and smiled.

It would be days before anyone noticed the exchange.

He closed the case and looked at his watch. Forty-seven seconds remained. He was right on schedule. A quick check of his tools—he had a habit of losing them—then he headed for the adjacent Expressionists Gallery, hurried through it, and gave himself a mental pat on the back for his self-control. But at the hall's exit he stopped abruptly and swore softly.

Maybe he should reconsider the plan.

Getting into the museum hadn't been easy. There were fences, spotlights, guards, alarms. On the roof, which sloped more than he'd estimated, he'd nearly slipped and broken his neck, and jumping into the building, he'd pulled a back muscle, the one stretching from his ribs to his shoulder on the right side, and he'd done something to his left knee. Both would probably hurt like hell for days.

All in all, a lot of trouble for just one diamond.

On the other hand, he hadn't really planned on stealing anything other than the diamond, which meant he hadn't figured out how to take anything else safely. Which meant he should keep on walking. If he were smart.

On the other hand, when would he have a chance like this again?

He backtracked ten feet and looked up. Of all the paintings in the room this was the best. Late-summer fields and hedges under a churning sky. Amber yellows, torquoise blues, grass greens slashed here and there by startling red roofs. A small but perfect painting. And he wanted it.

Swearing again, he reached up and lifted the oil from its hook. For one second the silence held; then, in a frenzy, the alarms began to clang. He heard a guard shout, then footsteps pounding toward him. Snow said, "Jesus Christ," tucked the painting under his arm, and started running.

Outside it was dark. The smell of rain clung to the air and clouds blocked the moon. He leaped over a low hedge and groaned as the painting bounced up and jabbed his stomach. For the first time all evening he felt sweat on his forehead, his pulse thundering.

In the distance sirens wailed.

At the wrought-iron gate, he slid the painting through the bars, then grabbed a spire in each hand. Adrenaline and lights blasting on in the museum sent him scrambling over. Snatching up the oil, he scampered down the sidewalk, keeping in the shadows. At the end of the block his aging compact waited like a conspirator beneath a tree.

He slowed down and looked back over his shoulder. Dogs were running around the grounds, howling wildly, but there were no guards in sight. They were still inside, he guessed, scouring the galleries. He laughed softly.

He was an idiot to have taken the Van Gogh. But the painting held all the stillness, all the pained acceptance of that one moment when summer becomes fall. How could he leave it behind?

It was impossible, he admitted, yanking the door open.

The sirens were closer. He had another minute or two, but that was all he needed. He ducked into the front and his heart stopped. On the passenger side a woman was sitting comfortably, angled toward him, one arm stretched across the seat back. He recognized her at once. She was the red-haired woman he'd seen at the last series of his public lectures, listening attentively, taking notes in a steno book. She usually sat in the last row, but he'd always noticed her. Botticelli hair. A Renoir mouth. Sea-green eyes. To not notice her you'd have to be dead.

He hoisted the painting into the back, smiled wryly, and said, "You'll have to excuse me, I'm in a bit of a rush," and appreciated the wry way she smiled back.

"You'd better start the car if you want to miss them. Put your seat belt on, drive the speed limit, and talk like we've been married twenty years."

He stopped smiling. He could ask questions, but something in her attitude told him he'd be wasting his time. Keeping his eyes on her, he started the engine and pulled away from the curb. "What do people who've been married twenty years talk about?" he said.

"How to pay for the kids' college educations, what to eat for dinner, and where the other sock is. Watch the road, okay?"

"Ah, a cynic."

"A pitfall of my line of work." She gestured at a tree-lined street. "Turn there. Use the signal."

He made the turn and saw in the mirror a chain of blue-and-whites hurtling down the road they'd left. "Now that that's solved," he said, "what do we talk about?"

"How about the contents of your left pocket, Dr. Snow?"

He felt his heart flip, then start hammering. He glanced sideways, caught her watching him, and thought, Christ, she knows, only it wasn't possible. Making himself relax, he forced another smile. "Maybe you'd like to tell me who you are?"

"The name is Starr." She opened her badge and held it up for view. "Detective Rachel Starr, L.A. Police Department."

"I see." He told himself to keep cool. Back at the museum she could've cuffed him, but she hadn't. If he kept cool, he might slide out of this. "Since when are police detectives interested in art?"

"What do you mean?"

"You've been coming to my lectures."

"It's a large hall. I didn't think you noticed me."

"In a crowded stadium I'd notice you, Detective."

She didn't react to the compliment. Okay, he thought. A woman who looked like her was probably used to compliments, especially from thieves and hustlers.

She dropped the badge into her bag and said, "Your last lecture was particularly interesting."

"Really?" he said, trying to remember what the lecture was about. Ahead the road divided into two branches. "Which one do I take?"

"The left. Though I disagreed with your views."

"Did you?" he said, having no idea at all what his views had been since they usually occurred to him as he was lecturing and were in many ways dependent upon his mood, how his day had been, and what he'd eaten for dinner. "In what way?"

"You were wrong about the Elgin Marbles. The British had no right to cart off pieces of the Parthenon."

"The Elgin Marbles. Of course. Why didn't the British have that right?"

"Because it wasn't theirs to cart off."

"I see. You'd prefer they'd left the friezes for the Turks to take pot shots at?"

"The marbles should have stayed in Greece, where they belonged. The British were thieves."

"It was somewhat more complicated than that, Detective."

"No, it wasn't. It was really very simple. Stealing's stealing." They were now on Little Santa Monica near Westwood. Just ahead, over a dingy bar, a neon sign spelled ACES. Rachel said, "Stop over there."

There were more neon signs in the window advertising beer and a neon clock that said it was 11:30.

"For any particular reason?"

"You and I have some things to talk about."

"One of them being the contents of my left coat pocket?"

"You're very swift, Dr. Snow."

The place was dark and smelled of cigarettes, stale beer, and ammonia. A bar lined one wall, backed by mirrors reflecting the stash of liquor and slotted glasses above the bar-top. In a corner two teenagers in aviator jackets and boots were shooting pool, and near the bar a bald man was swiping at a table with a rag.

"Hey, Freddie," Rachel said.

The man looked up and grinned. "Hey, Rachel. It's been a while."

"How's business?" She slid into a booth, took off her jacket, and waved a hand at Snow to sit.

"Not bad. Quiet tonight. The fight's started at the Forum." He circled behind the counter, giving it a wipe-down as he walked its length. "So, what can I get you?"

"Beer for me."

"You got it." He turned to Snow. "How about you?"

"Beer sounds good."

"Coming up." Freddie reached overhead for glasses.

When the drinks were poured, Rachel went to get them. Snow

watched while she and the man spoke quietly, then smiled pleasantly as the bartender scowled his way. Rachel brought back the beers.

"The man's sending me dirty looks," Snow said as she sat down. "What did you tell him I was? A hatchet murderer?"

She almost smiled then. Snow had wondered if she could and what she might look like if she did. And what she looked like, he realized, could break the strongest man's heart.

"Not quite," she said. "I told him you steal alms from St. Clement's down the street. The money that's supposed to go to the poor children in South America. He didn't like that. Freddie's very fond of children."

He gave a small toast with his bottle. "That was clever of you."

"I thought so, too." She took a sip of her beer. "Actually, I was careful in what I said. That way, if you do try to leave before we're done, he won't kill you, he'll just break your legs."

"I appreciate it." Snow took another look at the man. Freddie was cutting lemons, but his eyes flicked up now and then, glinting, Doberman eyes, to check him over. "I want you to know I have no illusions about getting past the fellow."

"Then we can get down to business."

"Which is?"

"The emerald-cut diamond in your pocket and the Van Gogh oil in your car."

Snow was silent and didn't let his face show any of the amazement he felt. After all these years of not being caught, how had this woman figured him out? "You're very good," he said. "Even I wasn't sure if I'd take the painting. How'd you know?"

"I've been watching you."

"Really? Since when?"

"Every time you visited the museum."

"I see," he said casually, but his pulse had picked up speed again. He'd cased the gallery four times since the special exhibition had been installed. He hadn't spotted her once.

"At first, I thought you'd take the emerald pin—the one in the case nearest the exit—but after a while, I realized it was the pink diamond you wanted."

"Perceptive of you. What about the painting? How did you know it was the Van Gogh?"

"A lucky guess, Professor, but not a hard one, really. It's no secret that you admire his work."

Snow swirled his glass, letting the liquid wash the edges. She was watching him the way a cat watches a trapped bird, and he didn't enjoy the feeling. "All right," he said, making himself relax. "What exactly do you want from me? You've had enough time to arrest me, yet you haven't, which gives me the idea you have something else in mind."

"I'm not going to arrest you, Dr. Snow. Not this time anyway, if you cooperate. You're a thief and I don't like thieves, but at the moment I'm in need of one. That's why you're with me and not in the county jail."

"Why do you need a thief?"

She leaned forward slightly, and for the first time Snow noticed she wasn't wearing makeup and that a small scar cut across her upper lip, flattening it slightly.

She said, "Five days ago a police officer was killed. I believe I know who was behind his murder. I need a thief to help me catch the man."

"Why a thief? Why not a fellow officer of the law?"

"For the moment that's my business."

Taking the beer with him, Snow sat back. The room was hot and airless and, courtesy of the pool players, rap music was playing on the jukebox. All he wanted, Snow thought, was a smooth and fast way out. "Fine. I'm in complete agreement," he said reasonably. "To tell you the truth, I think this is entirely your business, so I'll just finish this off and be—"

"You're not going anywhere, Professor."

"Look, Detective. I wish you all the best in your endeavor. I'd like to help you, I really would, but at the moment I haven't time to take on any new projects. So I'm afraid I'll have to pass on the offer."

"And I'm afraid you'll have to put your other projects on hold."

"I'd like to," he told her, trying to sound even more reasonable, "but it won't be possible. I'm in the middle of a term. I have numerous students clamoring for aesthetic knowledge. I can't disappoint them."

"I'm sure they'll survive."

"But I'd feel I'd failed them. Then there's the L.A. County Museum catalogue that I've promised to edit. I'm already several months behind on that."

"Then a few more weeks won't matter."

"And a new series of public lectures start in March. I need time to prepare."

"Use your class notes, Professor."

Realizing he was getting nowhere, Snow put down his drink and gave her a level look. "Detective Starr, I'm sorry a police officer was killed, I really am, but I'm not the one to help you catch the murderer."

"I disagree." She sighed as though she were reaching the end of the line humoring him. "Okay. Let me see if I can make this more interesting to you, despite your busy schedule. How does this sound? About eight months ago a Cartier diamond necklace was stolen from a New York gem broker named Victor Chang."

Snow felt his eyes react, a slight, caught-off-guard narrowing.

"During the theft of the necklace," she went on, "Chang was killed. I believe the man who had him killed also ordered the police officer's death. The suspect's name is Jacob Tong. Jacob Tong. Victor Chang. Those names mean anything to you?"

"Should they?"

"Victor Chang brokered jewelry that you stole, Dr. Snow. For a fee, he dumped your goods on the market, a very lucrative arrangement for you. You must have been quite annoyed when he was murdered. And I bet you weren't real happy about losing the necklace either. I hear it was worth close to a half-million dollars. Maybe you'd like to settle the score with whoever killed Chang and stole it?"

"I don't know anything about a Cartier necklace," Snow said and took another slow swallow of beer.

"Yeah?" she said, and he could tell she didn't believe him. "Well, listen up anyway. The same necklace was mentioned in papers taken from the safe of a guy named Danny Tai. It was one in a long list of jewelry pieces stolen in the L.A. area."

"Who's Tai?"

"Someone who works for Tong."

"This is all very interesting, but none of it means anything to me."

"No? Then how about this? Jacob Tong owns several jewelry stores. He sells only expensive pieces to a select clientele. Clients who might appreciate the value of a signed Cartier diamond necklace and who could afford to pay for it. That's what we think is going on, Professor. We suspect Tong heads a jewelry theft ring and that he dumps stolen goods into the legitimate market through his stores. The Cartier necklace Victor Chang was killed for appeared on the list of gem pieces stolen by that ring. So who do you think was responsible for Chang's death? Who probably has the Cartier necklace sitting in one of his vaults right now? My guess is Jacob Tong." She took a beat. "You remembering the necklace now? Sixty carats of square-cut diamonds set in an Art Deco mounting?"

Snow shook out a cigarette, tamped it down, and looked through the window at the street. What he was remembering was Victor Chang's body wedged between two bloody beds in a sunlit room of the Beverly Hills Hotel. What he was feeling was the loss. "I might be," he said blandly and turned back to her. "All right. Let's say I do remember it. Let's say I somehow help you catch this Tong. Let's say he still has my necklace . . ." Something in the way her head came up stopped him and he smiled dryly. "It was a bluff, wasn't it, Detective? You weren't sure if the necklace was mine or not."

Taking a matchbook that said FREDDIE'S out of the ashtray, Rachel struck a match and held it toward him. For a moment their eyes locked, then she shook out the flame and said, "I was fairly sure."

"You're a shrewd woman, Detective. Remind me to remember that." He took a thoughtful drag. "Okay. Let's say this Tong does have the necklace. If I help you, do I get it back?"

"If we recover the necklace, it goes back to its rightful owner.

And you're not the rightful owner, Dr. Snow. But I'll tell you the deal I'm prepared to make. You return the diamond and the painting and you help me apprehend Tong, and I don't say a word about what happened tonight."

"I help you and I get to walk, that's it?"

"That's it."

"How do you explain returning the goods?"

"That's my problem. I'll work it out."

"What if I say no?"

"You get handcuffed and taken to the station."

Snow tapped off an ash and shook his head. "This is not a very good way to start a relationship, Rachel."

"No? Well, let me set something straight. For openers," she said, her voice going dead cold, "you can call me Detective Starr. And we're not having a relationship. Relationship implies equals. We're not equals. If you decide to help me, I'll be calling the shots. All of them. If you decide not to help, you'll find yourself behind bars for five to ten years. Got it?"

"As you said, I'm very swift."

"Then make up your mind."

"You're not offering many options."

"Make up your mind, Doctor."

"I've never liked jail. . . ."

"I didn't think so." She reached for her coat. "I'll need you for two weeks. Make arrangements to clear your schedule."

"Two weeks beginning when?"

"Day after tomorrow."

"Sorry, that's impossible."

"Make it possible," she countered. "Do whatever you have to." Taking out several bills, she weighted them down with the beer glass and stood. "This one's on me."

When Snow came out, she was standing in the light of the neon sign, slapping her arms to keep warm. She was a tall, lean woman, with long legs and good hips. Strong-looking, like she could take care of herself. She glanced his way and he could read in her eyes what she thought of him. He was scum. Dressed up in nice clothes, employed by a nice college, giving nice lectures, but still scum. Then she glanced away, checking the lot, and he saw something else. Something she tried to hide. Something that was lonely.

She stuck out a hand. "I'll take the diamond now."

"Of course." He reached into a pocket and gave her the stone. "Now that we've taken care of business, can I offer you a ride?"

"My car's over there." She indicated the brown station wagon parked in the corner.

"You were sure of yourself," he said.

"Actually, Professor, I was sure of you. Now I'll take the painting."

"The painting. I almost forgot." He unlocked the back door. The canvas was on the floor propped against the seat. Even in the unlit lot he could see dabs and swirls of oil leaping from the surface, demanding a response. The best art always did. Though he'd made plans for the money it would bring, the diamond was easy to give up. But the painting was another matter. Losing it was a kind of torture.

He hunched inside, drew out the canvas, and reluctantly passed it to her. "The man who owns this doesn't deserve to."

"No one person deserves to own something like this." It had started raining again and she brought the work to her chest and drew her coat carefully around it. "Tomorrow an airplane ticket will be delivered to your office for a Wednesday-afternoon flight to Honolulu. The time and flight number will be on the envelope. Bring an extra suitcase of clothes and be on time. Good night, Dr. Snow."

"One last question, Detective. For my own curiosity. I've seen you at my lectures for a few months now. Is that how long you've been watching me?"

"About that."

"I've been watching you, too."

"Have you?"

"You like the aisle seat, if I remember right. Last row, closest to the door. That must be your police training. You use a fountain pen—black, I think—and a gray steno pad. You take voluminous notes and you listen attentively, even gravely, as though what I have to say should be taken seriously, which I feel I should tell you, it shouldn't be."

"That it?"

"Not quite." He settled against the car's hood, enjoying the thin mist blowing around in the night wind and the presence of the woman. "You have an extraordinary face. Very fine. Very beautiful. Never in a million years did I think you were a cop."

"Now you know."

"Now I know."

"I'll see you in two days, Professor. Don't be late." She took a step, then stopped. "One other thing. If you have any thoughts about leaving town before then, I'd advise you to forget them."

"I'm not going anywhere."

"I imagine you have tools. Bring them with you."

He frowned and said, "What are we going to be doing in Honolulu, Detective?"

"If we're lucky, Dr. Snow, stealing."

FOUR

THE HOUSE WAS THE last on the road that dead-ended at the top of the canyon. The driveway wound down a quarter of a mile through thick stands of eucalyptus and pine before angling upward again and coming to a stop at the cliff's edge. There a simple redwood structure served as a garage.

On the far side of the garage a covered lift was attached to the side of the canyon. It dropped twenty feet to a natural ledge. Built into this ledge and soaring over it was a house of steel beams and glass. Another lift, this one in the hall off the living room, connected the house to a second ledge some thirty feet below, this one a man-made steel platform. The studio was here, sitting on the rim, nothing blocking the view of craggy valleys and the Pacific Ocean. Between the studio and the mountainside were the gardens, the teahouse, and the carp ponds crossed with the red lacquer bridges Snow had brought with him from Hong Kong.

At one 1:00 A.M. Tuesday morning every light in the building was on. Myles McDonnell, rolling his wheelchair back and forth, was slapping slabs of clay onto a massive sculpture of a reclining woman.

Snow was watching him.

McDonnell was a gnomelike man, brawny in the arms and chest, but with thin, withered legs. His hair was pure white Einsteinlike frizz. "I don't like the idea, Nicholas," the old man grumbled. "It stinks, to put it bluntly. Like a goddamn pot of oysters on a ripe day."

"I think it could work."

"Work? It's foolish and risky, and I will not let you do it." Dunking his hands in a pot of water, he began scraping off clay.

"I've already made up my mind," Snow said.

The old man's head shot up. "Then, damn it all, why are you wasting my time? Bothering me while I'm trying to to work? Asking my advice with no intention in the world of using it?"

"I wanted your opinion."

"That is unmitigated crap from a bull. You wanted my approval, Nicholas. My blessing. Which, let me be absolutely clear, I am not giving you."

"Calm down, Myles. Remember your heart."

"I am perfectly calm and my heart is perfectly fine." The old man spun his chair around and wheeled it furiously toward an oak table near the window. He swept a coat, a plaid cap, a photograph of a reclining-woman sculpture by Rodin, a glass, a bottle of champagne—one snitched, Snow observed, from the case of Dom Perignon he'd hidden in the cellar—off the table and dumped them into his lap. "Where's my bloody cigar?" he growled.

"The lady's smoking it," Snow said.

"What?"

He nodded at the sculpture.

"Oh, yes. Right, right." The old man wheeled back and snatched the cigar from where he had stuck it between the woman's lips. "Now I'm too upset to work any longer. I want to go back to the house."

"All right. I'll get the lights."

"My concentration's ruined, you realize that, don't you? I despise it when my concentration's ruined."

"I know, Myles." Snow snapped off the lights.

"I need peace and quiet and serenity. The artistic impulse is a delicate one. It can't be disturbed. It can't be worried. It must be free of agitation."

"Yes, Myles," Snow said as he closed the door behind them.

The air was icy and damp. Snow separated McDonnell's coat from the other things in his lap and placed it around his friend's shoulders. Then he pushed the chair through the bonsai garden and over the largest bridge spanning the carp pond. As they passed the teahouse, McDonnell raised a hand and said, "Let's sit here awhile."

"It's too cold."

"Don't baby me, Nicholas. These old bones have seen the North Pole and more. Go on, roll me up."

"I don't think we should," Snow said, but he was already easing the chair over the ramp he'd built years before, when McDonnell became paralyzed. He turned it so the old man could see the gold carp swimming in the pool. For a while neither spoke.

Then McDonnell said, "Victor loved it here."

"Yes."

"I'd look out from the studio and see him sitting here as blissful as a child, thinking or plotting God knows what."

Snow put his hand on McDonnell's shoulder.

"I miss our chess games," the old man said. "Victor was a worthy opponent."

"You claimed he cheated, as I recall."

"And he did. But so shrewdly. And with such great class."

Snow smiled.

A white carp speckled with gold wound around a lily pad, then wiggled away.

"You rarely talk about him, Nicholas. It's been months and months and we never mention his name." When Snow didn't answer, McDonnell went on, "Do you remember the pond in Hong Kong? The gold carp, the water lilies?"

"Yes," Snow said and thought of the elaborate waterways in the courtyard of his family's home. Waterfalls and waterwheels and a dozen arching bridges. He thought of Victor Chang teaching him, making him stare into the water until only the water existed. "I remember it, Myles."

"When I think of Victor, I think of him in that garden. We met there that summer when you were ten. Do you remember?"

Myles the struggling artist making his living as a gardener. His white hair bright yellow then. His legs strong. His eyes a brilliant blue, full of wit and hunger. "Yes."

"Victor Chang gave me my life, Nicholas. Until I knew him I was without purpose. Adrift." The man touched Snow's hand and said quietly, "I miss him as much as you do. I am filled with rage at the thought of his death. But if you seek revenge, you destroy what we stand for. What Victor stood for. He wouldn't want this man's blood on your hands. And he wouldn't want you to endanger yourself. Too many people rely on you. You haven't the right to take foolish chances."

"I'll be all right."

"Will you? This policewoman you're going with. Why are you trusting her? What makes you think she'll let you walk away when it's over?"

"Because she said she would."

"My God, Nicholas. She says she will and you believe her?"

"Yes."

"Why?"

"Her eyes."

"Her eyes? What about her bloody eyes?"

"I don't think they lie."

McDonnell glanced up and snorted. "I think you better tell me what the lady looks like."

"Tall. Copper-red hair. Pale green eyes."

"Uh-huh." The old man uncapped the champagne.

"It's strictly business, Myles."

"I hope to God it is. I spend years sending beautiful women your way to absolutely no avail, and now you tumble for a female cop."

"I haven't tumbled."

"Haven't you? Then what's that vague, moony look on your face?"

"Hunger. I haven't eaten since lunch."

"Bloody cow crap, Nicholas." McDonnell took a swig of champagne, wiped the back of his hand across his mouth, then let out a sigh. "I don't think I have to tell you about our situation or our priorities or the care we must take."

"No."

"Then forget this plan of yours. We have more important business."

"I can't forget it. I've spent months looking for Victor's killer. Now I may have found him. You expect me to walk away?"

"Yes," McDonnell shouted, slapping the arm of the wheelchair. "I expect you to walk away. I expect you to do the one thing you are bound to do. Go on with our work as Victor would have wanted."

Snow shook his head. "I can't."

After a moment the old man nodded. He seemed to fall back, shrink into the chair, exhausted. "Go on, then. Go on. But be careful, Nicky. I feel danger. A great deal of danger."

There were two galleries in the house. A large one next to the parlor, which guests were welcome to wander through and which held an impressive collection of Impressionist and Post-impressionist paintings and drawings. Over the years scholars, appraisers, artists, and other collectors had studied the collection and left believing Prof. Nicholas Snow possessed one of the finest gatherings of late-nineteenth- and early-twentieth-century art. Not one of them realized that every piece on every wall in the gallery was a fake fabricated by the hands and genius of Myles McDonnell.

The second gallery was in a small, windowless room off the wine cellar in the basement. It was locked at all times with a bolt Snow himself had designed based on his knowledge of the insufficiency of available security devices. Only he and McDonnell had keys. Only their closest friends were allowed in. On the walls were twenty carefully chosen paintings: Monets, Pissarros, Gauguins, Signacs, Morisots, Cézannes, a Degas, and a Van Gogh. All were examples of the artists' finest work. All were worth millions. All were stolen.

These were the ones Snow refused to part with.

He leaned back in the chair. Except for the lights over each painting, the room was dark. There was no sound but his own breathing. His eyes roamed over the canvases, stopping on the Van Gogh. The one he'd taken tonight would've hung beside it if the lady detective hadn't caught him.

How the hell had she caught him? he wondered. He'd been a thief for twenty-two years, and this was the first time he'd made a mistake. The first time he'd been caught. He didn't like the feeling. Like someone had yanked back the curtains and seen what the play was really about, someone who could now shut down the whole production if she chose to. He felt vulnerable. He liked that feeling even less.

Myles was right about trusting her. She knew he was a thief. She would start asking more questions, start poking around—wasn't that what cops did?—and endanger their work. Which meant Detective Starr, as beautiful as she was, beautiful enough to make something inside him grow absolutely still, was a problem he'd sooner or later have to take care of.

Rachel slid back the closet door and began throwing clothes into two suitcases that lay open on the bed. She was careful to split the same items equally between the two bags. One case would go with her to the surveillance apartment. One would remain in the hotel room along with Snow's so if Tong had them checked out, they'd look like tourists staying in Waikiki.

On the phone, when she'd told Pono Smith about Johnny Haid, he'd offered his help without being asked. He'd understood when she told him that this was her own case, on her own time; L.A.P.D. had nothing to do with it and neither would the Honolulu Police Department until she was ready to pull them in. She'd also told him the truth about Nicholas Snow, and Smith hadn't backed off. He'd nosed around and, learning that Tong was throwing a fund-raising party for the local art museum, he'd arranged with an artist friend to get two invitations. The party would be the opening scene, she thought, locking the bags. The beginning of setting up the Asian.

She carried the suitcases to the front door, then looked back over the room. She'd lived in this second-floor apartment for ten years, but there was still a tentative feel to it, like she was just visiting and might leave at any time. The walls were bare, though a couple of framed prints leaned against the wall behind the couch. There were no plants, no knickknacks. She could have a pet if she wanted one, it was in the lease, but she didn't. Even a bowl of goldfish felt like a hook, a commitment. She didn't like commitments. She'd learned in a half-dozen foster homes not to count on them. She didn't count on anyone and she didn't want anyone or anything counting on her. It was simpler that way.

She started thinking of Snow as she walked back to the bedroom. Last night she'd wanted to make him nervous. Shake him. But he'd been cool. He looked different up close. Better-looking. Not in any way handsome, but there was something interesting about his face, something that made you like it more the longer you looked at it. He had a good smile, maybe that was it. And smart eyes. They had a smile in them, too, but behind the smile there was calculation.

She'd have to watch that.

She didn't want to admit it, but she'd been pleased when he'd said she was beautiful. How had he put it? In a crowded stadium he'd have noticed her? Okay, it was a line, and she'd heard a thousand of them, but the way he'd said it, like it wasn't a line, had gotten to her.

She'd have to watch that, too.

Something else. He'd believed her when she said she'd let him off. Rachel opened her dresser and shook her head. Yeah, he had his Ph.D., but he was still dumb. Sure she was going to let him walk. Sure she'd look the other way. Sure she wouldn't throw his Ph.D. ass in jail when this was over. Like hell she wouldn't. She took out Johnny Haid's yellow handkerchief, held it a moment, then put it in her pocket and went back to the living room.

So she'd let Snow trust her, Rachel thought, turning off the lamp. Let him think she'd keep her word. If he didn't know better, was that her fault? What it was was his own dumb luck.

Crooks lied to cops. And cops lied right back.

It was the oldest game in town.

FIVE

KALAKAUA AVENUE ON WEDNESDAY evening was a stew of cars, tourists, gaudy storefronts, and hustlers with perfect tans. A burning red sunset streaked the sky and gleamed off the ocean. Palm trees lining the sidewalks rustled in the wind. On both sides of the street the wall of hotels was lit up, ready for the nightly party. Pono Smith inched the white sedan forward and braked it as the light changed and a noisy crowd looking for fun herded across the street.

Rachel glanced over at Smith and said, "Traffic always like this?"

Pono Smith hadn't changed much in five years. Maybe he'd put on some weight, but at his height he could handle it. He still had the same calm eyes, the quick smile. About seven, eight years back, before he'd partnered with Johnny Haid, she and Smith had worked drug cases together. He'd been a good cop, very bright, fast at figuring out scams.

"Yeah, it's crazy," he said. "Getting worse all the time. You'd think we were in L.A."

"You liked driving around L.A. When we rode together, you always took the wheel."

"You know why? I'll tell you. The way you drove scared the shit out of me." He found Snow in the rearview mirror. "You ever seen her drive, Professor?"

"Not yet," Snow said. "What's it like?"

"It's like riding around with a wild woman. She used to do sixty in the city. Everywhere we went, it was like we were in the Indianapolis Five Hundred. I took the wheel because I didn't want to die."

Rachel smiled, remembering how nervous Smith used to get. "You should've said something."

"I did. Maybe three thousand times." The crosswalk cleared and he pointed at a low pink building ahead of them with turrets and awnings. "See that? That's the Royal Hawaiian. I got you booked there for two weeks."

"Very nice," Snow said. "Reminds me of a villa I visited last summer on the Riviera."

"Don't get your hopes up, Professor," Rachel said. "Only our extra luggage is staying there. You and me, we're booked into a surveillance apartment." She glanced back at Smith. "When can we get into the place?"

"Right now. We'll register you at the Royal Hawaiian, dump the bags, and head over there. My cousin Moses should have the equipment set up by now."

"This is the cousin who's with the Honolulu Police Department?"

"That's the one."

"He's knows to keep what we're up to from the department?"

"He knows."

"And he's willing to go along?"

Smith nodded and started smiling. "He's a young, crazy cop, just like we used to be."

"What kind of equipment did he get?"

"Couple of high-powered scopes, a recorder, some mikes, a video setup. Also the revolver you asked for."

The light turned green and Smith stepped on the gas. He turned off Kalakaua and took the car past a row of shops before curving around a drive lined with Japanese lanterns and palm trees. He brought the car to a stop in front of the hotel's entrance. Marble steps covered with a thick purple carpet led up to a vaulted entrance. Beyond it, Rachel could see a plush lobby surrounded by expensive shops. Off to their right a smooth lawn banked with clipped shrubbery and flowers rolled down to white sand and blue-green water.

"Okay," Smith said, shutting down the engine and signaling a porter. "Take a good look and eat your hearts out, 'cause this is where you're not staying."

An hour later they were standing in a nineteenth-floor apartment in the heart of Honolulu. From it they could see traffic swing past on Nimitz Highway, following the curve of the sea, the top half of the Aloha Tower with its lit clock, and rows of rectangular piers reaching into the dark waters of Honolulu Harbor. They could also clearly see the eighteenth floor of the office building directly across Alakea Street from them.

"Tong's suite's the one with the white blinds," Smith said. "Over there's his office and that side's where he lives. He owns about half the floor."

"The view's good from here," Rachel said.

"Yeah, we lucked out. Better to be above him than below." Smith moved to a makeshift shelf set a few feet back from the window. He raised a mounted scope, focused it, and said, "Take a look at this." Then he stepped aside to give her room. "It's like being in Tong's office. Once we get the bugs in, we'll have it made."

"What kind of recorder did your cousin get? Voice-activated?"

"Yep. And we got some high-speed video film for nighttime. What else?" He turned and gave the room a quick once-over. "Well, we got for you one boxy little apartment painted a funny shade of green. One run-down couch, a beat-up card table, two folding chairs. There's a bed in the other room, but I got my doubts about it. Linens in that closet over there."

"What about those invitations to Tong's party?"

"Oh, yeah." He handed her an envelope and settled against a cabinet.

Rachel pulled out the card and read it. "Where is this place?"

"Three-eleven Round Top Drive? It's an estate at the top of Tantalus. That's a mountain two, maybe three miles from here. Very ritzy address. Overlooks the whole city. Pretty incredible view. Only old money lives up there."

"Whose place is it?" Snow asked. "Tong's?"

Smith shook his head. "It belongs to Cooper Kincaid. He owns Kincaid Inc. For generations, since before the 1880s, the family's been into sugar and real estate, the two big ones in the islands. So we're definitely talking old money."

"Why's Tong having the party there?" Rachel said. "Are they friends or what?"

"They're both patrons of the arts. Both own important collections. And both sit on the board of the Honolulu Art Museum. I don't know if that makes them friends. That's something you two can start finding out tomorrow night." Smith shoved himself off the cabinet. "Look, I'm outta here. I'll be in touch tomorrow. Let me know how you want to work getting the bugs in."

"Let me think about it."

"Right. But the sooner the better," he pointed out.

"I know."

When Smith was gone they started unpacking, splitting up the closet space and the dresser drawers, choosing sides of the sink and laying out soaps, shaving creams, lotions, toothbrushes in even rows. Snow was neater than she was. He refolded his clothes before he stuck them in the drawer; hung his pants together, then his shirts by color, then his coats; put all his shoes in a line on the floor; draped his ties over a hanger. She got impatient waiting for him but hid it.

When he was finally done, she took a long shower, then put a green robe on over her pajamas. In the front room she found him by the window watching Tong's apartment. "Tong show up yet?" she said.

"No."

She saw him check her over, doing it quickly, not making it obvious, and wondered for a second what he was thinking, but it was hard to read his face. That was something she'd noticed about him. A lot of people, most straight people, in fact, couldn't hide their thoughts. They hung like signs on their foreheads. Even crooks weren't that good. You could always see something if you looked hard enough. But Snow's face was like a smooth blank. No clues anywhere, and it bothered her.

Taking a seat on the couch, she said, "This is what we're going to be doing, Professor," and waited until he turned and gave her his full attention. "Tomorrow night when we go to this party, I want you to meet Tong and impress the hell out of him as a learned professor of art history and a collector of fine art. That means dropping names, bragging, bullshitting him, doing whatever it takes to get noticed in a crowd of five, six hundred people. You with me?"

Snow nodded and for a second there was something hard in his eyes that caught her attention. Then it disappeared.

"Okay," she said. "Somewhere along the way you swing the conversation over to his business. His turn to do some bull-shitting. After he gets it out of his system, you bring it up that you have a gemstone you're interested in selling to a reputable broker. Don't make a big deal out of it. Don't give too many details. Keep him curious."

"Then what?"

"Then what will probably happen is this: Tong will agree to take a look at the gemstone. He'll set up an appointment with you. Before the appointment, he'll make some calls, check you out. You have a classy reputation, Professor. That's why I wanted you along. When Tong checks, he'll find you live well, have good taste in art and jewelry and an impressive collection of paintings. He'll find you interesting, figure maybe you've got something worth taking a look at. So we'll have him where he's the one who wants to see you."

"One small detail," Snow pointed out. "If and when we do see each other, what do I sell him?"

"This." Her purse was near her on the floor. She rummaged through it, passed him a velvet bag, and waited while he looked inside, then looked at her like he was seeing her in a new way.

"You kept it," he said.

"For this job. Afterward it goes back to the Camden Gallery."

She took the bag, made sure the pink diamond was still in it, then said, "The theft of this made a splash even in the Honolulu papers. Tong will know what he's looking at. If he makes a move to buy it, we've got him on a stolen-goods charge."

"Wait a minute. I want him on more than that."

"So do I, Professor. If he's the one, I want Tong in jail for murder. But we have to take it step by step. First we see how he reacts to the pink diamond. How he plays it. Does he make an offer to buy it or does he act shocked and call the police? If he acts shocked then we have a problem."

"What are the chances he'll go that way?"

"He could if he thinks it's a setup. Police push hot goods to see who bites. If Tong tends to be suspicious, he might think that's what's going on. Again, that's why your reputation's important. He'll probably figure wealthy art collectors don't dirty themselves working with cops."

"What if he makes an offer to buy the stone?" Snow said.

"Then we'll know the chances are pretty good he's the one heading the stolen jewelry ring and not simply some businessman who doesn't know what his employees are up to. We'll also know he's the one responsible for the murders of Johnny Haid and Victor Chang.

"So if he does make an offer," Rachel went on, "what you do is put him off for a few days, tell him you have to think about it. At that point, if it comes to that, you each know something about the other. You know he buys stolen goods. He knows that either, one, you buy stolen goods and that's how you got the piece, or two, that you're a thief. But the best way for it to go is for him to think you do the stealing."

"Why?"

"Because before he died, Johnny Haid was trying to break a jewelry ring run by Danny Tai. What I'm guessing is they like to hire freelancers. Guys who'll pull three, four jobs for them, make some nice money, and move on. What we want is for Tong to hire you for the same kind of work."

"If he does?"

"If he does, we can set him up. Get him on videotape hiring you to pull a job for him. Then let the local police watch him accept stolen goods from you. After that, we blow open his whole operation, here and in L.A. And we nail him for the deaths of Haid and Chang."

Parting the curtains a few inches, Snow took another look at Tong's apartment. "Why was Haid killed?" he said.

"The way he got hit, I know it was a setup. My guess is they found out he was a cop."

"How?"

"I don't know."

"What if they find out you're a cop? What are the chances I end up like your friend?"

"If Tong checks me, all he'll find is that I'm a freelance writer with art as my special area of interest. It's a tight cover. There should be no—"

"How tight?"

"As tight as it can get."

"As tight as Haid's?"

She caught his point and said, "Life doesn't give guarantees."

"That's why I like to hedge my bets."

"So do I. Don't worry, Professor. If I can keep you alive, I will."

"I'd appreciate it," he said dryly.

"The last thing we get straight is why I'm with you. What we'll tell Tong is we're here together on a holiday. We let him think we're lovers. That way, where you go, I go."

"Do you know I'm a thief?"

She thought about it a moment, then said, "Let's make the stealing your secret. Something you and Tong have in common. Something that separates you from the straights." She could feel the tension that had driven her since Haid's death change into exhaustion. She rose and stuck her hands in the pockets of her robe. "Anything else, Snow?"

For a moment he didn't move and she wondered if he'd heard her. Then he let the curtain go, turned, and his eyes found hers. There was something unexpected in the way he studied her. It made her heart start pounding; she could feel it at the base of her throat like a small, agitated hammer. She felt suddenly as if she were standing somewhere high and dangerous, where the air was thin and hard to breathe. "If there's nothing else," she said, keeping her eyes firmly on his and forcing herself to sound calm, "let's call it a night."

"Who sleeps where?" Snow asked.

"You got a quarter?"

He grinned. "So you're a gambler, Detective."

"Sometimes. When I have to be." She took the coin, flipped it, and covered it with her palm. "Your call."

"Heads."

She raised her hand. "You lose, Professor. Enjoy the couch."

At midnight in the bedroom of his apartment, Jacob Tong poured a pale yellow wine into a crystal goblet, then lit a thin cigarette, puffed on it once, and left it burning in an ashtray. He was a thin, smoothly handsome man with milk-white skin and light brown eyes that were strange for an Asian. Over red satin pajamas he wore a gold velvet robe, which he closed and tied as he padded across the white carpet to the desk near his bed. For a moment he studied the phone, then, smiling coldly, picked it up and punched in numbers. While the connection was being made, he tasted the Chablis.

At the other end of the line Danny Tai was in bed with his wife. It was late, but neither was sleeping. The jangle of the phone made them jump. Tai's wife, clutching at the blankets, began to tremble.

After four rings, Tai warily picked up the receiver and said, "Hello?"

"Hello, Danny. It's Jacob. How are you?"

"Fine, Mr. Tong."

"I'm happy to hear that." Tong sat on the edge of the bed and crossed his narrow ankles. "And how is your wife? And your little girls?"

"They are all fine, Mr. Tong."

"You're very lucky to have a family, Danny. To have people who care about you. I hope you realize that. You must take good care of them. Make sure nothing happens to hurt them."

Tai said nothing, but the receiver in his hand grew damp.

"You were supposed to call me this afternoon. I waited a long time for your call."

"I know, Mr. Tong. I'm very sorry. I was busy and when I could call I worried it was too late and I might disturb you."

"You are very considerate. I appreciate it. So. Have you any news for me?"

"Not yet, Mr. Tong."

"That's too bad."

"My men are still looking," Tai added quickly. "They'll find the witness. You have my word."

"All right, Danny. I value your word." Tong loosened his tie and drew it off. "Because I do, you have one more day to keep it."

"Thank you, Mr. Tong."

"Call me tomorrow evening. And this time, don't make me wait." Abruptly he hung up and punched in Robert Moon's number. "It's Tong," he said when the phone was answered. "Tai is useless to us. Take care of him now. When you're done, put him where he won't be found."

He hung up, walked over to the window, and gazed at the harbor. In the moonlight the water shimmered. Several small boats crowded the wooden docks. He liked the way the piers curved into the ocean, and he liked the low, sagging warehouses and the narrow alleys twisting between them. They reminded him of Hong Kong. If he stared long enough, he could almost believe he was home.

Suddenly his head jerked up.

He looked across the street at the dark apartment building.

He felt someone in it, awake like he was.

Someone who was watching him.

SIX

IT WAS YOUR TYPICAL upper-class art party, Rachel thought. Guests dressed to the nines, flashing their jewelry and their pedigrees. Booze flowing easily, the smell of money in the air. The smell of privilege. On a raised platform, on a white baby grand, a delicate-looking blond man was playing "Rhapsody in Blue," one of her favorites, only she could barely hear the music, the room was humming so loudly with voices.

It was a spacious room, decorated with slick, gray, armless furniture, smoked-glass tables, and gray rugs on a gray wood floor. Track lights circled the ceiling, directed at the abstract paintings and sculptures that filled the walls and cabinets. On both sides, glass doors opened onto verandas, one facing the city, the other overlooking a wide lawn and a tree-lined drive that curved into the road leading down the mountain. For the party, all the doors were open, and the air drifting in was warm.

Rachel glanced around for Snow, wondering if he'd managed to hook up with Tong yet, and, not spotting him, decided to make her way toward the music. She hated crowds but loved Gershwin. And the piano player wasn't half bad.

"And what do you think of it?" an angular woman in a long blue dress asked, catching Rachel's arm as she passed.

"What do I think of what?"

"That." With a cigarette dangling precariously out of its holder, the woman made a sloppy gesture at an elaborate ice carving of flowers and flying birds. "Tell me, do you like it or not?"

Rachel said, "It's very interesting," then wondered how much longer the woman would manage to stay upright.

"There," the woman slurred happily, flouncing back to the group of four elderly men with whom she'd been arguing, pulling Rachel with her. "You see? She thinks it's very interesting. She didn't say tacky. Or tasteless. She said interesting." The woman turned back to Rachel. "These academic snobs have been telling me that ice is not a proper medium. They think it's . . . it's . . . what did you say it was, Benjamin?" She tugged on the tuxedo collar of the most conservative-looking man in the group.

The man replied patiently, "I said it wasn't serious enough, Claire," and at the same time struggled to disengage her fingers.

"Exactly. That's exactly what he said," she went on, releasing the lapel and swinging back to Rachel. "Not serious enough. But what I want to know is, who the hell are they to tell the rest of us what is and isn't serious?" She leaned into Rachel's shoulder and mumbled confidentially, "I mean, aren't you just sick of small-minded, stuffy old men telling us what is and isn't art? I know I am. I am sick to death of the dictates of dried-up old weasels—"

"Claire."

The woman's body tightened and she quieted at once as a blond man quickly approached. When he put his arm around her waist, she shuddered and looked helplessly at Rachel. "I don't want to go to my room," she said. "Please don't let him make me."

"Be quiet, Claire." He smiled apologetically at Rachel, then motioned to one of the maids serving drinks. "Take Mrs. Kincaid to her room. See that she takes her medication."

"No," the woman whimpered, starting to squirm. "I don't want to go."

The man tightened his hold and gave her a shake. "Don't make a fuss, Claire."

"I won't go. I won't."

"You're not doing this to me tonight," he hissed, then thrust her firmly toward the maid. "Take her upstairs. Right now."

Outside of the man's arms the woman seemed to compose herself. She smoothed her dress, gathered her dignity, and looked straight at Rachel. "You see," she said without emotion, "the truth is my husband doesn't love me. I've tried to make him, but I can't because he's in—"

"Will you be quiet?" the man snapped, cutting her off. Then to the maid he said, "And will you for God's sake get her out of here?"

As the maid guided Claire out, the man said, "I apologize for my wife's behavior. She's not well."

"Will she be all right?"

"She'll take her pills and go to sleep. All this excitement is too much for her." He looked restlessly around. He was a plump man of medium height with thinning blond hair and washed-out blue eyes, probably in his late thirties. His mouth was soft and petulant like a young girl's.

"This is your home?" Rachel said.

"All mine."

"It's very beautiful."

"Thank you." He smiled unhappily.

"The artwork's extraordinary."

"Do you think so? So many people don't like anything painted after 1900. If they're not given realistic little images that tell a realistic little story, they get very annoyed."

"I like the Moderns," Rachel said.

"Do you? How delightful. Tell me why."

"I suppose because the finest art illuminates its own time. I'm interested in the world we live in, not one that died centuries ago."

"So am I." The man's smile was happier. "I'm Cooper Kincaid, by the way."

"Caitlin West."

They shook hands, and Kincaid said, "Are you a collector?"

"I'd like to be, but I can't afford it. Actually, I'm a writer. I write articles on art."

"If you were a collector, who would you collect?"

Rachel smiled. "That's an interesting question. I think for the early Moderns, Jasper Johns, definitely. Rothko, of course. And Stella. For more recent artists, Longo and some of Salle's earliest work. Also Schnabel."

"Your tastes and mine are almost identical." He again restlessly scanned the room, then said, "Look, I don't know about you, but I find all of this boring as hell. Would you like to see my real collection? My little treasures? I think you would be able to appreciate them."

"Yes, very much."

"Good. Follow me." He led her out of the living room and along a long, thickly carpeted hall, stopping halfway down it at the only closed door. He unlocked it and twisted on the light. "After you."

She stepped into a large room that was half gallery, half library. On the walls between the bookcases were Rothkos, Stills, Nolands, Newmans looking almost sedate beside the vibrant canvases of Schnabel and Longo and Salle.

Kincaid let her glance around a moment, then said, "What do you think?"

This is one of the best collections I've seen, and I've seen many."

"Thank you. Go on, take a spin around. I don't invite many people in here." He threw himself on the couch.

"Why not?"

"I can't bear ignorance. Or the lack of taste. Or small-mindedness."

"Perfectly good reasons."

Kincaid was quiet a moment, then he tossed his head back and laughed. "They sure as hell are, aren't they?"

Rachel took her time circling the room and learned two things about Kincaid: he had money and he had taste. Even his more eccentric choices worked. It was clear he wasn't a dabbler. The works before her made up a serious collection.

"I like the way you look at art," he said as she returned to the couch."

"How is that?"

"Like you're looking at the paintings and not simply seeing your own preconceptions. Most people do that. They expect to understand what they look at. To fit it into neat and tidy mental concepts. When they can't, when the art demands a kind of surrender of the intellectual process, they find it unbearable." He paused, then said, "So tell me. What sort of articles do you write?"

"Interviews mostly. With artists and collectors." She began to smile. "I think, Mr. Kincaid, that I'm coming up with a terrific idea."

"Please call me Cooper. And what idea is that?"

"I'm here on a holiday. I had no intention of working, but now that I see your collection, I think an article on Honolulu art collectors would be fascinating. If I decide to go with the idea, would you let me interview you?"

He straightened up, clearly flattered. "Of course. It would be my pleasure. If you like, I'd also be happy to introduce you to some of the other local collectors."

"Would you?"

"Sure. We're all pals. It's a tight little group in a tight little town. Only three or four of us are the big guns when it comes to art collecting here."

"Who would you say is the biggest?"

"We're all fairly equal. It's what we collect that differs. I like the Moderns, the Abstract Expressionists in particular. Parker Anderson goes for the Old Masters. And Jacob Tong tends toward the Impressionists, though he also has some excellent Oriental pieces. We each despise the others' tastes, but we try to be good-natured about it.

"I suppose," Kincaid went on, leaning sideways and finding a bottle of brandy in the cabinet beside the couch, "if I were to be absolutely honest, I'd have to say Jacob's collection is worth the most, though he's very secretive about its value. He keeps all his paintings locked up in a tiny room, never shows them to anyone. People are always speculating on what he has. But I've seen them. Many times. They are quite extraordinary," he added reluctantly.

"You and Mr. Tong are friends?"

"Friends? Not quite," he said, his voice suddenly strained. "I think it would be more accurate to call us associates. Jacob doesn't have friends." Suddenly Kincaid's gaze flew to the doorway.

Rachel followed it.

An exceptionally beautiful Chinese woman stood there like an ivory carving. Flawless skin. Blue-black hair woven into an intricate knot on her neck. A slim body encased in a cream-colored silk sheath.

Kincaid rose immediately, in his haste almost dropping his brandy. "Excuse me," he said, "but there's someone I have to talk to."

"Of course."

She followed him out, taking one last look at the Rothko by the door. It was simple stuff—one square yard of blue squares on blue—but she figured it had cost about fifteen years of her salary. She wondered what it was like to be rich enough to hang fifteen years of a cop's salary on a wall in a locked room.

After locking the door, Kincaid said, "Contact me at my office about the article. It's in the directory. Kincaid Inc." Without waiting for a reply and without making introductions, he took the Asian woman's arm and guided her down the hall in the direction away from the party.

"There was another case similar to the stolen Goya," Snow said. He and the Asian were standing near the open doors leading to the veranda. The crisscrossing lights of the city could be seen far below.

"Which is that?" Tong said.

"In Tokyo, in the fifties, a Renoir was taken from a wealthy collector. The thief asked for a ransom, then changed his mind and said he'd return the Renoir if the collector donated it to the Tokyo Museum. It seems he felt the museum needed an example of the artist's work."

"As good a reason as any for stealing a painting."

"Altruism? Yes, it's the one justifiable reason for theft."

"Perhaps," the other man said, but without conviction. "It's warm in here. Shall we get some air?"

Snow nodded and followed him outside. Tong was sleek in the way wealthy Asians often were. Expensive suit. Expensive watch. A piece of jade on his left finger worth thirty thousand dollars. His face was pale and hairless. His hair was pure black and combed straight back from a high forehead. The way he walked, as though he were half gliding, the way he held his body elegantly erect as he moved, reminded Snow of his father's business partners—three Chinese gentlemen who would come every Sunday to their Hong Kong home for dinner, wearing pointed shoes and felt hats, with linen handkerchiefs folded meticulously in their silk suit pockets. They were polite and cultured and civilized. Except for the eyes. Their eyes, Snow remembered, were as cold as death.

Like Tong's were.

They walked to the railing and looked down on the city. A patchwork of lights flowed to the solid dark of the sea. Overhead the moon drifted in and out of swiftly moving clouds.

Tong said, "You're quite versed, Professor, in the history of stolen art and jewels."

"I have an interest in the subject."

"A somewhat strange pursuit for a scholar."

"Maybe. But the notion of ownership is a curious one."

"In what way?"

"It comes down to the question of who should own art." Snow deliberately let a professorial note enter his tone. "Museums, which allow everyone to view the work? Private citizens because they're lucky enough to afford the price of beauty? Or persons with the power to simply take what they want?"

"Don't persons with power usually take what they want?"

"Usually," Snow agreed. "The question is, is it moral?"

"In the case of power," Tong said, turning to face Snow, "perhaps morality is not an issue."

"Morality is always an issue."

"Is it? I think for some, Dr. Snow, but not for all." He looked back at the view. "Now tell me about your collection. What does it emphasize?"

"The Impressionists and Postimpressionists."

"So does mine." Tong smiled. "We are clearly both men of taste. Have you any Van Goghs?"

"One."

"I have two."

Now Snow smiled. "Gauguins?"

"One."

"Two," Snow said.

Tong laughed with pleasure, then fingered a vine hanging from the overhead latticework. "How long will you be in Honolulu, Dr. Snow?"

"Two weeks."

"Then you'll be here for the showing of the Martinos Collection."

"The José Martinos Collection?"

"You're familiar with it?"

"Who isn't?"

"Yes, it's quite a gathering of art and gems."

"Possibly the best in private hands," Snow said.

"You may be right. Particularly the gemstones. Several of them are one of a kind. Have you ever seen them?"

"Years ago. They were on display at the London Art Museum."

"Then you haven't seen José's latest acquisition. The Red Heart diamond. Are you familiar with the stone?"

Snow nodded. "A seven-carat blood-red diamond carved into the shape of a heart. But I thought Fairchild in England owned it."

"He did. A year ago he sold it to Martinos for an undisclosed sum."

"And it's included in the collection you're showing here?"

"Yes. If you have the time, we're having an opening reception on Sunday. You and your traveling companion must come and take a look. You can be my special guests."

"We'd like that very much."

"Excellent." He stepped back from the railing. "Well, as much as I'd like to continue our conversation, I suppose I must see to the others." He held out a slender hand. "I am very happy we met, Professor."

Snow shook his hand, then said, "There is one thing I wanted to discuss with you."

"Of course."

"I've heard that you broker jewelry between private parties."

"On occasion."

"Do you ever handle large pieces?"

Suddenly the Asian's mouth thinned as though he felt insulted. "The larger the better, Dr. Snow. As a matter of fact, two days ago I sold a ruby necklace worth a half million dollars. My clients, you understand, look for, and buy, only the best."

"Then I have something you might be interested in seeing."

"I'd be glad to look at anything you have."

"Perhaps tomorrow?"

"Around four?" He handed Snow an ivory-colored business card. "My address."

"I'll be there at four." Snow pocketed the card and glanced back at the crowded room. Rachel was making her way through the throng, angling sideways, weaving around clusters of guests, until she noticed him on the veranda and tipped her head in a brief acknowledgment. With an odd pleasure he watched her emerge finally from the crush of people, step outside, and walk toward him, her hips defined under dove-gray silk, her hair a loose tumble of waves, the jade pendants dangling from her earlobes mimicking the color of her eyes. Smoothly, as though she'd done it a hundred times, she slipped her arm through his, pressed close, and smiled at Tong.

Snow liked the way she felt against him.

He made the introductions, then Rachel said, "What were you two talking about?"

"I was just inviting you and Dr. Snow to an opening reception at the Honolulu Art Museum," Tong said.

"How kind of you."

"Then I'll see you both there. Now you'll have to excuse me. I really must make the rounds."

The moment Tong re-entered the living room Rachel dropped her arm. "Everything's set with the showing?"

"We do it tomorrow."

"Good. Let's get the hell out of here. I hate parties."

SEVEN

AT TEN O'CLOCK FRIDAY morning, Capt. James Towers walked into Artie Lee's pawnshop in Chinatown. At a jeweler's bench Artie Lee was poking a screwdriver into a watch, working it around with his pudgy fingers. He had a magnifying glass hooked in front of one eye.

"What's going on, Artie?" Towers said, and Lee's gaze flicked up, then dropped uninterestedly back to the watch. "Okay, screw the friendly bullshit. What do you know about Danny Tai?"

"I hear he cooks good mu shu pork."

Towers smiled perfunctorily. "You always were a real comedian, Artie."

The man shrugged. "What do I have to tell? I don't owe you."

Towers took one step, caught the neck of Lee's shirt, and hauled the man out from behind the bench. "What's the word on Tai?"

"The word is, Captain," Lee said calmly, his eyes contemptuous, "that his troubles are over. There's only peace and silence in his life from now on."

Towers let him go, giving him a shove backward. "Tai's dead?"
"That's what the fish say."
"Who did it?"
"I don't know."
"Bullshit."
"Suit yourself."
"Who's taking over?"
"Taking over what?" the man asked innocently. "You must know something I don't know, Captain."
"Don't jerk me around. You know everything that goes down in Chinktown."
"Not this time."
"Why not?"
"The winds are changing. The first shall be last."
"What the fuck does that mean?"
"It means, Captain," the man said, picking up the watch again, "you should watch your back."

As Snow crossed the office, he noted the contents of the jewelry cases lining three walls. Diamonds in one, rubies, emeralds, sapphires in another, every shade and shape of jade in the third. "Very impressive," he said.
"Thank you." Tong assessed him a moment, then pushed forward an ivory cigarette box. "You smoke, as I remember."
"Yes." In the case were thin brown Chinese cigarettes that Snow recalled from Hong Kong. He took one and let Tong light it. "Excellent," he murmured.
"In life often the smallest things give the most pleasure. This is my pleasure. I began smoking these as a young boy in Hong Kong, and once a week I have them flown in. An expensive habit, I will admit, but well worth the cost. Now tell me," Tong said, angling his head so that his eyes became thoughtful slits, "what are your pleasures, Nicholas?"
"Mine are mostly visual." He knocked an ash neatly against the lip of a white jade ashtray. "I can remember as a child sitting for hours before a painting I admired."
"And did you always prefer the Impressionists?"

"No, that preference came later, after certain events encouraged me to seek the lightness of those artists. In the beginning," he went on, "I was partial to Medieval art, then, of course, Rembrandt. At that time I believed only a spiritual base could give value to a painting."

"What changed your mind?"

"I learned that the spiritual is found indirectly. I began searching for the subtle."

A brief frown altered Tong's face. "You're a curious man, Professor. Quite unlike most Westerners I meet. You did say pleasures. What else besides paintings?"

"Gems. My mother owned a rather impressive jewelry collection, and when I was very young—no more than three or four—I'd make her lay the jewels across her bed. It was a world of color and translucence I could lose myself in. I was intrigued that all that beauty came from beneath the earth. Of course, their monetary value also caught my interest."

Tong laughed, then rested his chin on folded hands. "You share my love of beautiful objects and their value. That arouses my curiosity. What is it you've brought to show me?"

Snow reached into his coat for the pouch and at the same time palmed a microphone. "This," he said, and slid the bag forward. With his other hand he right-sided the transmitter and stuck it under the desk close to the leg.

Tong picked up the bag and tipped it. Like a piece of light the diamond dropped into his hand. He stared at it for a moment, then said, "I've never seen this depth of color in a pink diamond. Let me see it in the sun." Taking tweezers and a loupe he went to the window and turned the stone over and over, examining it from all sides. "Amazing," he finally whispered.

Snow said, "Yes, it is," and reached for another brown cigarette.

It was half smoked by the time Tong returned.

"Diamonds like this are rare," the Asian said. "In fact, I know of only one twelve-carat pink diamond of such intense color. It belongs to a collector name Joseph Hanover. That particular stone was on loan to the Camden Gallery in Los Angeles for a special showing of important jewelry pieces. The odd thing is a week ago it was stolen."

"It was?" Snow said and blew out smoke.

"I read in the papers that the police are completely baffled by the theft. Whoever took it was very clever." He leaned back, his gaze flat and cool. "Tell me if I'm wrong, but I think this is that stone, Nicholas."

Snow waited a beat, then smiled. "You're not wrong," he said.

"Then logic tells me you are either an acquaintance of the thief or the thief himself. In either case, you've taken a serious risk in bringing this to me. I might report you to the authorities."

"You might," Snow said without concern.

"It would, of course, be the honorable thing to do."

"It would. I suppose the question is, are you an honorable man?"

"I have my moments."

"And is this one of them?"

Rolling back his chair, Tong scrutinized Snow across the wider space. Then he said, "How much do you want for the piece?"

"Five hundred thousand. Firm."

"Absolutely firm?"

"Yes."

"You're asking over top dollar."

Snow said, "If you were selling it to another dealer, yes. But you deal retail. You'd be selling it to a private client. At a half million, you could make fifty percent. One hundred percent if you have someone who's been waiting for a stone like this."

"The problem is I don't, and because of the circumstances I can't make a lot of calls." Tong shook his head, looking as though he were trying to figure out an angle and not coming up with one. "I'll have to think about it."

"Take until tomorrow. Let me know at the opening."

"All right."

"Until then." Snow put the diamond back in the bag and began to get up.

"There is something I would like to know, Professor."
"What?"
"Why did you come to me?"
"Because of who you are. Your reputation. The clients you deal with. I wanted to meet you. To see if we could do business together. I thought this"—he tossed and caught the bag—"might make an interesting introduction."
"Certainly a memorable one."
"You'll let me know tomorrow one way or the other?"
"Yes."
"Fine." He pocketed the bag and stood.
"Tell me this," Tong said, rising along with him. "For my own curiosity. Which are you? The acquaintance or the thief?"
"I work alone, Jacob. Always alone. It's an old habit."

Tong swung his chair slowly back and forth.
Nicholas Snow.
Unreadable eyes. Impenetrable mind. Very disturbing. He rubbed a finger across his lower lip, then pressed the first button on the intercom.
At once, a small, muscular Asian in a black suit and lightly tinted glasses came in. "Yes, Mr. Tong?"
"I want you to check out this Professor Nicholas Snow and the woman with him, Gregory. They're staying at the Royal Hawaiian. Take a look through their room. Then make some calls to Los Angeles. Find out if they are who they say they are."
"Yes, Mr. Tong."
"But not to Captain Towers." Carefully he mashed the cigarette. "The captain's being phased out."

At 9:30 Friday night, Andrew Solomon used his own key to open the wrought-iron gate fronting the offices of Kincaid Inc. Instead of following the covered walkway that led directly to the main entrance, he veered across the courtyard and cut through the open garage, coming out on the far side of the building, where rarely used metal stairs led to the second landing. He took these and used another key to unlock the narrow door at the top, pushed it quietly open, then waited a moment for his eyes to adjust and his heart to calm down.

He was a small, slender man with wispy gray hair and dainty hands. High up on a thin nose he wore thick horn-rimmed glasses. Behind them, his eyes were perpetually worried. When he could see the shape of the hall, he forced himself to move. As he passed the old man's office—Walter's office—Solomon's nervousness gave way to a pang of anger. Why had the old man died? he wondered bitterly. Why had he left the business to the son? Everything was different now, bad now, and he didn't like it. Kincaid Senior would never have stood for what the boy was doing to the company. Not the wild spending, not the son's insolence toward the company's oldest, most loyal shipping clerk. He was more than a clerk really. A confidant. A friend. That's how it had been between him and Walter.

But he also felt a pang of guilt. What he was doing could ruin Kincaid Inc. When the old man was alive Solomon would've given his life for the company—in fact, he had, hadn't he?—but with the boy in charge, he could do this, squelch the guilt and do it.

After Cooper's office he passed the staff room and the manager's office, then his own. When he reached the accounting department, he unlocked the door, snapped on a flashlight, and went straight to the filing cabinet beside the computer. In the bottom drawer he found the income and expense files for the last two years. He pulled these out along with the spreadsheets and laid them on the floor.

Yes, there it was. He hadn't made a mistake. He flipped to the next sheet. There again. To be sure what he thought was going on was really going on, he'd have to compare these figures with shipping records for the same period. He folded the printouts and stuck them in his pocket. Then he shut off the light, closed the door behind him, and stood in the hall.

It was 9:40. In five minutes the night watchman would be making his rounds. It was too late to do more. The shipping records would have to wait until tomorrow. He could go in during lunch when everyone was out and take them. Yes, that was a good plan. That's what he would do.

Solomon hurried back down the hall and peeked out the door. No watchman. Carefully he stepped down the stairs so his shoes wouldn't click against the metal, then retraced his path through the garage and courtyard, slipped out the gate, and moved as fast as he could toward the street where he'd left his car.

Rachel had done her first stakeout with Haid. This was six months after her graduation from the academy, when she was still young enough and dumb enough to think it would be like the movies. You sat in a comfortable car a block away from the mark, watched a building, and after a while the bad guys showed like they were supposed to and you got out of your car and nailed them.

Only it hadn't happened exactly that way, Rachel remembered.

They'd spent three days in a Toyota freezing their butts off, getting leg cramps, eating stale sandwiches and staler doughnuts, drinking enough coffee to keep their hands shaking for days. She'd lost fifty bucks playing low-ball with Johnny, won it back shooting craps in a shoebox, and lost it again in a couple of hands of gin.

By the time the lieutenant pulled them off the stakeout, they'd stopped speaking to each other and both were coming down with colds. And the guys who were supposed to rip off a warehouse full of designer handbags never showed.

So much for the movies.

Snow put her coffee on the table and joined her on the couch. She was checking Tong's place with the scope.

"Anything yet?" he asked.

"He's still not home." She pushed the scope aside and rubbed at the stiffness in her neck. "You sure there's no way he'll go the five hundred thousand tomorrow?"

"Not unless he finds a ready client. I don't think he'll buy it outright."

"Why not? It's a one-of-a-kind piece. He could decide to put it in stock and sell it later."

"It's too much money," Snow explained. "At five hundred grand it's just about top dollar. There's not enough room for him to move. He'd have to tie up a lot of cash and hope he can find a buyer fairly quickly. In the meantime, he's paying interest or losing interest. So unless he comes up with a customer, I don't think he'll go for it. He might make an offer, but if he does I can turn him down."

"You'll have to go to the opening wired. I want whatever gets said on tape."

Snow nodded.

Rachel drank some of the coffee, thinking. Then she said, "I want you to start setting up Tong tomorrow. Let him know you're considering pulling some jobs here. Ask a couple of questions about the territory, what's available. But keep it low-key. Just enough to make him start thinking about using you."

Behind them a voice came over the recorder. Rachel swung the scope around.

"Is it him?" Snow said.

"Yeah. He's in the office on the phone." She reached back and turned up the volume. In a few seconds they caught on that Tong was speaking to a woman, making arrangements to show her a pair of jade earrings the next day. He asked if her mother was back from Hong Kong, listened, then hung up.

"What's he doing now?"

"Taking off his jacket—a white tux, must've gone someplace fancy—now he's crossing the room"—she paused a moment—"and going into his apartment." She watched for another minute. "I don't think he plans on helping us out and opening the blinds. We need a mike in there."

"Can it be done?"

"Maybe from the outside. Use a high-powered bug. The problem is, his unit's not up against any other apartment. If it was, we could go into the other apartment and place the mike on a common wall. The way it is, the only outside wall's the corridor, and it's wide open. We put something on it and it'll be seen."

"Why don't I go in?"

"I don't want to chance it. We can live without the extra microphone. Your job's to find out if he hires thieves. That's the priority. In the meantime, it doesn't look like anything's happening tonight, so let's get some sleep. Who's got the bed?"

"You."

"Yeah? Good. See you in the morning."

An hour later, still wide awake, Rachel slipped into the kitchen to get a drink. She was pouring it, being as quiet as possible, when Snow switched on the lamp and said, "Can't you sleep?"

"No." She lifted the bottle. "I thought this might help. Sorry if I woke you."

"You didn't."

"Want some?"

"Thanks."

She poured him a glass and carried it over, then, out of habit, looked at Tong's apartment. It was closed up and dark.

"You always have trouble sleeping?" Snow said.

"Not always." She shrugged and gave a quick smile that she saw surprised him. "But most of the time I do. I'm used to it." She took a sip, glanced at him, then back at the window. After a few silent moments she said, "Well, I guess I'll give the bed another try."

"You ever play poker, Detective?"

"What?"

"You know, cards? Jacks-back, low-ball. You ever play a few hands?"

"Now and then."

"For money?"

"On occasion."

"Good. Have a seat." He picked up a deck from the table, shuffled it twice, noticed she was standing. "Sit down," he said and began dealing.

She watched him, the way his hands moved, the way the light was hitting his face, and realized she didn't want to go back to the empty bedroom. She said, "Before I take that seat, I ought to tell you something."

"What?"

"I'm a lousy sport. I'm not kidding. I hate to lose."

"Don't worry. So do I. Pick up your cards."

"Just remember, I warned you." She got comfortable and

checked her hand. He'd given her a pair of queens and the rest was garbage. "What are we playing?" she said.

"Name it."

"Jacks-back?"

He nodded and shifted cards around.

"Let me have three. What's the pot?"

"Dollar in, dollar a raise?"

"Fine."

Both found their wallets and tossed money on the cushion between them, then Snow dealt her three more cards. One was a queen and she could barely hold in a smile.

"Raise it one," he said.

"Wait a second." Her head came up sharply. "What're you doing upping the bet? You didn't take any cards."

"Don't need any. You putting in a dollar or not?"

"Don't rush me, all right? I'm thinking." Biting her lip thoughtfully, she threw in a dollar, then after a moment added another. "It's going to cost you one to see what I've got."

He added three and smiled. "It'll cost you two."

"Look, Snow," she said irritably, "I've been around. I know all the tricks. And not taking cards is the oldest trick of all."

"Is it?" he said, then casually nodded at the pot. "You're short two bucks. You staying in or not?"

"Jesus." She made a show of pulling out more money, then flinging it down. "Okay. Let's see this great pat hand."

Snow spread the cards. Three jacks and two tens lined up by color. He picked up the cash and grinned. "Sorry."

"Don't be." She reached for the deck and began shuffling it vigorously. "The night's still young, Professor."

A hour later Rachel was ahead forty dollars and they had switched from scotch to brandy. She felt up and loose, sharp but at the same time on the brink of being drunk. She also felt lucky. Snow was dealing, concentrating on the cards, telling her while he tossed them back and forth about a game he'd played in Monte Carlo, an all-night, high-stakes match against two wealthy English dwarfs, a Middle Eastern prince, and one of the most successful call girls in Paris. On one hand he'd pulled an ace-high straight and picked up fifty grand.

"Did you take it and walk?"

"Of course," Snow said. "The dwarfs weren't happy, but the prince didn't give a damn. To him it was pocket money."

"What about the call girl?"

"She called it a night and invited me to her room."

"Did you go?"

"No. Can you go high?"

"Can't. Let me have two. Why not?"

"She would've robbed me and I needed the money for something else. And I don't believe in casual sex."

"What?" Rachel gave a hooting laugh, then coughed, then shook her head. "Christ, I think that's the first time I've ever heard a man say that."

"Is it?"

"Most men believe the casualer the better."

"I'm not most men."

"Yeah," she agreed, studying him. "Maybe not." All at once, she didn't feel drunk anymore. All she felt was the same sensation of standing somewhere high and dangerous she'd felt with him before. Part of her wanted to step back onto safer ground; part of her—the crazy, reckless part—wanted to step over the edge and see what was there. Just as suddenly, the sensation floated off, like a cloud blown away by a light wind, and she felt safely drunk again. "Okay," she said, carefully counting out dollar bills, "I am now raising the pot by three big ones."

Snow matched the bet and increased it by three, which made her look up suspiciously. Before she could comment Snow said, "How long have you been a cop, Detective Starr?"

"A cop? Let's see. Eleven, no, twelve years. Joined right out of college. Couldn't wait to save the world." She gave a short, cynical laugh. "Talk about being dumb. What's the bet?"

"Three to stay in."

"Right. Anyway, it took about six months for me to figure out the world didn't want to be saved. You want a refill?" She was pouring more brandy into her glass, and when Snow nodded, she filled his. "I almost quit then."

"Why didn't you?"

"Johnny Haid talked to me. Sat me down in a bar one night and got me to see that if all the good guys—that's me, by the way—gave up, the war was lost. So I stayed. Only I'll tell you something, Snow." She slouched toward him, lowered her voice confidentially, aware that she was feeling punchier now, slurring some of her words, but not really caring. "The good guys hang in there, but I think we've lost the war. What I'm doing, what all cops are doing, is we're pretending things are still okay, you know? That there's still a point to putting on our uniforms and a reason to hit the streets every day. We do this so the citizens don't get too nervous." She sat back and tried to concentrate. "Whose bet is it anyway?"

"Yours."

"Right. I'm folding. Good God, take a look at this hand. It's my deal?"

"Your deal."

She scooped up the cards, shuffled them clumsily, and caught Snow smiling. "What?" she said.

"You're really soused."

"No," she said, shaking her head and frowning as though annoyed by his error. "To be absolutely accurate, Professor, I'm slightly soused, which is just the way I like to be. So pick up your cards. Let's play."

"I think you should call it a night, Detective."

"I'm fine. Perfectly fine. I can handle a few drinks." She pushed the cards at him insistently. "Go on. Pick them up."

With a shrug, Snow gave in and looked at his hand. "All right. Let me have two."

"Two coming up." Having got her way, she felt friendly again. "Will you tell me something, Snow?"

"If I can."

"Why the hell do you steal? I don't understand it. I mean, you have a good job, a respectable reputation, a comfortable income. Why steal?"

"I enjoy it."

"You enjoy it?" She gave another hooting laugh. "I think you're the first thief I've known who's ever said that."

"A lot of us feel that way. Most don't admit it."

"You mean it's not the money?"

"The money's part of it. Half of it. But it's more than that."

"What else?"

"It's the getting in and getting out, it's being somewhere you're not supposed to be and knowing you might not get away with it, and getting away with it. That's the—I don't know—the high, I suppose you'd call it."

"And that's what you like?"

Snow smiled slyly. "That and the money."

"Right. Your bet."

"Raise it five." He lifted his drink. "My turn to ask a question."

"Go ahead."

"You ever been married?"

She lifted her eyes. "No. What about you?"

"No."

"Why not?"

"No time. Never met the right woman. You?"

"No time. Never met the right man."

"What if you did, Detective?"

"Meet the right man? Uh-uh. I don't think it's in my cards, Snow."

"Why not?

She dealt herself three new cards and took a deep breath. "Because I've been alone too long. I'm stubborn and opinionated. I'm not good at compromising. You know, that whole fifty-fifty bit that makes for good relationships? I'm a lousy cook. I hate to clean. I don't want kids or a picket fence or a two-car garage. I've seen too much—most of it enough to kill your faith in the human race—and I drink too much, and I get mean hangovers. I don't trust too many people—hell, I don't like too many people, and mostly, I don't give a damn if anyone likes me. You see what I mean, Snow? Not in my cards." She looked back at her hand. "So whose bet is it anyway?"

"Mine. And my bet, Detective Starr, is you're not half as tough as you pretend to be."

"No?" She spread out her cards to show three aces and two kings. "How's that for tough?"

Snow laughed as she reached for the pot. "Not bad."

"Your deal."

He didn't pick up the cards. For a moment, he simply watched her, then he reached over and ran the back of his hand down her cheek.

What she first felt was surprise—that he would touch her; that she would like the feeling as much as she did. Then the thoughts came in a crazy rush: that she wanted him, but he was a thief; that they were alike, but they couldn't be; that her mind was clear, but she was drunk. For an instant she could see them together, her and Snow. Only it would never happen, she told herself. Never. Because he was a crook. A greedy, cheating, sonofabitch crook she was dumping in jail once she was done with him.

She got up unsteadily, picked up the bottle of brandy, and said coolly, "You were right, Professor. It's late and I'm drunk and I think it's time I called it a night."

EIGHT

IT WAS 8:00 A.M. in Los Angeles and sunny, with the temperature hovering around seventy. In Chinatown, Capt. James Towers pulled into a red zone and parked behind a delivery van. After hunting around in the glove compartment, he found his POLICE ON DUTY sign and propped it on the dashboard. Then he crossed the street.

From the front door, the Moon Noodle Factory looked like a small operation. A twenty-by-twenty-foot space lined with wooden racks piled with packages of dried noodles, a short counter with an aging brass cash register on top and, in a corner, a grimy Coke machine.

A woman in an apron was sitting behind the counter filing her nails and looking, Towers thought, like she couldn't care less about selling noodles. When she saw him she nodded. "Mr. Moon is expecting you."

Towers opened the sagging screen door behind her, walked down a short hall and into a noisy kitchen. Six workers streaked with flour and sweat were rolling out dough. Towers skirted them and entered a longer hall. On the left side of the corridor was a closed door. Behind it, he knew, was the room where the Moon Noodle Factory's real business took place. After that the hall made a bend to the right and went straight into Moon's office.

Towers walked in and looked nonchalantly around, checking to see if any of the creeps who worked for the man were hiding in the shadows, but the place looked clean.

Robert Moon was sitting in a red velvet chair playing solitaire. From the expression on his face, Towers knew he took the game seriously. Moon was big for a Chinese, husky, especially in the shoulders and arms, as though he worked out with weights. He had thick eyelids and lips—looked a lot like a toad, Towers thought—and no hair except for a scraggly beard on his chin.

Moon stopped flipping cards and said, "What is it you want, Captain?"

Towers walked right up to the desk. "I want to know what the fuck's going on," he said, "that's what I want."

Taking his time, Moon placed a queen on a king. "What do you mean?"

"Tai's dead and I wasn't told about it. I had to find out on my own."

"His death wasn't your concern."

"Since when? I've always been told things before."

The other man turned over three cards and tossed a black four on a red five. "Some changes are being made. When they're completed, you'll be informed."

"What kinds of changes?" Towers asked tightly.

"Just changes."

"How long will it take?"

"It's hard to say. A little while."

"A little while? Listen, Moon, I placed the order for the dope right on schedule like Tong asked me to. It's sitting on a boat off Guaymas waiting for our payment. I have Tommy Morales here and his people in Mexico asking me about their money and they're not asking real nicely, you know what I mean?"

"We understand that." The Asian flipped three more cards. "Be patient."

"Hey, pal, tell them to be patient. They're giving me two days to pull my end of the deal or else. Can I get the money in forty-eight hours or not?"

"I'll have to talk to Honolulu."

"I've been trying for a goddamn week to talk to Honolulu," he shot back, giving the desk a hard shove. The cards scattered everywhere, and Towers liked the anger that flashed through Moon's eyes. "Look, I want to know this afternoon when and where I'll get the cash. You tell Honolulu that."

"If I can reach Mr. Tong."

"Make a point of reaching him," Towers growled. "This is not some fucking game I'm playing here. The Mexicans are my contact. I need the money to pay them or I'm in deep shit, and if I'm in deep shit, then believe me, so are you. You tell Jacob Tong that. And tell him I want to know what's happening. You tell him to give me a call. Got it?"

"I'll see what I can do." The Asian stared hard into Tong's eyes, not hiding his hatred, then blinked lazily and returned to his cards. "You know the way out, don't you?"

"Yeah, don't get up, you son of a bitch. I know it."

"Wake up!"

Rachel felt the blanket being pulled back, cool air, and someone's hand on her shoulder, shaking her. She flopped over, covered her face with her arms, and groaned. A jackhammer was beating in her brain and she was an inch away from losing whatever control she had over her stomach. "Christ." She gave a blind shove at the hand. "Go away."

"C'mon, Detective. Up. Something's going on at Tong's."

She took her arms off her face and Snow came spinning dizzily into view. "Where?"

"At Tong's. Remember him? Let's go." He hauled her off the mattress.

"Okay, okay. Will you stop shouting? I can hear. What time is it anyway?"

"About one o'clock."

"In the afternoon? Why the hell didn't you wake me?"

"After last night, I thought you needed the sleep."

"Shit." She grabbed her clothes off a chair, yanked on her jeans, and followed him into the living room.

Voices were coming over the recorder.

Rachel picked up the binoculars and the hangover died. "That's Cooper Kincaid, the guy who threw the party," she said. "Turn up the recorder. And flip on the video camera. We might want this on tape."

In Tong's office, Kincaid was pacing back and forth while Tong slouched lazily in his chair.

"He knows something," Kincaid said.

"What does he know?"

"I'm not sure. Something." Seeing Tong idly setting his watch, Kincaid stopped abruptly and said peevishly, "Am I boring you, Jacob?"

Tong gave the stem another slow turn. "Just tell me what happened."

"Okay. Andrew Solomon walks into my office this morning —doesn't even knock, the little worm—and says he wants to discuss a business matter with me. I don't know what it is, Jacob, but I don't like the man. Never have, all the years he's been with us. Dad liked him, though. They were real buddies. I could never figure it out."

"What was the business matter, Cooper?" Tong said impatiently.

"All he said was, 'Mr. Kincaid, I know about the misplaced containers and I know about the money.' I said to him very innocently, 'What are you talking about, Andy?' and he gives me this look like he knows what I'm trying to do and says this isn't a good place to talk, he'll call me later. In the meantime, he wants me to keep in mind that he'll be needing some cash."

"What else?"

"What else?" Kincaid shouted. "That's not enough? He's blackmailing me."

"Correction. He's trying to blackmail you."

"What's the difference?"

"The difference is whether you let him get away with it. Right now he thinks he has something on you. That's all. Don't admit to anything and what can he do?"

"What if he does have something?"
"What could he have?"
"I don't know." He waved his hand loosely. "Company records, something."
"I told you to clean up your books, Cooper."
"I know. I intended to. I didn't think anyone would—"
"You didn't think, period. That's the problem." Tong glared disdainfully at Kincaid, then chose a cigarette and snapped on the lighter. "When Mr. Solomon contacts you again, find out what he thinks he knows."
"All right. Then what?"
"If he can cause us trouble, we'll take care of him."
"Wait a minute. What does that mean?"
"Take a guess, Cooper."
"Christ," Kincaid said, shaking his head miserably. "I never meant for it to go this far."
"We go as far as we have to."
"This is the last shipment, Jacob. I've had enough. It's too risky."
"We'll see."
"I mean it. This is it. No more. I'll talk to Ivory about it."
"Do as you please." He glanced at his watch. "You have to leave now. I have a client coming."
"I mean it. I want out, Jacob. I don't like what's going on."
"Neither do I."

"We're following him." Rachel caught her jacket off the card table and her bag off the pass-through counter. "C'mon, c'mon, let's go."

Within minutes they were speeding down the circular garage, brakes squealing, wheels skidding. Coming around the last turn, she jerked the gearshift back into first and gunned the gas. The outer wheels lifted, the car slid, missing a thick stone post by inches, then righted itself and exploded onto the street.

Snow said, "Smith wasn't lying about your driving." A second later a silver Cadillac pulled out of Tong's building. "It's Kincaid."

Rachel let three cars pass, then pulled in behind him. The

Cadillac made a left on Merchant Street, moving through a row of steel-and-glass buildings fronted by palm trees. Four blocks later, at Nuuanu, it made a right. The high-rises gave way to low, turn-of-the-century stone structures. Ahead of them, in the distance, they could see the slope of a valley and the jagged ridgeline of dark green mountains. Kincaid drove two more blocks, then turned into a parking lot. Rachel waited until Kincaid got out of his car, then drove in just in time to see him run across the street and go into a shop called the Gallery Ivoire.

She had the car door half open when Kincaid came out with a woman. They stood in an alcove between two bay windows filled with abstract paintings and framed posters. Kincaid was doing all the talking. He looked even more agitated now than he had at Tong's.

"That's the Chinese woman I saw at the party," Rachel said. "The one he left with."

"Whatever he's asking her," Snow pointed out, "she's telling him no."

"Seems that way. Which means whatever Kincaid's involved in with Tong, he's not getting out of, at least for now." She nodded back at the alcove. "Take a look at that."

The woman had started struggling in Kincaid's hold but was trying to keep it low-key enough not to draw attention. Finally she yanked free, said something that made Kincaid shut up with astonishment, and strode back into her store, slamming the door in his face.

He seemed about to follow, then changed his mind and hurried back to his car. He started to open the door, stopped, hit the roof, and looked back at the gallery. After taking a few steps in that direction, he stopped again as if he couldn't make up his mind. Finally he turned back to the Cadillac, banged the roof one more time, got in, and sped off.

"Unhappy man."

Rachel said, "I think we just got lucky, Professor."

Thomas Morales didn't look Mexican, with his blond hair, green eyes, and lightly tanned skin. He looked, Towers thought, like a real American. But when he opened his mouth anyone could tell he was south-of-the-border, despite the law degree and the thousand-dollar suit and the Rolex watch and the Lamborghini.

Morales had an office in Beverly Hills where he specialized in theatrical law. Some of his clients were big Hollywood names. When Towers walked in on Saturday afternoon, dripping with rain, a familiar-looking blond woman was sitting in the waiting area, paging through a fashion magazine, one of her shapely, high-heeled feet thumping against the coffee table. She was chewing gum and on her, Towers decided, it looked sexy.

"Tommy's with someone," she said, smiling and giving him a once-over at the same time.

"I'll wait," he said.

"Is it raining again? I'm so bored with the rain."

"Weatherman thinks more thundershowers."

"Oh, damn." She kept chewing, lips slightly parted, giving her a pouty look. "I hope you don't have a lot to talk about with Tommy because I'm starving and he's taking me to dinner."

"All I need is five minutes." He was staring at her breasts; he couldn't help it. They were huge and creamy and in imminent danger of tumbling out of her low-cut suit, which, if they did, Towers admitted, would be the high point of an otherwise lousy day.

"Oh, good. I'm Didi, by the way. Didi Hollister." She paused as though expecting him to recognize the name, which he didn't. "You a friend of Tommy's?"

"Business acquaintance."

"Really? That's how Tommy and I met. He handles my contracts. You know, looks them over, makes sure I'm being taken care of, stuff like that. 'Course, now we're more than acquaintances." She wiggled a little, then crossed her legs and looked toward Morales's closed door. "God, I wish he'd hurry up."

As though he'd heard her, Morales came out into the hall. Another familiar-looking blonde was with him. She appeared to have been crying. "Don't worry about anything," Morales was saying, patting her arm. "Leave everything to me."

"All right." The blonde dabbed a lacy handkerchief at her

nose. "I can't tell you how much I appreciate what you're doing for me, Mr. Morales."

"I want you to call me Tommy."

"Tommy." She said it breathlessly and reached for his hand. "You'll be in touch?"

"In the next day or so."

"I'm looking forward to it." She held on to his hand a moment longer, smiled as if no one else were in the room, and walked out.

The second the door closed, Didi said, "Who is she, Tommy?"

"She's a new client." He raised his brows questioningly at Towers. "Did we have an appointment?"

"No. This is a drop-in visit. I need to talk to you."

"She was flirting with you. I don't like that, Tommy."

Morales's gaze flicked back to the woman. "I told you before, Didi," he said evenly, "don't push it." He rolled his eyes at Towers as if to say, The shit men have to put up with, and Towers gave him a sympathetic smile.

"I saw the way she was looking at you, fluttering those fake lashes."

"She's a client. That's all."

"That's all it better be."

"We'll talk about it later, sweetie."

"And I'm hungry, Tommy."

"I'll keep it short," Towers said.

"She's driving me crazy," Morales grumbled as he shut the door. "Wants to be with me twenty-four hours a day. Keeps calling me, checking up on me. You know why I don't dump her?" He sat and motioned Towers to do the same. "Take a guess."

"Her tits?"

"It's that obvious?"

"Yeah," Towers said and smiled.

"In a month or two when they start to bore me, I'll get rid of her. You want a drink?"

"No thanks."

"So. Are you here to give me the cash?"

"I don't have it yet," Towers said, not letting any weakness into his voice. If the Mexican heard weakness, he'd be on him like a snake.

"Time's running out, my friend."

"I'll have it." He made himself sound irritated. "I still got forty-eight hours."

The other man turned his wrist. "Forty-five."

"Forty-five, forty-eight, what the hell's the difference? Anyway, I'm here for something else."

"What?"

"Tong and Moon had Danny Tai killed."

"You're kidding," Morales said, sounding genuinely surprised. "When was this?"

"Thursday night, I think. Body hasn't turned up yet. Probably never will."

"Why'd they hit him?"

"He was making some on the side. And he brought a cop in by mistake."

Morales nodded. "I heard about the cop. Real messy business."

"He was one of mine."

Morales tilted back his chair and looked troubled. "Then you got problems, my friend."

"Nothing I can't handle."

"Good, because I don't want any hassles with the payment."

"There won't be. I've been doing business with you for a long time. I always pay my bills, right? I want you to do something for me."

The Mexican smiled. "You're asking me for a favor?"

"You could call it that. Someone was with the cop when he was killed. Saw the whole scene and got away."

"Bad luck for you," Morales said, again looking concerned.

"Ask around. See if there's any word on the street who was working with Haid."

"Why me? You have as many contacts as I do."

"I want to keep it low."

Morales considered him a moment, then said, "All right." He

lowered his chair. "Check back tomorrow. And remember. Favors get returned."

"I'll remember." Towers stood and put his hands in his pockets. Even in here it was cold.

"You don't look so good," the other man said.

"It's this goddamn weather," Towers said and sneezed.

"Well, take care of yourself, Captain. You and I, we take a trip to Mexico in two days. I want you to be healthy. I want you to have a good time."

Towers said, "Don't worry, I'll be fine," and started for the door.

"And, Captain," Morales added, "have the money, okay? I don't want problems. I get real down when I have problems."

"I'll bring the cash. You have my word."

"And I'll bring Didi. Maybe one night, I'll let you have her. You'd like that?"

"Yeah, that'd be great." He gave Morales a look as though he couldn't wait.

But walking through the reception room he didn't glance at the woman or remember she was there. His mind was on the million dollars he had to come up with in forty-five hours to keep his word and maybe his life.

NINE

ANDREW SOLOMON'S COTTAGE WAS on an unpaved, tree-lined road off Kahala Avenue. It was the last of six small beach houses and the least cared for. The paint was a weathered gray, the steps sagged, the yard was overgrown and strewn with the rusting parts of old cars.

Rachel was parked a half block away. It was ten on Sunday morning, and for two hours she had been waiting for the man to leave so she could check the house for whatever it was he had on Cooper Kincaid. With the sun angling higher, she flipped down the visor, then opened the Thermos and filled a cup. As she sipped the coffee, she thought of Snow and realized she'd been thinking of him off and on all morning. Irritably she threw the Thermos back in the glove compartment and slammed it shut. She didn't need the man walking around in her mind, getting in her way. All she needed was for the shipping clerk to give her a break and get the hell out of his house.

As she was thinking this, the door to the cottage opened and a man came out and walked rapidly to the garage. He was wearing a brown suit, the same color as the ten-year-old Volvo that was parked half in and half out of the open-sided structure.

He looked as if he was going to church except that he was nervous, glancing around furtively as he struggled to get the key into the lock.

Anytime someone was nervous, Rachel found it interesting. She decided to change her plans and see what the man was up to.

She let him make the turn onto Kahala Avenue before starting the engine. Keeping a block between them, she followed him past the sprawling mansions half hidden by lush shrubbery overlooking the sea, past a lighthouse, then around the rocky slope of Diamond Head and into Waikiki. They wound along a wide park on a road shaded with ironwoods, then crossed Kapahulu Avenue and got onto the Ala Wai and stayed on it until McCully. As they made their turn, she was one car behind, then she dropped back, letting another car pull between them. At Punahou, they made a left and headed toward the mountains.

One mountain in particular.

Now she knew where they were going.

Solomon spent twenty minutes inside Cooper Kincaid's home, then rushed out looking furious, threw himself into the car, and sped back down the hill. She followed the Volvo along the outskirts of Honolulu and into Nuuanu Valley. A mile in, Solomon swung into the parking lot of what looked like a hospital but that turned out to be, when she drove past the sign on the entrance gate, the Banyan Convalescent Home.

On the street Rachel found a place to park with a clear view of the convalescent home's driveway, and waited. An hour later, finished with the Thermos of coffee, bored with playing Vegas solitaire on the front seat, she told herself she should have checked the house like she had planned to.

Suddenly the Volvo came out of the driveway and raced by her.

She didn't catch up with it until five blocks later when Solomon pulled into a small shopping plaza. She pulled in after him, then drove around while he parked and got out. He was crossing the lot when he stopped and turned and looked straight at her, and kept looking at her with so much fear in his eyes she thought of getting out and talking to him, thought of breaking her cover and offering her help in exchange for what he knew. Only the big question, of course, was could she trust him? Or would he tell Kincaid about her? She didn't know enough about the man to risk his choice. Breaking eye contact with him, Rachel kept driving, right out of the lot and down the road until she was out of his sight.

By the time she swung around in a service station, caught a red light, and came back up the street, Solomon and the Volvo were gone.

Pono Smith said, "You're sure he made you?"

"I'm sure. But I don't know if he got the license."

"We better dump the car anyway and get a new one."

"Yeah, okay," Rachel agreed. Smith was in the kitchen. She and Snow were on the other side of the pass-through counter. She said, "What was your cousin Moses able to find on the guy from H.P.D. files?"

"Andrew Solomon's a sixty-one-year-old shipping clerk. He's been with Kincaid Inc. for thirty-five years. He and Kincaid Senior were friends, but the word is he and Cooper don't get along. He rents that beach cottage you tailed him from. Has no family except for a retarded younger sister. She's the one he was visiting in the convalescent home. She's been there about two years, ever since she had a stroke. The place isn't cheap. Around forty grand a year, not counting medical care. Add another twenty thousand for that, minimum, and she's costing Solomon a lot of money."

"Good reason for blackmail."

"Uh-huh."

"What about Cooper Kincaid's girlfriend? Anything on her?"

"Her name's Ivory Lin-Cho, and she does own the Gallery Ivoire. I got somebody you can talk to about her." He scribbled an address on a card. "Name's Kwai Jones. Runs a high-class whorehouse in Chinatown. Seems she knew Ivory Lin-Cho back in Hong Kong."

"You trying to tell me Lin-Cho was in the business?"

"That's what Moses heard."

"How?"

"Chinatown was my cousin's first beat. He made friends there. When he asked around about her, someone said to talk to Kwai Jones. Kwai owes Moses a big favor, so she's willing to chat."

"When?"

"Monday. It's all set. She's expecting you." He looked at Snow. "How are you working it tonight with Tong?"

"I'll be wired. If he makes an offer on the diamond we'll have it on tape."

"Won't mean shit in a court of law," Smith said, "but at least we'll know what league he's playing in. What if he doesn't make an offer?"

"Then I'll sell him something else."

"What's that?"

"Me."

The Honolulu Art Museum sat in the heart of the city, a few blocks south of a mountain-chain of apartment buildings. The architecture was Spanish. Thick stone walls. A red tile roof. Arched doorways leading into a grassy central courtyard. When Snow and Rachel arrived, guests were milling about the lawn and the wide veranda and inner yard. Snow handed Tong's card to a tuxedoed guard.

"Mr. Tong is expecting you," the guard said. "Please follow me." He led them through a side door, down a private hall, and out into a sculpture-filled yard crossed with a red ribbon. Beyond the ribbon stood the new wing, a hexagonal structure of glass and chrome. "Mr. Tong's in there. You can go on in."

The room had thirty-foot ceilings, white marble floors, and predominantly nineteenth- and twentieth-century art on the walls.

"Quite an impressive collection for a small museum," Rachel said.

"Not bad. A bit dull. Except for that," Snow said, and guided her across the room to a large canvas slashed with blues and reds and grays.

"You like de Kooning?" she asked.

"Not particularly. But this isn't a de Kooning."

"What do you mean?"

"I mean I watched this being painted. Look here and here. Myles was never happy with these sections. Whined about it a lot."

"Hold it. You're telling me somebody other than de Kooning painted this?"

"Myles McDonnell did."

"Who the hell's Myles McDonnell?"

"A friend of mine."

"And this is his work?"

"Yes."

She looked at the oil again and said, "I don't believe you."

"It's the truth."

"I know a little bit about de Kooning's style. His choice of color, his brushwork, his attitude. They're all in this painting."

"Myles is very good."

"If he really painted this, then he's a genius."

"I'll tell him you said that. He'll appreciate it."

She stepped nearer to the canvas, scanned it silently, wondering if she was being conned. "Did your friend really do this, Snow?"

"Yes."

She looked around at him and knew suddenly that he wasn't lying. "Christ. Who else does he copy?"

"He's particularly good with the Impressionists, but he can knock off the Old Masters and the Moderns almost as well."

"What happens to the originals?"

"I beg your pardon?"

"The originals. If your friend makes copies, what do you do with the real paintings?"

To gain a few seconds he smiled, and she could see in his eyes he was figuring a way around the question. He strolled over to a Pollock, said, "I've never liked his paintings much, have you?" and then turned along with her as brisk footsteps tapped against the hardwood floor.

From around a massive bronze sculpture Jacob Tong appeared, dressed in a white linen suit and white shoes. "So this is our little museum, Professor," he said. "What do you think?"

"I'm impressed."

"Good. Then I'm assured the others will be, too. Now come. José's collection is in the special exhibition room. We can look at it in private before the others arrive." He let Snow go first and fell into step beside Rachel. "Cooper tells me you're a writer, Miss West."

"Yes."

"And that you write about art."

She nodded.

"Tell me," he said. "What do you think of those?"

"The Rembrandt sketches? They're very fine."

"Why?"

She stopped and began smiling. "Is this a test of some sort?"

"Please indulge me and answer the question."

"All right. They're exceptional because of the economy of the line, the almost Oriental simplicity, and the deep spirituality in every brushstroke."

"Yes, exactly." He appraised her another moment, then made up his mind. "Cooper says you're interested in writing an article on our collections. I would like you to do so."

"So it was a test," she said, and Tong laughed.

"Yes, I suppose it was."

They began walking again.

"To do the article, I'd need to interview you and Mr. Kincaid and take some time viewing your collections."

"An interview with you would be most welcomed. And both our collections would be at your disposal. All we ask in return is that mention be made of this new wing. That sort of publicity does wonders when we ask for future contributions."

"Of course."

"Shall we start tomorrow? The sooner the better, don't you think? Let's say in the afternoon. Nicholas, you'll come as well," Tong added, leading Rachel into a semidarkened gallery, dramatically lit with spotlights. "Perhaps you'll find my small assortment of artwork amusing."

Snow, standing transfixed in front of a jewelry case, could only nod in assent.

Rachel said, "Tomorrow afternoon will be fine."

"Around three? Good." He slipped his hand around her arm.

"Our friend seems entranced. Shall we see what's captured him?"

"That," Snow murmured when they were beside him.

In the center of the case, gleaming in folds of white velvet, was a blood-red stone carved into the shape of a heart.

"My God," Rachel whispered.

"The Martinos diamond." Snow couldn't keep the awe out of his voice. "Known simply as the Red Heart. It shouldn't exist, but it does."

"A red diamond is one of the rarest gems in the world," Tong explained. "This one is close to priceless. Perhaps it is priceless. José was extremely generous to include it in the show."

"Is it safe here?" Rachel asked.

"Quite safe. The case is completely wired, and during viewing hours there will be armed guards around it. After hours, it goes into a vault in the basement. The system of alarms in this museum is considered foolproof."

"There you are, Jacob." Ivory Lin-Cho was standing under one of the spotlights in the center of the room dressed in cream silk and pearls. Tonight her hair hung past her shoulders like a sleek black sheet. As she walked toward them, the dress flowed around her legs like waves.

When she reached them, Tong took her arm almost possessively. "Ivory, I want you to meet our special guests, Professor Nicholas Snow and Caitlin West."

"We're very honored to have you here tonight," she said, looking only at Snow. Jacob," she continued, her eyes still on Snow, "Cooper is in the office. He wants to speak to you before the building opens."

"Tell him I'll see him later."

"He says it's very important. Perhaps you should talk to him now."

"Everything is important to—" He stopped and sighed. "All right. Nicholas, Miss West, please excuse me. Ivory will take care of you while I'm gone."

"Perhaps you'd like to see the Monet?" the Chinese woman said. "A pond scene, small, but very beautiful. It's this way."

* * *

"How much does he want?" Tong said. He was leaning against a desk in a windowless office lined with books. Kincaid was slumped in a nearby chair.

"He says a hundred thousand, but who knows? Maybe he'll keep asking for more. Why shouldn't he? He's got me by the goddamn balls."

"What did you tell him?"

"What do you think? I did my outraged act. I said he was crazy. I said I didn't have that kind of cash, he should know that. You know what he told me? He told me to sell my paintings. My paintings, Jacob. Of all the unbelievable gall."

"Tell me again what kind of proof he claims to have."

"Papers, some kind of papers," Kincaid replied impatiently. "Accounting sheets, shipping records, God knows what else. He knows about the containers, too. Not the details but the general picture. This has to be the last shipment."

"How long is he giving you?"

"Three days. He wants the money on Wednesday."

"What did you say to that?"

"I told you. I said he was crazy. Asking me to sell my paintings. I don't give a damn what he needs the money for."

"What do you mean?"

Kincaid's mouth twisted bitterly. "This is all altruism, Jacob. The money's not for him. He has a sister. I don't remember her name. Eileen, Arlene, something like that. A retard. A few years ago she had a stroke, can you believe it? Now she's in a convalescent home. Can't talk or walk or do anything. A real vegetable. He wants my money to take care of her."

"Convalescent homes are expensive. One hundred thousand won't last long."

"You think I don't know that?" Kincaid said. "This is just the beginning. He's going to keep nailing me until the woman dies."

"What do you want me to do?"

"Whatever it takes, isn't that how you put it? I want him out of my life."

"All right. He's out of it."

"Just like that?"

"Just like that."

"Okay." Kincaid nodded, then stared at the floor a couple of yards ahead of his polished black shoes. "Okay," he said again, but there was no energy in it.

Tong said, "I have to get back to the party," and rebuttoned his coat as he stood. "Don't worry about anything. It's under control."

The oak staircase spiraled down to a cavernous hall. Snow was following Tong, their footsteps echoing against the thick stucco walls. "What's down here?" he said.

"Storage rooms, some offices, the staff library. We can talk in here." The Asian unlocked a door and let Snow go first, then locked the door behind them. "So we won't be disturbed." Tong waited for Snow to sit, then settled into the chair opposite him. "I want you to know, Nicholas, that I think the pink diamond is exquisite. However, at the moment I have no need for it. Please understand that I made several calls to various contacts advising them of its availability. However, for the present, there's no interest in it at the offered price. Under other circumstances," Tong continued, "I would buy it for my own stock. At the moment, regretfully, my capital is tied up."

"Well." As though the meeting was over, Snow stood. "Another time, perhaps."

Tong said, "Please wait a moment," and motioned Snow back to the chair. "Let me be honest, Professor. I find you very interesting. A respected teacher, a highly paid lecturer, an authority on art. Yet also a thief. Why?"

"For the money, of course."

Tong calculated him a moment, then relaxed and smiled. "Of course."

"I enjoy owning beautiful objects. When something presents itself on the market, and I want it, I like having the money to pay for it. Teaching is very satisfying, Jacob, but it doesn't buy Van Goghs. Or diamonds. So I steal."

"How long have you been a thief?"
"More than twenty years."
"And you've never been caught?"
"Never."
"What kinds of places can you break into?"
"Whatever's there. Banks. Galleries. Homes. Luxury condos with state-of-the-art security."
"What about museums?"
Snow nodded. "I've gone into museums."
"How many?"
"Six or seven."
"How difficult is it?"
"Depends on the museum. There was one in the south of France, very charming, with a nice gathering of eighteenth- and nineteenth-century art. There were no alarms at all. It took me ten seconds to get inside and another minute to take two Gauguins and one Matisse off their hooks and leave through the back door. On the other hand, a museum in Switzerland took two hours to break."
Tong said, "The Swiss are a careful people," then grew quiet, measuring Snow again. He said, "I have a proposition for you, Nicholas."
"What kind of proposition?"
"I want to hire you."
Snow glanced at the books lining the walls, working out in his mind how he was going to handle this. He decided to play hard to get. "Sorry, I don't work for anyone."
"You misunderstand me. The deal is strictly freelance. Two independent businessmen working together on a project of mutual interest."
"I don't think so. I told you before, I like working alone."
"On this you could make a half million dollars."
Snow's eyes came up. "Nice round figure."
"Round enough to interest you?"
"Maybe. What's being stolen?"
"The Red Heart."
He gave a low whistle. "You don't fool around, do you?"

"Are you interested, Professor?"
Snow waited a second, then leaned forward and nodded. "I'm interested."
"Good. Tomorrow we'll make our plans."

Rachel was waiting for Snow when he came out of the new wing.
"Let's talk over there," he said and they made their way to the dark lawn of the sculpture garden, Snow pulling out his cigarettes as soon as they got there.
"How did it go?" Rachel asked.
"He turned down the pink diamond. Said he couldn't afford it at the moment."
"That's it?"
"Not exactly. He made me an offer."
"What kind of an offer?"
Snow pulled deeply on the cigarette, then blew out the smoke. "He offered me a half million dollars to steal the Red Heart."
"What?"
"Five hundred thousand if I can get the Martinos diamond."
"Jesus Christ."
"Now we know who killed our friends," he said quietly, then looked sharply past her.
"What is it?"
"Tong and his lady friend are watching us." He dropped the cigarette, reached forward, and pulled Rachel into his arms.
"What the hell are you doing?"
"Kissing you, since we're supposed to be lovers." Dropping his hands to her hips, Snow put his mouth on hers, keeping the pressure gentle, not pushing anything, not making any moves, and still Rachel felt something inside her leap, out of her control. For a second she wanted to struggle, then, without thinking, she brought her arms up around his waist, waited a second, and let her mouth move on his. She felt him grow still and knew she'd startled him. Then he began kissing her, harder now, and the leap happened again, only stronger this time, her heart going crazy.
From somewhere nearby came voices and laughter, the click

of shoes on the stone pathway. They pulled apart, Rachel turning immediately to look for Tong because she needed a moment to steady herself. When she turned back, Snow was lighting a new cigarette and she saw that his hand was shaking. So it wasn't just her, she thought.

"Tong and Lin-Cho are gone," she said and he nodded. "Tong just took his first step toward the trap," she added. "We should get back to the party." Without waiting for him, Rachel started across the yard.

TEN

IN IVORY LIN-CHO'S APARTMENT, Tong was stretched out on white satin sheets, watching her in the dresser mirror as she brushed her hair. She was still wearing the cream silk dress she'd worn to the museum opening, only now the back was unbuttoned and he could see the milky whiteness of her shoulders.

"Who is he, Jacob?" she said.

"I'm not sure."

"Can he be trusted?"

"I'm not sure of that either. He was checked by my people in L.A. So was the woman. And I had Gregory Chee look through their hotel room. Both appear to be who they say they are. And yet . . ."

She put the brush down and faced him. "What?"

"There's something about him."

"What?"

"Something . . . elusive."

"And it troubles you?"

"Yes."

She crossed to the bed and lay beside him, resting her cheek against his chest. "Then why are you using him?"

"I need the Martinos diamond. Lee Chan no longer wants the Tokyo emerald. When he learned the Red Heart was out of José's vault, he wanted nothing else."

"Then bring in someone from L.A. One of our own people."

"I can't. Tai's death has been a disruption. Who can and can't be trusted is still unsettled. Better to use a stranger."

"What happens to the professor after he steals the diamond?"

"I haven't made up my mind. Maybe he and I will do more business. Maybe he will have to die. I don't know." He stared at the ceiling. "Our friend Cooper is getting nervous. I'm concerned."

"Don't be. I can handle him."

"Yes." He trailed his hands down her back to her thighs and heard her breathe in sharply. "I'm sure you can."

"Don't do that, Jacob."

"Why not?"

"Because it's . . ." She groaned as he slipped his fingers between her legs.

"Tell me."

"Unbearable." Twisting, she found his mouth and kissed him, and he thought of the first time he'd seen her in Lee Chan's living room, her black hair tumbling to her waist, her skin as fine as the ivory she was named for, her features as pure as any sculpture. He had wanted her. Until that moment, he had never wanted another human being.

Her arms slipped around him. She whispered, "I love that. Don't stop. Don't."

"Does Cooper touch you like this?"

"No."

"Why not?"

"I won't let him."

"Why?"

"Because he's not you." Suddenly her body tightened. "Jacob, please. Yes. Please. Like that."

He felt her shudder, wave after wave, and held her tighter. When she stilled, he buried his face in her hair and said softly,

"When we are done with Kincaid, I will kill him. Very slowly, very painfully, for even touching you at all."

Gregory Chee swung the black Porsche onto Andrew Solomon's street, cutting the engine as he neared the house. The cottage was dark, but the man's car was in the garage. Chee unbuttoned his coat but didn't take it off even though it was a hot night. Then he reached under the seat for the .45 fixed with a silencer.

As he crossed the lawn, he could hear the ocean softly hitting the shore, could smell the sweet, heavy scent of flowers. He thought, Not a bad place to die, and walked up the stairs.

The gun made a swift, popping sound as it knocked out the lock. Chee pushed in the door. A wide picture window let in light from the streetlamp. He gave the room a glance, dismissed it, and started down a short hall, checking the room on the right, the room on the left, finding nothing, going to the last room, where a faint pool of light spilled from under the closed door. He took a step back, then rammed forward, catching the door with the flat of his shoe, slamming it open with a ripping sound.

A small lamp was on and Chee could see the man in the bed jump up and clutch at the covers with a look on his face like any second he might crap in his pants. Solomon was small, skinny, pasty white like a slug, and Chee felt a rush of loathing, which was good; he needed that feeling to do what he had to do. He gave the mattress a hard kick. "Get up!"

Solomon clambered off, almost falling on his face, his legs were shaking so badly. "What . . . what do you want?"

"Where are the papers?"

"What papers?"

"The ones you took from the Kincaid offices."

"I don't know what you're—"

Chee slapped his mouth and Solomon curled over, whimpering.

"I'm going to ask you one more time," Chee said, "and if

you don't give me the papers, I'm going to put a bullet in your face."

"They're not here! I swear it!"

"Then where are they?"

"I put them in . . . in . . ." He began weeping, holding his hands over his eyes.

Chee stuck the gun next to his nose. "Where?"

"In my sister's room. In the convalescent home. But I can't get them until morning."

"Get dressed."

"Please. I'll give them to you tomorrow. I swear to God."

Chee picked up the pants and shirt draped over the back of a chair near the bed and threw the clothing on the floor near Solomon's feet. "Put them on. And don't take all night. We're going for a drive."

Kwai Jones lived in a suite of rooms above a bar and a tattoo shop on North Hotel Street. The parlor resembled a lush Victorian sitting room. Red velvet curtains with gold tassels hung from the windows. Wine-colored carpets covered the floor. On the walls were paintings of lions in violent poses. It was the middle of the afternoon, but the heavy drapes were drawn, the only light coming from dozens of flickering candles and a pair of small oil lamps.

Kwai Jones was sitting in a high-backed brocade chair looking peeved. "I am talking to you," she said in a clipped British accent, "because Moses Kahana asked me to and for no other reason."

She was about seventy-five, Rachel guessed, and still voluptuous, with a seen-it-all, done-it-all look in her eyes. She had jet-black hair and startlingly white skin except for circles of rouge on her cheeks and inch-wide streaks of iridescent blue smeared on her eyelids. She was half-Chinese but didn't look it.

Kwai Jones said, "Go ahead. Ask your questions."

"How long have you known Ivory Lin-Cho?" Rachel said.

"I met her fifteen years ago in Hong Kong."

"How?"

"She was living in the streets. I took her in, cleaned her up, gave her work. She was sixteen."

"What kind of work?"

The woman smiled dryly as if to say, Why ask what you already know? "I employed her as a prostitute."

"For how long?"

"She stayed with me six years. During that time I taught her everything. When she came to me, she was a filthy street whore, no better than a dog. I taught her how to dress, how to move, how to speak, how to please a man. I paid for her classes. French, English, history, art. I developed her mind. I understood her potential. I nurtured it."

"What do you mean, her potential?"

"I mean her uniqueness." Kwai sipped at her tea, then rested the cup on the lace doily draped over the arm of the chair. "I will explain something. Every ten years or so one woman comes along who has everything. Beauty, brains, elegance. But, above all, she has the uncanny ability to attract men, to fulfill their deepest desires and dreams. I saw this in Ivory when I brought her in. I did all I could to develop her capacities."

"Why?" Rachel said. "What was in it for you?"

"Perhaps I did it out of the kindness of my heart," the other woman answered. "That is a possibility, isn't it?"

"It's a possibility."

"I enjoy thinking it was part of the reason."

"Okay, what was the other part?"

"Money, of course. We live in a capitalistic world. It was a good business plan to develop Ivory's skills. Much like training a racehorse, or educating a brilliant student, hoping in the end the training and education will pay off."

"Did it?"

"She brought a lot of business to my house," Kwai Jones said, looking momentarily nostalgic. "All the men wanted her even though I charged for her five times the normal fee. But for the money she brought in," the woman added bitterly, "she got the best of everything. The finest clothes, the best jewelry, her own room, her own car. I did everything I could for her, spoiled her as I would have spoiled my own daughter. I even planned to bring her into the management of the business. Had she stayed with me, everything that was mine would have been hers. But she chose to leave."

"Why?"

"Something better came along."

"What was that?"

"Her prince."

"What do you mean?"

"Her prince, her savior," the woman explained irritably. "That's what the girls in the trade call the man who takes them out. Their prince. When Ivory was twenty-two, she quit my establishment and left Hong Kong."

"Any idea who the prince was?" Snow asked.

The woman's eyes glittered with resentment. "It was an old man. A very rich old man who was also a little strange. He used to come to my place and sit in the front room and watch the men and women go upstairs. That's all. He never touched any of my girls. All he wanted was to watch. Until Ivory appeared. Then I think he fell in love. Only I don't think he touched her either. He didn't like people coming too close."

"What did he do with her?" Rachel said.

"She was very beautiful. He liked to look at her."

"He gave her money for looking?"

"A lot of money."

"What was his name?"

"Lee Chan. Some people call him Tiger Lee Chan. He makes Green Jade Balm. Sells it all over the world. Makes millions every year. He's the one who stole Ivory from me. I think he still helps her, though she doesn't need it."

"Why not?"

"I've heard she has a new prince. I've heard he takes good care of her."

"Do you know who he is?" Rachel said.

"No."

"But you think she's still involved with Chan?"

"Yes. Why not? Ivory always was greedy. Why have only one prince when she can have two?"

* * *

Priscilla Belmont kicked her legs slowly in the churning water of the hot tub, letting the jet stream of bubbles foam around her breasts. She was thinking about Capt. James Towers and about the mink coat she'd seen on Rodeo Drive. What would it take to make him spring for it? Especially with the way he'd been acting lately. Grouchy and preoccupied. Like a real prick.

Maybe one wild, kinky evening in that hotel in Westwood that he was always dragging her off to. She hated it there, but he loved it. Loved the vibrating beds and the dirty movies on TV and the overhead mirrors. Loved her in those black-and-orange lingerie numbers he was always buying and making her wear.

Still, one night for a whole mink coat was a pretty good deal. She could handle it. And in his own way Jimmy was a sweetheart. When he wasn't acting like a prick.

The phone began ringing. She stretched her arms along the tub's rim, leaned her head back, and imagined herself strutting around in the new coat. They'd have to go somewhere nice for dinner. Maybe Ma Maison if they could swing reservations.

The phone kept ringing.

"Cilla, will you answer the goddamn telephone?" Towers was standing in the back doorway, taking off his coat. "I got a headache. The sound's driving me nuts."

"Okay, darling." So he was still in a lousy mood. So this was going to be a great afternoon, with him getting on her case for every little thing. Terrific. She hoisted herself out of the water and ambled over to the patio table. "Hello? Yes, he's here. One moment, please." She waved the phone. "It's for you, Jimmy."

Towers came down the steps. "Who the hell is it?" he whispered.

She palmed the receiver. "How should I know? Some man."

"Shit. Why'd you tell him I was here?"

"Because I didn't know I wasn't supposed to."

"Christ." He grabbed the phone. "Yeah?"

"It's Morales."

He said, "Hey, Tommy, how ya doing?" then swallowed hard and pulled off his tie, using it to wipe his face. He felt lousy, hot and cold, like he was coming down with the flu. "Look, Tommy, I'm still working on the money. I might need a little more time. A few—"

"This isn't about the money," Morales said.

"What, then?" Towers said, collapsing with relief onto a pool chair.

"That favor you asked me? I think I got a lead on your witness."

"Yeah? That's great. Lemme get something to write on." He stuffed the tie in a pocket, switched the phone to his other ear. "Okay, shoot."

"What I got is this. Haid was living in a place called the Palm Motel in Santa Monica. Guy who owned it, guy named William Pratt, was found dead four days ago in a warehouse near the airport. Word is, some of your Chinese friends paid some visits, asking him questions about Haid's visitors. Word is the guy didn't talk. But other people live in the building. They might have seen something. Might be worth talking to them."

"It's a good idea. Thanks for the info."

"Anytime. Now, what were you saying about more time?"

Towers felt the sweat break out on his face. "Maybe I'll need another day to get the cash together."

"What's the problem?"

"No problem. It's taking a little longer than we thought, that's all.

"Don't bullshit me, Jimmy."

"I'm not. Twenty-four hours. That's all I need. See what you can do on your end, okay? As a favor to me."

"You're the one owes me the favor."

"So I'll owe you two."

The line was silent for ten seconds. Then Morales said, "I'll make some calls, get back to you."

"Thanks."

Morales hung up and Towers leaned back and closed his eyes.

"You okay?" Priscilla said.

"Do I look okay?" he snapped. "Jesus, look at me."

"What's wrong, honey?"

"The whole fucking world is wrong, that's what's wrong."

"Oh." She slipped back into the hot tub.

Maybe she would wait until later to ask about the mink.

ELEVEN

THE PALM MOTEL OFFICE was padlocked and a handwritten sign was posted on the door.

CLOSED UNTIL FURTHER NOTICE
FOR RENTALS, SEE #12

Half-opened venetian blinds hung lopsidedly in the window. Towers stooped to peer through them. There was a TV on the counter, a girlie calendar on the wall, a floor fan next to an empty bookshelf, newspapers and beer bottles on the couch. Everything was generally neat, no signs of struggle or violence except for the bash marks on the door.

On the other side of a narrow strip of lawn was a row of duplexes. He cut across the soggy grass, making jumps for the driest spots to save his shoes, and checked the numbers posted on the jambs. Number 12 was the one closest to the pool. A television was blaring inside and he heard the sounds of cooking. Towers took out his badge and knocked twice.

From inside a man's voice called, "Hold on a sec. This stuff's burning."

Cupping his fingers, Towers blew into them to warm them, then stamped his feet while looking over the grounds. One-story duplexes painted light blue and brown lined up in an L shape around a pool sheeted with scum and yellow leaves. A half-filled parking lot with a neon sign in the corner flashed PALM MOTEL, then VACANCY, off and on in orange letters.

The door behind him was pulled back and a husky black man in overalls and an undershirt said, "Sorry to keep you waiting. You looking for a room?"

Towers showed his badge. "Towers, L.A.P.D."

"Oh. You gotta be here about Johnny Haid and Billy, right?" The man stroked his crewcut hair. "Might as well come in. Let me take my food off the burner," he said, shutting off the television. "You want something to drink?"

"No thanks."

The man came back, popping a can of Coke. "Okay. What can I tell you?"

"First off, what's your name?"

"Fred Waters."

"Have you spoken to the police before, Mr. Waters?"

"Sure. After Johnny's body was found, there were cops all over the place, asking questions. Then, after Billy got killed, some other cops came around. I told them what I knew, which wasn't much. Johnny Haid was a policeman, so you could understand why somebody might've killed him. These days, the way things are, it's dangerous being a cop. But Billy, he just owned this place. He never bothered nobody. Who'd want to murder him?"

"That's why I'm here, Mr. Waters. To try to figure that out. If you don't mind, I'd like to ask you some questions about both men. You might remember something now you didn't think of before."

"Sure, go ahead."

"Let's start with Haid. How well did you know him?"

"Not real well. Enough to say hello, shoot the bull about football sometimes, that's about it."

"Did he have visitors, people stopping by who you noticed?"

"You mean someone who looked like they might kill him?"

Waters scratched his neck. "Don't think so. He kept to himself, you know? Nice guy, but a loner. Didn't play cards with the rest of us. Didn't go out with friends. Didn't have no one coming over except . . ." The man scratched his neck again.

"Except?"

"Well, I just remembered. There was that woman who came around sometimes. She'd go into his place, come out maybe a half hour later. Not regular visits. But I sure as hell don't think she—"

"What did she look like?" Towers cut in.

"Well, let's see. Tall. Real pretty. And this hair." The man gave a disbelieving whistle. "She'd wear it free sometimes, you know? Oh, man. Long and red and wavy."

Towers straightened. "Red hair?"

"Yeah. Not bright red. Darker, like . . . like, I don't know, wood or something."

"How often did she come around?"

"Like I said, now and then. Once a month maybe. Maybe less. Drove this brown station wagon. Hey." The man snapped his fingers. "I just remembered. The night Johnny got shot, I saw her car."

"You're sure?"

"Yeah, I'm sure. She used to park it in the gas station after the place closed in the evening. I remember seeing it that night 'cause I took out the garbage and Billy keeps the cans behind the office and from there you can see the service station. I saw the brown wagon and I remember thinking what a lucky son of a gun Johnny was, having a lady like that. Then, boom, the next day I hear he's dead. But she couldn't have . . ."

"Why didn't you tell the police about the car and the woman?"

"I didn't think about it till now." The man rubbed the back of his head sheepishly. "I get forgetful sometimes, you know? Can't remember worth a damn. It's getting worse the older I get."

Towers tried to smile sympathetically. "I understand. You've been a big help, Mr. Waters. I may have other questions later on. Where can I reach you if I do?"

"Right here. I retired from the railroad ten years ago. Don't like to travel no more, so I stick close to home. You need me, you just knock on my door."

The traffic was light on Sunday and Towers drove fast, every muscle in his body taut. It took him less than twenty minutes to reach headquarters. He went directly to the personnel office. It was after hours and no one was working. Hitting the light switch, he headed for the filing cabinets.

Rachel Starr's folder was the last one under *S*.

He carried it to the nearest desk. The top page was her vacation clearance. He skimmed it until he reached the address on the bottom and a notation that where she was staying had no phone. Towers scrawled down the address, a route number in the Salem area, replaced the file, and went upstairs to his own office. On his private line he made a call to an old friend who worked for the Salem sheriff's department.

An hour later the friend called back and said, "Checked the place out, Jim. Completely deserted. No one's used it for months."

"Any messages?" Snow asked as Rachel let the door of the phone booth swing shut. Twice a day she checked with the front desk of the Royal Hawaiian, giving the desk clerk the impression that they were in the hotel.

"You got a call from your friend McDonnell. 'Returning your call,' the clerk said. What's that about?"

"I need a special tool to get into the museum. I want him to send it."

"Next time check with me first before you make personal calls," she said curtly, then wondered what was going on with her. Since the kiss in the museum garden, she'd been in a lousy mood. Maybe, she admitted, because a bad mood was safer than sorting out whatever it was Snow really made her feel. She checked the time. "We should get over to Tong's."

When they arrived, Tong was dressed in loose white trousers and a red kimono. He went behind his desk and pressed a spot on the wall. A panel moved back, revealing three carpeted stairs and a long hallway. At the hall's end he pressed another spot on the wall. A second door slid silently back. "My gallery," he said, moving into it.

Spotlights came on and struck the walls. Rachel stepped inside and gazed around, speechless. On the walls were incredible paintings. A Gauguin. A Matisse. A Cézanne. Another wall held an enormous Monet lily pond. A third, Vlamincks, Cassatts, pastels by Degas. On the fourth were two small Van Goghs. Without a word, she began to walk around the room.

What seemed like a long while later, she felt Tong lightly touch her arm. "Shall we join the professor?" he said.

Snow was on the other side of the gallery, utterly still, staring at the larger Van Gogh. He didn't move as she and Tong came up beside him.

"You like my Vincent?" the Asian said.

Snow gave one short nod and let his eyes return to the painting. "How long have you owned it?" he said.

"Nearly a year. A friend in Paris decided to sell it, and because I've wanted it for as long as we've been friends, he gave me first refusal. Come. Let's be comfortable." He motioned them to a gathering of chairs in the center of the room. "Now," he said to Rachel when they were seated, "what do you need to know about me for your article?"

For the next hour she questioned him on his preferences in art, his aesthetics, and the history of the collection. They talked about his choices for future acquisitions and his involvement in the Honolulu art community. Finally Rachel said, "Tell me, Jacob, which was the first painting you owned? Which one started the collection?"

"That one." He pointed at the oil directly in front of Snow. It was a Paris street scene done in winter at twilight. "I will tell you about it," he said, "but this story is personal and not for publication. Is that agreeable?"

"I'll keep it off the record."

"It was my father's. Obviously it's not an important work, but he loved it very much. My father's family lived in Peking," Tong went on. "Before the Revolution they were very wealthy jewelers. After the Revolution everything was taken from them—home, possessions, business. My father was too young and too ambitious to be a Communist. He decided to flee to Hong Kong, where he could remake the family's fortune.

"The family had hidden a few jewels from the authorities. They were special pieces, valuable pieces. It was decided to give them to my father for his new life. The problem, of course, became one of getting the jewels out of China. Hiding the gems in his satchel was too risky. Then my father thought of his painting. It was small enough to carry, and the frame large enough to hold the jewels. A chamber was dug into the frame and the gems hidden inside. For precaution, my father painted over the hated Western art, replacing the Paris scene with a rather amateurish rendering of mountains and clouds and tiger lilies."

"Was he ever stopped?" Rachel said.

"Three times. And searched three times. And frightened for his life three times. But each time he was allowed to go. A week after the last search, my father carried the jewels across the water into Hong Kong. And that is how my collection was started."

"It would make a great article," Rachel said, and the Asian smiled his agreement.

"But I can count on you to keep it to yourself?"

"Yes. Reluctantly."

"Very good. Now, Nicholas and I have some private matters to discuss. Perhaps you would like to look at the paintings a bit longer?"

"I would." She glanced from him to Snow with enough curiosity to convince the Asian she knew nothing.

Tong rose. "Shall we go to my office, Dr. Snow?"

They got back to the apartment a few minutes after six. The sun was setting, clouds were on fire across the sky and in the windows of Tong's building.

He was there now, Rachel thought. With his paintings and his jewels. Safe, comfortable, above the law, thinking he could get away with anything, even murder.

Her grip tightened on the curtains.

"You all right?" Snow said.

He was standing beside her, but she hadn't heard him come up. She felt her pulse quicken and tried to pass it off as nerves, but she knew she was lying.

"Are you?" Snow repeated.

"I want to get Tong, that's all. When the two of you were talking, why didn't you get him to set the date for taking the Red Heart?"

"I tried, but he said some arrangements still have to be made. He said he'd be in touch."

"When's that going to be? We need that date, Snow. And we need to know when and where he plans to pay you. We can't take it to the local police until the whole deal's set."

"I'm aware of that."

"Jesus, I hate this waiting around." She started past him and Snow caught her arm. "Okay, what's going on?"

She pulled free and glared at him. "What do you mean, what's going on?"

"You've been in a rotten mood for days. I'd like to know why."

"Look, Snow. You're here to help me get Tong. That's all. My moods are none of your goddamn business. All you have to worry about is how—" The phone rang and she grabbed it on the first ring. "Yeah, Pono, we're back. It went well. We— What?" Her voice rose sharply. "When? Goddammit! Where was he found?"

"What is it?" Snow said.

She covered the mouthpiece. "Andrew Solomon's dead." Then she said into the phone, "That's what they think? No. No way. What did it say?" She listened, shaking her head. "No, we don't take it to H.P.D. Because it's too soon, that's why. I don't care. Listen, have the cops been to his place yet? And what? Nothing? Okay, let me know whatever Moses can dig up. And something else. Ask your cousin to look up someone named Tiger Lee Chan. Hong Kong national with ties to Honolulu. I need whatever he can get. Right. Talk to you later."

She hung up, remained still for a long moment, then slammed her fist into the couch. "He was killed sometime this morning. They're calling it a suicide."

"Why?"

"They found a note, handwritten, saying he was depressed. It asked his insurance company to look after his sister."

"Where was he found?"

"In a car near the airport. Shot in the head. Pono says the gun used was found in his hand. Only his prints were on it. And the suicide note was on the seat beside him."

"Neat."

"Very neat. Pono wants to give the Honolulu police what we've got on videotape."

"What about you?"

She didn't answer right away. She was thinking of Solomon. How it had crossed her mind to warn him about Kincaid and Tong. How she'd put it off, afraid of breaking her cover. How he was dead now because of it.

She said quietly, "We don't give Tong up until we can put him away for life."

TWELVE

AT NOON IN LOS ANGELES, Towers was in bed with his mistress getting his back massaged. While Priscilla kneaded his muscles, he was wondering how everything in his life had suddenly gone sour. Tong was playing games with him, Moon was stonewalling him, Rachel Starr wasn't where she was supposed to be, and in thirty minutes, when his extra twenty-four hours were up, Morales would start applying real pressure.

And Thomas Morales was too crazy a son of a bitch to have hanging on your back. He liked peeling off faces, Towers had heard. He liked doing it when the owner of the face was still alive and could scream.

He had other troubles as well. More and more the wife was nagging him. And the girlfriend wanted a fur coat and a wild night in the Crazy Hearts Motel, where even the toilet was shaped like a heart. Movies, vibrating beds, slinky lingerie. It wore him out thinking about it.

Maybe this would be his last deal. Maybe he'd get out while he was still in one piece, before anything happened to the job or the pension. He hadn't stayed a cop for twenty-three years to lose his pension in the end. The idea made him feel a little better.

Then the phone rang.

"I'm not here," he said quickly.

"Okay, honey." Priscilla lifted the receiver. "Hello? I'm sorry, he's not here. May I take a message? Well, he usually calls in during the day." Suddenly her eyes widened. "I beg your pardon? No, I won't tell Jimmy anything of the sort. Who is this? Hello? *Hello?*" She shot Towers a peevish look. "He hung up."

"What did he want?"

"Who the hell is Didi?"

"What?" Towers rolled over. "What are you talking about?"

"The man on the phone said to ask you where the money is and to tell you Didi can't wait to go to bed with you."

"Cilla, will you hold on a second?" He made a grab at her arm as she flounced off the bed.

"Let me go, you bastard!"

"Cilla, c'mon. I don't even know a Didi."

"That man seemed to think you did." She was breathing quickly, chest heaving. "You better not be cheating on me, Jimmy."

"I'm not, I'm not. Christ." He sat up, wrapping the sheet around his stomach. "You're enough woman for two men. Why would I want anyone but you?"

"Don't think a little flattery will make everything all right."

"It's not flattery, it's the truth. Now, c'mon, Cilla. Don't gimme a hard time."

"A hard time? I wait here all day and all night for you. Whenever you want me, I'm here. I don't see other people. I don't do anything, go anywhere. I've never cheated on you. I've never even thought of cheating on you." She began to cry. "Because I love you. Because you're my whole world, Jimmy. And now this happens."

"Okay, sweetheart." He pulled her into his arms and stroked her back soothingly. "It's all right, baby. There's nobody but you, I swear to God that's the truth."

"Is it?" She sniffled and eyed him. "I don't know if I'll ever be able to really trust you again."

"Don't say that." Towers rubbed his hands up and down her arms. She felt soft and she smelled good, and even if she was a pain in the neck sometimes, they had fun together. Jesus, did they have fun together. "What can I do to make you belive me? Tell Jimmy what he can do."

Priscilla shrugged and let out a tiny sob. "I don't know."

"Well, I think I do. Want to know what Jimmy has in mind? How about a nice fur coat? Would that make my little baby happy again?" He pulled her closer and snuggled against her breasts. "Would it?" After a long moment he felt her nod. "Then Jimmy's buying it for his sweetheart. Is that good? Does that make her happy?"

One more trembling sniffle, then a breathy "Uh-huh."

"What do you say?"

"Thank you, Jimmy."

"Now look what you've done. Got me all worked up."

With a laugh, Priscilla pushed him back into the satin sheets. "Then let baby take care of you," she murmured.

Towers groaned.

Moving on top of him, Priscilla decided that today must be her lucky day.

The nurse was thin and blond and was chain-smoking filterless Camels. They were in the cafeteria of the Banyan Convalescent Home, where Andrew Solomon's sister was a resident. Rachel was sitting closest to the door that led out to a garden. The breakfast rush was over and the place was quiet.

It had taken only a quick flip of Rachel's L.A.P.D. badge to convince the nurse that she and Snow were local police working on the Solomon case. Like most people, the woman had barely glanced at the badge before agreeing to talk.

"We'd like to go over what happened yesterday morning one more time with you, Ms. Barrows. Sometimes on these follow-up interviews, people remember something they didn't recall earlier."

The nurse nodded and crushed out her cigarette, reaching immediately into the pack for another. "Well, Mr. Solomon stopped by around seven-thirty. I was surprised to see him because he usually visits Ellen—that's his sister—in the afternoons."

"How did he seem?"

"Worried. Nervous. He usually dresses very neatly. You know, coat and tie and pinstripe shirt, but yesterday he looked disheveled, liked he'd gotten out of bed and dragged on anything."

"Did he speak to you?"

"Yes. He said he wanted to see Ellen. He was abrupt, which was strange because Mr. Solomon is always very polite. A real gentleman."

"Did he say anything else?"

"I asked him if something was wrong and he said no. I asked him why he'd changed his visiting hours, and he didn't answer. He was quite worked up. He slipped around me and ran down the hall to Ellen's room."

"Did you see him talking to her?"

"No. Another patient needed me. By the time I left that patient's room, Mr. Solomon was leaving. I saw him come out of Ellen's room and head for the stairs that go to the lobby."

"He was alone?"

"Yes."

"How did he look?"

"Afraid. He looked afraid. And he had his arms up against his chest like he was carrying something."

"Any idea what?"

"Some papers, I think."

"You didn't notice anyone waiting for him in the lounge area or outside?"

"Well, that's hard to say. We have so many visitors. I suppose any one of them might have been with Mr. Solomon." She tapped off an ash. "Detective, I'd like to know why you're asking these questions. I heard on the news that Mr. Solomon committed suicide."

"Whenever a violent death occurs we have to investigate."

"Oh." The nurse let out a weary breath. "It's really too bad, his dying. He was a nice man. Funny, you see somebody every day and you never really know what they're like. What their lives are like. How sad they are. Maybe if someone had known . . ." She shrugged. "It's a hell of world, isn't it?"

"Yes," Rachel said. "It is."

Two hours after promising Priscilla a new fur coat, Towers was back in his office, making a call to Robert Moon on his private line. "Look, I know he's in," he said to the woman on the other end. "Tell him to get on."

"I'm sorry. Mr. Moon is not in his office."

"Then where the fuck is he?"

"He's out of town for two days." Her tone remained blandly polite. "If you'd like to leave a message . . ."

"Yeah. Tell him this is Towers. Tell him I don't like getting screwed. Tell him he made a million-dollar commitment to me and he'd better keep it. You writing this down?"

"Yes, sir."

"And then what? We get off the phone and you dump it in the garbage?"

"I'll make sure that Mr. Moon receives it."

"Yeah, of course you will." Towers banged down the receiver.

The phone rang immediately.

"Towers."

"This is Morales. You have my money?"

Towers felt his stomach knot, his hand go clammy. Definitely he was getting too old for this. He loosened his tie. "Tommy. How are you?"

"Cut the bullshit," Morales said coldly. "I expected you an hour ago. I don't like to wait. I got better things to do with my life."

"Coupla things came up. I can't get away."

"Then I'll come to you."

"No." Hating the fear he heard in his voice, Towers slowed himself down. "What I mean is, that's not such a good idea, Tommy. Anybody seeing us together."

"Why not? I'm a lawyer. Cops and lawyers get together all the time. Maybe I should come over right now, what d'you think?"

"Gimme another hour. I've got a few appointments to take care of, then I can get out of here."

"Okay, Captain. Because I like you, I'll give you an hour. Be here by three. Sharp. Don't make me wait, you dig?"

Morales hung up and Towers held the receiver in midair for a moment, waiting for his heart to calm down. He felt like he was sliding fast into a sewer, like his whole life was going down some dark, smelly hole and he couldn't stop it. Swearing, he dropped the phone into place, then jumped when it rang immediately. He took a breath and picked it up. "Towers here."

"It's Artie Lee."

Sinking back in his chair, Towers sighed. All he needed to cap off a rotten day was a call from the pawnbroker. "Yeah, Lee, what's up?"

"I heard some news you might find interesting."

"What kind of news?"

"News pertaining to you, Captain."

"Go on."

Lee gave a small laugh. "Excuse me, Captain, but the last time I checked, we weren't friends. Why would I be giving you what I know for free?"

"What's the price?" Towers said gruffly.

"There's a man in Chinatown. His name's Tuck Au. He owns a laundry called the Golden Lily. In the front he washes clothes. In the back he sells dope. He almost killed my son. I want him off the street."

"I can arrange a raid."

"He has friends. He gets arrested, the next day he's miraculously free. That doesn't happen this time, Captain."

"I'll see what I can do."

"No. No seeing what you can do. You do it."

"You're pretty sure of yourself, Lee. You better have something good."

"You'll take care of Au?"

"He's taken care of, okay? Now, what've you got?"

"Two things. One, Tong's ending his business arrangement with you and Morales."

"What's that mean?"
"He's going to start getting his drugs from somebody else."
"Who?"
"A dealer from Hong Kong named Tiger Lee Chan. What I understand is Tong wants to work only with Chinese from now on."
"That right?" Towers spun his chair toward the window and glared at the muddy sky. "Maybe that's what the bastard wants, but it's not what he's getting. What else have you got?"
"You're going to be hit."
Towers felt his mouth go dry. "When?"
"Soon. Take care of Au, Captain. And yourself."
Towers didn't pack. He figured whatever he needed he could buy in Honolulu. He didn't call his wife or Priscilla. Why leave a trail or set it up where they could have problems? Get out, but don't run. Never run.
No, what he planned to do, assuming he was right and Tong was behind the planned hit, was take the party right to the man himself. Show the Asian he had balls. Show him James Towers II wasn't some jerk who could be scared off. In fact, maybe he'd do a little scaring of his own.
He had ammunition. Wasn't that what knowledge was? Mental ammunition for nailing the other guy? He knew about Rachel Starr. He'd bet his goddamn silver Lincoln Continental she was with Haid the night he'd been killed. He'd bet the Continental and the boat he was going to buy that right this second she was in Honolulu and tracking Tong. What he wanted to know was, how had she linked Tong to Tai? Had Haid found out about Tong? And if he had, who else had he known about?
Towers was standing to the right of the snack bar near the departure gate. He was standing with his back to the wall and a row of phone booths on his left, leaving only two sides exposed. He kept watching the crowd for Asians because if Tong was setting him up he'd keep it Oriental, that was the way the man worked.
He was sweating, Towers discovered. Under his suit he could feel his shirt sticking to his chest. He could feel his blood pump-

ing, the constriction in his lungs. He didn't want to admit it, but he felt like a coward standing close to the wall, using a bunch of stupid telephones for protection.

A voice came over the sound system announcing an arrival from New York, and suddenly he was thinking about the beginning. How he was going to be the best there was, the finest cop in New York City. How he was going to save the whole world. How he was going to be a hero.

Some fucking hero.

Nowadays what he felt most of the time was emptiness and regret. Only what could he do? Some roads you can't backtrack to the beginning. You get on and you keep going, and one day it hits you the road wasn't the one you meant to take, only by then it was all too goddamn late.

Yeah, he thought, checking his left again.

All too goddamn late.

THIRTEEN

"WE BRING IN H.P.D. now," Pono said. "Not tomorrow, not next week. Now."

"And give them what?" Rachel demanded. "Illegal tapes? The D.A.'ll love that. Hell, Tong would love it. He'd laugh all the way out of court with his expensive lawyer."

"We're talking murder, Rachel. A man's dead," Pono said. "We've got on videotape a conversation between Tong and Kincaid about taking care of Solomon and now Solomon's dead."

"If Tong finds out we're on to him that's it for our case. He'll walk away from Solomon's murder and Johnny's and from whatever else he's into. He'll bide his time and become very careful. We'll never get him. Look," she added. "Let me play this out. Let me see where it goes. If it looks like someone else could get hurt, I'll call in H.P.D."

"Sure you will."

"You have my word."

"I know you. We worked together, remember? I broke the rules with you once before. Turned out bad all around."

"If you're worried about your cousin being in on this, take him out."

"It's not only Moses . . ."

"If you're worried about yourself, I understand. You've done plenty. I appreciate it. But maybe it's time you quit. Before there's trouble."

"C'mon, Rachel. I'm not saying I want out. I'm saying a man got killed. Maybe it didn't have to happen. Maybe it's time to bring some other people in so it doesn't happen again."

Rachel said quietly, "You want to get out now, Pono, get out now. I'll understand."

"Take a look at who walked into Tong's," Snow interrupted. "Better turn on the camera."

How many times had he seen the woman standing by his desk, Tong wondered. Hundreds, easily, in the last six years, yet each time her beauty awed him. That she had been a whore delighted him. Corruption within the most refined beauty. He was a man who appreciated dichotomies.

He leaned back in his chair and watched as she unbuttoned her silk blouse and tossed it aside, unzipped her skirt and stepped out of it, pulled the pins from her hair and shook it free. When she stepped around the desk and stood in front of him, she wore only a sheer slip, high heels and a strand of pearls.

Tong kept his face completely calm while she studied it. Then, without a word, she kissed him, open-mouthed and hungrily, and Tong couldn't stop the rush of hunger. He thought of it as weakness, what the woman could make him feel. For a moment he held her, then to prove to himself he could, eased her back. "Business first."

"All right, Jacob." With a patient smile, Ivory settled on the corner of the desk, letting the slip ride up to the top of her legs. "Business first."

"When will Lee Chan arrive?"

"Within the week. A deal in China is holding him up."

"That works out well for us. It will give us time to obtain the Red Heart." He let his gaze drift over the firm curve of her thigh, then looked up when she laughed softly.

"How much more business is there, Jacob?"

"The papers Gregory Chee took off Solomon. Did he deliver them to you?"

"Yes, they're in my gallery safe."

"Mr. Solomon could have caused us a good deal of trouble. He knew about the containers."

"How?"

"Cooper wasn't smart enough to hide what was going on. How is he taking the clerk's death, by the way?"

"It upset him." She began lazily swinging her leg, aware that the motion fascinated Tong. "He started drinking."

"The loss of a friend is always upsetting. He'll get over it."

"He's been drinking too much lately. I think it could cause problems."

"Your job is to keep Kincaid in line."

She stopped swinging her leg. "I don't like the job anymore, Jacob. I don't like him touching me."

"A little while longer and it will be over."

She reached out and stroked his mouth with her thumb. "Are we through with business now?"

"Yes."

"Good," she said, and slid into his lap.

"So they have more than art in common," Snow pointed out dryly.

Smith shot him a knowing look. "Lots more, I'd say."

"I'm going to Lin-Cho's gallery," Rachel said. "Solomon got killed because he had something on Cooper Kincaid. Something he figured out from the papers that are now in the lady's safe. Snow, you stay and watch the two of them."

"I'm going with you."

"No, you're not. I need you here."

He said, "You need me to get you into the safe," and picked his tool case off the table.

"Look, I know how to get into a—"

"You were always lousy breaking locks," Smith said. "Real lousy. If he knows safes, take him with you. I'll keep an eye on the lovebirds."

"You're not in this anymore."

"Says who? Did I quit?" He turned to Snow. "You hear me quit, Professor?"

"No."

"See? I'm still around. So get going."

"Pono . . ."

"Go on. If there's trouble I'll call the gallery. The old signal. Two rings, hang up, ring again."

She hesitated and Pono snatched up her black jacket and tossed it at her. "Get out of here, will you?"

With his hands holding the top rail, Snow swung his legs over the wire fence and dropped soundlessly to the ground. A second later, not as quietly, Rachel followed. They were in a narrow alley behind Ivory Lin-Cho's building. A single tree pitching over the fence streaked the ground with shadows.

Hugging the wall, they made their way to the middle door.

"Wait here." Snow flipped on a small flashlight and moved down the walkway. A moment later, just as the moon disappeared, the lights on the building snapped off.

Instinctively Rachel twisted around. "Snow?" She took a few steps, letting her eyes adjust. "Snow, where the hell are—"

"Right here." He touched her shoulder and she jerked around. "Sorry." He switched on the flashlight and she saw he was grinning. "Didn't mean to scare you."

"You didn't," she lied and added brusquely, "What about the alarms?"

"They're off."

"Then let's go in."

Hunching, he checked the lock, saw it was a cylinder job, and knew it would be easy. He laid his tools on the ground, chose a pick and an L-shaped tension bar, then handed her the light. "Keep it there."

The pick went into the keyway. He felt around for the first pin, found it, jiggled it up, and held it in place with the bar while he moved on to the next one. A minute later, with all five pins tensioned into place, he twisted the bar and the bolt snapped back.

The room was about thirty by fifty feet, broken into smaller spaces by freestanding dividers. Off to the right a staircase led to a basement. They looked quickly around and didn't spot the safe.

"Down there?" he said and Rachel nodded.

The basement was half the size of the gallery and musty-smelling. Artists' drawers, wooden crates, and metal shelving crisscrossed the floor. "I'll take this side," she said. "You cover over there."

It was Snow who found the safe wedged into a recess in the wall behind a stack of framed prints.

"It's an old one," he said, opening his tool case again. He took out a stethoscope and hung it around his neck. Before he used it, he tried some simple combinations based on even and odd numbers and the letters in Lin-Cho's name. When they didn't work, he made himself comfortable. Listening for the right clicks was going to take time.

Ten minutes later the phone rang twice, stopped, then rang again. Snow looked questioningly at Rachel but kept working the lock.

"It's Pono." She trailed the sound to a shelf near the stairs and lifted the receiver. "What's up?"

"Get the hell out right now. Tong and Lin-Cho are on their way."

"They already left?"

"About five seconds ago. Don't mess around. It's a three-minute drive from here to there."

"Okay, we're out." She hung up and hurried back to Snow. "We're leaving. Tong and Lin-Cho are on their way."

"Not right now. I almost have it."

"We're out of here. Right now. That's an order."

"I said no." Leaning closer, he pressed on the curved handle, gave the middle of the door a push, and dragged it back. "Get the camera ready."

"Dammit, we don't have time."

"Get the camera, Detective Starr." He pulled out a packet and shuffled it across the floor. "The papers Solomon took from Kincaid."

She looked at the pages, about ten sheets covered front and back. Too tempting to walk away from. "Damn you, Snow," she said and unsnapped the camera. Halfway through, she tore out the film and reloaded. "Start turning them over."

She shot the backs of the sheets, trying to keep the lens still enough not to blow the negatives, listening for sounds from upstairs, thinking something about Snow bothered the hell out of her, then thinking, This matters too much to him. When she was finished, she bundled the papers together and shoved them back into the safe. "Now can we leave?"

"Now seems a good time."

"When we get out of here, you and I have some things to talk about." She moved around him and started up the stairs. At the top she spotted Tong and Lin-Cho opening the main door and skittered down to where Snow was. "They're outside."

"Is the door open?"

"Almost."

"Okay. Stay down." He gave her a push that put her down low, then led the way back to the top of the stairs. Tong and Lin-Cho were standing just inside the entrance, working the light switch. The room was dark, but not dark enough to slip past them if they turned.

"Let's go," Snow whispered.

Grasping her wrist, he started across the carpeted floor, towing her along. Tong and Lin-Cho were still at the door but beginning to turn. Any second they'd be seen. Rachel thought, fighting an impulse to take her chances, get on her feet, and run. She gave another backward glance. Tong and Lin-Cho were still turning, but looking outside at the same time at the eaves, where the lights should have been on.

Snow hauled her forward.

The back exit was open. "You first," he said and gave a shove.

A second later, they were both outside. Rachel scrambled down the alley, grabbed the fence, and heaved herself over, turning in time to see Snow spring up and over in a catlike leap.

Amazing, she thought, then his arm came around her shoulder and they both started running.

* * *

Rachel poured herself a drink and slammed the bottle on the red-and-white Formica counter. Nothing changed in Snow's face. It stayed calm but alert. She decided she'd enjoy slapping it just to see what he'd do. She left him in the kitchen and went into the hall, taking a long swallow.

"Do we talk about it?" he said.

She swung back, hard enough to slosh the scotch out of the glass. "Okay, let's talk. What's this case mean to you?"

He thought a moment and said, "Reparation."

"Bullshit."

"Someone took a necklace of mine. I want to pay him back."

"It's more than that. It's personal. I saw it on your face in Lin-Cho's gallery. And it isn't the necklace, is it? You could steal any necklace you wanted. So what does that leave? It leaves Victor Chang." She moved into the doorway. "Who was he? A partner maybe? Your boss? More than your broker, right?"

"What does it matter?"

"Because I want to know."

"All right," he said quietly. "Victor Chang was my teacher and my friend. For the last eight months I've been looking for his killer. You came along and made it easy."

"You're out as of now."

"What?"

"Go back to L.A., Dr. Snow. Vengeance can get us killed. A half hour ago it almost got us caught."

"A half hour ago it got us proof, Detective."

"Proof? You don't want proof. You want to make Tong pay, isn't that it? What are your plans for him anyway?"

"What are yours?" he countered.

"Life in prison. Guaranteed."

"With parole in ten years, five off for good behavior. My way," he went on, "he gets justice."

She saw it in his eyes. Hard, cold, deadly. Not professor's eyes. Not even thief's eyes. "You plan to kill him, don't you?"

"I plan to see he pays for his crimes."

"I finish this myself. You leave tomorrow." She dumped her

glass on the counter, went into the living room, and heard him come around behind her.

"You need me," Snow said. "I can get the Red Heart."

"So can I."

"I don't think so. Tong gives the Honolulu Art Museum a great deal of money. In return they give him their trust. He has access to some interesting information, including four combinations needed to get into the vault where the Red Heart is stored. Tong gave me the numbers. You can't get in without them, so you can't get in without me."

"Give me the combinations, Professor."

"No."

Rachel thought again how much she'd enjoy hitting him.

"Tong expects me to steal the diamond," he went on. "He'd wonder what was going on if I left town."

"I don't like it. When it's personal, people make mistakes."

"When it's personal, I get better."

"Yeah? Back there you almost screwed up. What if they'd seen us?"

"They didn't. And if we're talking personal, what about one cop avenging another cop's death?"

"It's not the same."

"Why not?"

"This is my job."

"Is it? Then why doesn't L.A.P.D. know about it? Where's your organization? Your backup? I think you're on your own, Detective. I think this is very personal."

"Christ, what do I have to do to get rid of you?"

"You can't," he said. "I want Tong. We can do it together or separately, I don't care. Either way, I'll get him. If we do it together," he added, "you can keep an eye on me."

Rachel looked straight into his eyes, swore again, then said, "It goes my way, Snow. No stunts. No more stupid risks."

He nodded.

"And we take him in. Understood?"

"Understood."

She shook her head and let out a frustrated breath. "Why the hell don't I believe you?"

* * *

"It's sent out?" Snow kept his voice low so in the next room Rachel couldn't hear him talking.

"An hour ago. Our pilot friend has it. It'll be in the Express office by midday tomorrow."

"You included the drill? I told her that's what I'm expecting."

"I did. Don't lose it, by the way. I'm very fond of that tool. My first. Bought it in Hong Kong in that little place behind Chao Loon's, remember the one?"

"Yes, Myles." Snow sank back and worked the blanket over his legs. McDonnell's voice made home seem close. "How did the job come out?"

"How do you think? Brilliantly. Of course, it would have been better had you given me more time. And working from a photograph is not as simple as having the real thing in front of me. But the work will do." There was a pause and the sound of a pipe being lit. "I might as well tell you now. Thailand is asking for their money. They need it in ten days if we want the work to proceed on schedule."

"Tell them they'll get it."

"How go things with the lady cop?"

"Fine."

"Mmmm."

"What does that mean?"

"It means watch your step, Nicholas. Don't let lovely green eyes and burnished hair trip you up."

"I don't trip up, Myles."

"That's why I worry. There's always that first time." He inhaled, causing the tobacco to crackle. "Does she know what you're up to?"

"No."

"She won't like it when she finds out."

"We need the money. I just have to work it where she can't trace it back to me."

"How much longer will it take?"

"A few days. I'll call you when it's over."

"I'll wait to hear. Take care, Nicky."

"You too. And Myles."

"What?"

"Stay the bloody hell out of my Dom Perignon."

The old man chortled loudly and hung up.

Snow snapped off the lamp, stretched out his legs, and gazed at the ceiling. Not tripped up? he thought, letting his attention focus fully on the woman in the other room as it usually did late at night when he was alone. Not tripped up? He smiled a small, wry smile and shook his head.

FOURTEEN

IT WAS WARM, it wasn't raining, the air was clear, and the sky and the mountains were a vivid blue and green. This was definitely paradise, Towers thought. He took off his coat, draped it over the seat of the cab, and caught the driver's eye in the mirror. He smiled and said, "Weather like this all the time?"

"Most of the time," the driver answered. "You must've come from someplace cold. You got that coat."

"L.A., would you believe? Over a week now we've been freezing our asses." The driver was about twenty, a surfer-type, with muscled shoulders, blond hair, tanned skin, and snappy eyes looking for action. Towers said, "You from here?" but figured the kid was probably from Malibu.

"Nah. Florida. But I like it here better. Miami's a drag."

"No kidding?" Towers looked out the window. Alongside the road a grassy park stretched for blocks with all kinds of trees growing everywhere. After the grass came a ribbon of pure white sand, then the ocean rippling under the bright sun. When the cab went around a curve and pulled onto Kalakaua Avenue, he could feel the change in energy that comes with entering touristland. He could feel the pace pick up, the hustling going on, the scams in the air, the people hunting for whatever it was they couldn't find at home.

"Welcome to Waikiki," the driver said and gave a glance over his shoulder. "Tell me your hotel again."

"Sheraton."

"That's right." He stopped at a light and Towers caught the kid giving him a fast once-over in the mirror. As though he'd made up his mind about something, the driver leaned over, opened the glove compartment, then angled around, holding up a gold business card. "You need anything, give me a call. Girls, parties, something to make you feel good. Whatever." When Towers didn't take the card right away, the kid reached farther back and stuck it into his suit pocket. "Don't be shy, man."

He could pull him in, Towers thought. It'd be fun to do it just to see the kid's expression when he took out his badge. On the other hand, this wasn't his town. He had his own business to attend to. Let the local boys clean up their city. He patted his pocket. "I'll keep it in mind."

"That number's my machine. Call anytime. I'm always open."

Towers checked in at the front desk, studying the layout of the hotel while the clerk filled in a form. One wall was all glass and he could see the water changing from green to navy blue as it reached toward the horizon. Halfway out, a handful of sailboats moved smoothly between the breakers. This was the kind of place he could get used to, he thought as he signed the form and smiled back at the clerk.

On the way to the elevator he stopped at the hotel's sundries store, picked up a toothbrush and a razor, toothpaste, mouthwash, shampoo, shaving cream, deodorant, cologne—all in sample sizes—a roll of adhesive tape, a bottle of bourbon, and a couple of candy bars. Passing a men's shop, he decided he needed something more casual than his three-piece suit and overcoat, and went in.

He bought a pair of white slacks, pleased because he'd always wanted white slacks only he'd never had anywhere to wear them, a pair of lightweight khaki pants, a matching khaki jacket, and three Hawaiian shirts, one with palm trees, one with parrots, the third with seashells. He also bought underwear and beige loafers.

While the clerk was putting the clothes in a bag, Towers asked him if there was somewhere in the hotel that sold radios, tape recorders, that kind of thing, and the clerk told him to take a right when he got out of the shop and head down the corridor toward the beach. He'd find a gift shop two doors from the exit. Towers thanked him and paid cash.

In the gift shop he found exactly what he was looking for: a three-by-four-inch Sony tape recorder that fit neatly into the side pocket of his pants. He bought it, again paying cash, and went up to his room.

He stashed his haul, then found the phone book and carried it onto the veranda. Before he looked up the number he wanted, he ambled over to the railing and checked the view. He could see a kidney-shaped swimming pool and a half-dozen women, some of them not bad at all, lounging on deck chairs in skimpy swimsuits.

In the phone book he found Tong listed under Jacob Tong Jeweler, Inc. He went inside, dialed the number, and asked for him.

The woman who answered said Mr. Tong was out on an appointment. Towers said his name was Hank Gardner and that he had some nice jewelry pieces he was thinking of selling. Could she take a look and give him a ballpark idea of what they were worth? The woman said of course. He got directions to the office and hung up.

He got out of his suit and pulled on the khaki pants. He put the recorder in his left side pocket, plugged in the microphone, then opened the roll of adhesive tape. Tearing off six-inch strips, he anchored the mike to his chest, positioning it a few inches below where he estimated the top button of the shirt would be. He chose the parrot shirt, slipped into it, then slipped into the khaki jacket. In the full-length mirror beside the door, he checked himself out.

The recorder and microphone couldn't be seen. He shifted around for a side view. Nothing. No wires, no bumps. He walked back a few feet and fooled around with the collar, making the collar of the shirt fold over the jacket collar, pushing both back as far as possible so his chest showed. He thought he looked good. Casual, laidback, like nothing was worrying him.

He hadn't decided yet on his approach with Tong. Hard-ass or buddy-buddy. Pissed off or understanding. He decided he'd see the man face to face, then make up his mind. He also decided he wanted to surprise him. He'd get the secretary to tell him where Tong was, go there, and walk in on the man like it was an everyday situation. See what he did. Take it from there.

And get every goddamn word on tape.

Ten minutes before noon, Pono Smith arrived at the surveillance apartment. Between walking in the door and dumping the cartons of take-out Chinese food on the counter, he caught on that something was wrong between Rachel and Snow. Stakeout tension probably. After a few days of close living it wasn't unusual for people to get on each other's nerves.

He tossed Rachel a manila envelope. "Here're the photos of Andrew Solomon's papers. And this is what you wanted." He slid a package wrapped in brown paper toward Snow. "It was at the Express office when I got there."

Snow said thanks, took the package, but made no move to open it. Rachel glanced from it to him, then said to Smith, "You get a chance to look through these?"

"A quick once-over in the restaurant. Lots of dates and numbers. Couldn't make out what they mean."

"What about Lee Chan? Anything on him?"

"Not much more than you already know. He's a Hong Kong national. Manufacturers Green Jade Balm and makes a bundle from the stuff. Visits Honolulu maybe three times a year. Keeps a low profile. No available photographs. No criminal record of any sort."

"But somehow connected to Tong and Ivory Lin-Cho."

"Yeah."

"The question is how do these"—she lifted the photocopies and dropped them—"tie in to what's going on with Tong and Lee Chan? And how's Cooper Kincaid involved?"

"Good questions." He reached for the largest white carton. "Can we think about them over lunch?"

It was Rachel who finally made the connection between the numbers on Solomon's papers.

"Take a look at this," she said, sliding a page across the counter to Smith and waiting for him to pick it up. "Kincaid Inc. grows and processes sugar in the Philippines and ships it to Hawaii in numbered containers. Some of the containers remain in Honolulu, but the bulk of them go on to L.A. There were two deliveries of sugar in the past year. Look here. Solomon makes a note of two containers, one from each shipment."

"What about them?"

"Both came through Honolulu, got sent on to L.A., and disappeared."

"Stolen?"

"I don't think so. Check this. Copies of data from Kincaid Inc.'s accounting department. Financial statements and economic forecasts for the company dating from five years back when Cooper took over from his father. It seems Kincaid Inc. has been having financial problems. Losses from bad real estate investments and the drop in sugar prices. Cooper was having a tough time. Now take a look at this."

She handed Smith a letter and said, "A couple of years ago the Board of Directors was threatening to fire him. But within twelve months of that letter, the company begins making money again. From sugar. Even though sugar prices keep dropping. So Kincaid stays on."

Smith said, "How do you think he worked that?"

"I think we go back to Solomon," Rachel said. "Solomon was making a connection between the missing containers, the company's financial problems, and its mysterious economic recovery. Why?"

"The missing containers held something worth more than sugar?" Smith offered. "Something worth enough to save the company."

"That's my guess, too, Pono. So we have to ask ourselves: what did they hold?"

"Coming in from the Far East? What else? It's not chopsticks, so it has to be dope."

"I think so, too." She tossed the page she was holding onto the counter. "This gives us Kincaid. But how do we hook in Tong? And what about Lee Chan? How does he fit in?" She glanced from Smith to Snow. "That's what we've got to figure out. And I think we have to do it soon. If we don't—"

"Lee Chan manufactures more than Green Jade Balm," Snow said.

Rachel swung to face him. "What do you mean?"

"Lee Chan owns another company, not in his name but through a series of corporations, called Jade Tiger. It manufactures pharmaceuticals. Morphine base for hospitals, medicinal heroin for countries where it's legal."

"How do you know this?"

"I know it because I know Lee Chan."

"You know Lee Chan?" Her eyes widened angrily. "And when did you plan to tell us about it?"

"I've met the man twice," he said calmly. "Years ago."

"Would he remember you?"

"I don't think so."

"You don't think so. But if he does happen to remember, and he does happen to mention your name to Tong, then what?"

"Then we have a problem."

"How big a problem?"

"I was with Victor Chang when I met Chan."

"You were with—" Instead of finishing the sentence, she hit the table.

"Take it easy, Rachel," Smith said.

"What's the connection between Victor and Lee Chan, Snow?"

"It was a business relationship."

"What kind of business?"

"That's not important."

"I'll decide what's important. What kind of business?"

"I can't tell you."

"Goddammit." In one angry motion she got up, walked into the living room, and swore again.

Smith said, "Rachel, will you calm down?"

"I was an art student when I met Lee Chan," Snow said. He waited until she faced him, furious but listening. "Because I was studying art, he showed me some of the pieces he owned. There were extraordinary oil paintings—masterpieces that had been missing since the war—a few sculptures, and two religious icons that were beyond beauty. But the core of his collection was gemstones. Rare, one-of-a-kind gemstones."

She felt her expression change, her pulse speed up as she made the link. "Go on," she said coldly.

"I remember Chan saying once that very little in the world was unavailable to someone like him. And that what was unavailable was always the most desirable. He said acquiring the unacquirable was the one pleasure left to a man his age."

"He's here for the Red Heart," Rachel said.

"Yes, Detective," Snow agreed. "And paying for it with drugs."

The restaurant was in Chinatown, eight blocks from Tong's office. Towers decided to walk it, enjoy the warm air and the sweet breeze coming down from the hills. He was hoping that the rest of the job would be as easy as his visit to Tong's office. All he'd had to do was show the secretary his gun and she'd told him where Tong was.

He found the restaurant on the corner where Smith and Hotel streets intersected. It reminded him of a temple with its gold walls and red dragons and fancy latticework. The front doors were round, decorated with calligraphy, and set in under a frilly overhang. Towers buttoned his coat, crossed the street, and went inside.

The place wasn't busy. Waitresses were clearing the tables and setting them up for dinner. He could hear the cooks talking loudly in the kitchen, dishes clanking around in a sink. A sullen-looking teenage boy in a greasy apron was sweeping the aisles. When he saw Towers come in, the boy said, "We're closed. We don't open till five."

"I'm meeting some friends." Towers looked up at the smaller dining alcoves on the second floor. "Jacob Tong's party. Which room's he in?"

"Mr. Tong didn't say somebody else was coming."

"Maybe it slipped his mind. Which room?"

The boy glared belligerently, then, figuring it wasn't his problem, shrugged and turned away. "They're up there. Third door."

"Thanks."

Without answering, the boy began sweeping again.

At the top of the stairs, Towers paused, then moved quietly to the third door and took a fast look before stepping back. Tong and three other men were sitting around a long table drinking tea. Tong was facing the door. Towers switched on the recorder and undid the safety on his gun. Then he took a deep breath and walked in.

There was the briefest flicker of surprise on the Asian's face, quickly hidden. Tong said, "Hello, Jim."

"We need to talk, Jacob." He felt the other men ease around to watch him.

"At the moment, I have guests."

"Ask them to leave. You fellows don't mind, do you?"

"What's this about?" Tong said.

"I don't think you want to talk about it in front of your pals. If I were you, I'd tell them to go."

Tong was silent a moment, then his eyes darkened. "Gentlemen, you'll excuse us?"

The men looked from Towers to Tong, then began pushing back chairs.

When they were gone, Tong carefully folded his napkin and placed it on the table. "Moon's been trying to reach you."

"Oh yeah?" Towers sat and leaned comfortably back. "Why?"

"To explain about the money."

"Explain what?"

"The reason for the delay."

"What's the reason?"

"There were problems with the deal in Tokyo. The money didn't come through. But—"

"But what?"

"Other arrangements are being made. We should have the million within a week. As soon as we do—"

"Cut the bullshit, Jacob. I know what's going on." He waited a second, getting a small kick out of the way Tong's mouth remained half-open with surprise. Then he said, "I know you're screwing me on our drug deal. I know you're leaving me on a fucking meat platter for Morales to carve up and eat. I know all about your new friend Tiger Lee Chan."

"You seem to know a lot," Tong said coldly.

"I know my days of doing business with Morales are over. When I didn't come through with the cash yesterday, he lost face with his connections in Mexico City. The man does not like to lose face, you know what I mean? Morales is pissed with me and nothing'll change that." Without asking, he shook a cigarette out of Tong's case, lit it, and aimed the smoke at the Asian's face. "I'm not happy losing the two hundred thousand I was supposed to net on our deal, but what really hurts is all the money I might have made down the line and won't because Morales wants me dead."

"That is difficult," Tong said without sympathy.

"You think so? Well, that's a way of putting it. You know, I was supposed to fly down to Mexico with him today. Since that trip got canceled, I decided to come here and visit you." Towers took a beat and added tightly, "The way I figure it, you owe me, Jacob."

"What is it you want?"

"Money, what else? The two hundred thousand I would've made on our heroin deal and another two hundred thousand for me losing Morales as a connection. So, four hundred thousand total. That's cheap, by the way."

"You want me to give you four hundred thousand dollars? And what do you give me?"

"With everything's that's happened, I figure we're even. But just to show you I still consider us buddies, I'll give you something else."

"What?"

"Peace of mind."

"What do you mean, peace of mind?"

"I know who went in with Haid." He watched as Tong refilled his teacup and took a sip, trying not to appear too interested.

The Asian said, "You want four hundred thousand dollars for a name?"

"Yeah."

"Rather expensive."

"For peace of mind? I don't think so."

"It's a great deal of money. I'm not sure I can raise it."

Towers let out a disdainful laugh and picked up an almond cookie. Taking a bite, he said, "You can raise it. I think you better raise it," he added quietly.

"When would you want it?"

"Today. This afternoon at the latest."

"Impossible."

"Don't tell me impossible. You probably have twice that in your safe. Look, Jacob"—Towers leaned forward, pushing plates and bowls out of the way—"do us both a favor and give me the money. I think you need to know what I know."

Tong put down the teacup. He had an ugly look on his face that for a second got to Towers.

"What time this afternoon?" Tong said.

"Five o'clock."

"All right. Meet me at my office."

"I don't think so. I think it's better if we meet somewhere else."

"Where?"

"There's a restaurant in the Sheraton. Right on the beach. Bring the money in hundred-dollar bills. And put it in one of those zippered canvas sports bags, the smallest one it'll fit into."

"This name you have, Captain. I hope it's worth four hundred thousand dollars."

"Believe me," Towers said, "it is."

FIFTEEN

IT WAS THE SINGLE red brushstroke placed deep within the green that unified the painting. Snow stepped back another three feet and narrowed his eyes. A simple painting, one of Cézanne's lesser works yet quite powerful. He wondered how it would look beside the two Cézannes he already owned.

He didn't turn as Rachel came up beside him.

She said, "If you're making plans, Professor, forget them."

"Just admiring the work." He led her down a short flight of stairs and into the Honolulu Art Museum's next gallery. "Did you time it?"

Rachel nodded. "Following the main corridor, it takes forty-seven seconds to cross the basement and reach the vault where the Red Heart is kept. There are sensors on every other pillar, cameras every thirty feet."

"The sensors I can knock out. The cameras are a problem." He moved to the next canvas, looked at it briefly, then motioned Rachel to follow him out into the courtyard. Shrubs were planted around a square of grass. In the center, on a four-foot-high concrete platform, was a late-Roman statue of a woman. "Let's take a look at her."

They crossed the lawn and strolled slowly around the sculpture.

Snow said, "We'll come in from the roof the night we steal the diamond."

"Why?"

"We can avoid the alarms monitoring the outside doors and windows. The control box for that group is the hardest one to get at."

"Where is it?"

"Over there. To the left of the front gate. It's set into the building and protected by steel. I'd need time to drill it open."

Rachel glanced at the entrance. Near it, a guard stood at attention, talking with the woman behind the desk. "It's wide open from the street."

"Exactly. Hundreds of cars go by every hour. We'd definitely be seen. That's why it has to be the roof. We'll get on in back, use the trees planted against the building as cover, then work our way forward to this yard. Take a look up there."

There were two rooflines, both tiled in terra cotta, the higher one sloping toward the lower with a space of four feet between them. The lower roof continued the slope, stopping fifteen feet above the ground.

"It won't be hard to get down," he said and caught her wary expression. "We just have to time it so the guard is in the gallery."

"How do we do that?"

"Tong gave me a schedule."

"That was helpful of him."

"He wants the Martinos diamond. He's going to be as helpful as possible. Let's go," Snow added. "We've been here long enough."

On the other side of the street was a park the size of a city block with a fountain pluming out of a circular pool. They found a chair set off from the rest. Snow took a roll of paper out of his pocket, worked off the rubber band, and handed the sheet to Rachel. It was a neatly drawn map and the guards' schedule given to him by Tong.

"From beginning to end it's all timing," he said. "Let's take it from the top. The guards are inside the galleries until eleven fifty-seven. We get on the roof at eleven forty-seven. Three minutes to get from there to there. At eleven-fifty we're ready to drop into the yard. By eleven fifty-four we're on the ground and we've knocked off the alarms and sensors."

"How?"

"The control box is behind the front desk. I open it and punch in one of the combinations Tong gave me. Then we have three minutes to get through this door."

"Will it be locked?"

"Yes, but it's a cylinder job. Simple stuff. I'll need about twenty seconds to work it with an automatic pick. The door gets us into the galleries. We go through the Medieval Hall, cut across here"—he traced his finger across the map—"and come out in the back of the building. The curator's office is here. Across from it is a door that opens to the basement."

"Also locked?"

"Yes, but the same cylinder style. We cross the basement—figuring on the forty-seven seconds you clocked. By eleven fifty-seven we reach the hall you checked out. This is when it gets a little difficult. I have the combination that knocks off the sensors but not the cameras, which is why we have to move down that hall and open this door between eleven fifty-seven and midnight. That's when the guard watching the video screens goes to the front gate to let in his relief."

"How long before the relief gets back to the screens?"

"Three minutes, tops."

"We cross the hall and open the door. Then what?"

"By midnight we're in the room with the safe. Once we're in, we're secure. There are sensors in the room but no camera, and I have the numbers to take out the sensors."

"What about the safe?"

"It's wired, but I have the combination for that, too. After I neutralize the alarm, all we have to do is open the box and take the Red Heart.

"How long will that take?"

"Depends. If I can punch it, five minutes. If I have to peel and drill it, maybe twenty, twenty-five."

"That's a long time."

"Longer than you think. Once we get started, it'll seem like years."

"What about the other guards? How many are there?"

"Two. Each one has a specific route and spaced time clocks he has to punch. We're concerned with only one of them, the one who goes through the furniture galleries then down through the basement. He starts the route at midnight, covers the galleries first, taking thirty minutes. He's in the basement at twelve-thirty sharp, which gives us twenty-five minutes to open the safe, get the diamond, and get out of the building."

"How do we do that?"

"Get out? The only tricky part is getting back through the hall where the cameras are. We'll have to divert the guard. I'll talk to Tong about it. Something has to happen at twelve twenty-eight to get his attention off the screens."

"Like what?"

"A phone call maybe. One that'll keep him occupied for the ten seconds we need to get down the corridor."

"The cameras will be running. We'll be on tape."

"We'll use masks. Once we're out of the corridor, we'll head this way. There's a delivery door back here. It uses a separate alarm keyed from the inside. That takes the last combination Tong gave me. The door opens onto a short drive. It's ten seconds from there to the street, then another ninety seconds from the street to where we leave the car."

"And we're home free?"

"If everything goes right." He began rerolling the map, thinking, Never on any job did everything go right, but why tell her that? When he looked at her again, she was staring at the museum, the sunlight falling through the trees lighting up her hair. He'd known beautiful women, Snow thought, but no one quite like her. No one so unaware of her beauty. No one so serious or strong or solitary. For a second he let himself watch her, then looked away as she turned back to him.

"Do you think we can do it?" she asked.

"We have a good shot."

"But it's not a hundred percent."
"What is?"

Around three o'clock Towers decided to take someone with him when he met Tong.

He was leaning against the railing, eyeing a brunette in a pink bikini, when the idea came to him. He went to the closet, found the coat he'd worn in from L.A., and pulled out the taxi driver's gold business card. He dialed the number expecting a machine, but the kid was home.

Towers explained what he needed and the kid said sure, he'd make some calls, no problem at all, what time did Towers want the girl? Towers gave him the time and the place, thought about asking the price, then, not wanting to seem cheap, didn't.

Afterward he went back to the balcony. In the pool, the girl in the pink suit was doing laps, her short hair slicked back by the water into a neat black cap.

He felt a funny urge to call Cilla, an even funnier urge to call his wife. He was into something now that was cutting him off from them in a way more real than the ocean. An ocean you could fly over, get back to what you'd left. There was no turning around in what he was doing.

Around four-thirty there was a soft tapping on the door and he opened it to find a knockout blonde in a tight black mini-dress, one hip cocked out suggestively. The dress showed most of her thighs and three-quarters of her back. She had big breasts, long legs, and sleepy eyes.

"Should I come in?" she said.

"Yeah, sure." He watched while she moved to the center of the room, her body fluid, her hips rocking. Don't get into it, he told himself. She's a one-hour rental, that's all. "You want a drink?"

"That'd be nice." Her voice was breathy and girlish like Marilyn Monroe's. He couldn't decide if it was natural or a put-on.

"All I got's bourbon."

"I like bourbon. With a little water, if you don't mind."

He made drinks for both of them.

She sat on the chair by the television and crossed her legs.

He sat on the bed. "So, what's your name?" he said.

"Cheryl."

"Cheryl. Pretty name."

"Thank you."

One of her high heels had come loose, and she was swinging it so it hit her heel. She had nice feet. Small and soft, with high insteps. For a second Towers could see his mouth pressed into the curve. He drank some of his drink.

Cheryl said, "I'm not really sure what you want me to do. Sean said this wasn't a party."

"All I want is for you to have dinner with me."

"Just dinner, huh?"

"Right."

"Okay, if that's what you want." She checked the time. In the same little-girl voice but now with a working-girl edge, she said, "The meter started five minutes ago. I go by the hour. Anything over an hour you get a ten-minute grace period. After ten minutes you get charged the full hour."

"Sounds fair. What's the rate?"

"Two hundred per."

"That's the going over here?"

"It's higher than the going, but I'm worth it." She smiled and uncrossed her legs. "And you can change your mind anytime. I mean, you know, if you want more than dinner."

At ten minutes to five he and Cheryl walked into the restaurant. Towers asked the hostess for a table close to the entrance. From it they could see the swimming pool and the beach.

Towers said, "So, Cheryl, what do people do when they come to town?"

"Is this your first time in Hawaii?"

"Yeah."

"Well, you should definitely catch some of the shows. Don Ho's fun and Tavana's really wild. You know, lots of dancers and great music."

"What else?"

"Well, that depends on what you're looking for. I mean there're tour buses that hit all the tourist spots—Punchbowl, Pearl Harbor, the Polynesian Cultural Center."

"I don't like buses much."

"Neither do I."

He hooked an arm over the back of his chair. "So what do you like, Cheryl?"

"Nice cars. Good-looking men. Fun." She smiled, letting her thigh rub against his.

He smiled back.

They were still smiling at each other when Tong arrived at five o'clock sharp. He was alone, carrying the blue canvas bag in his left hand.

As usual, he was wearing his pretentious white suit that made him look, Towers thought, like a Chinese pimp, which, if rumor had it right, was how Tong had made his first fortune.

While Tong got settled at the table, Towers looked around. If anyone was with the man, they were good because he couldn't spot them. "You're right on time," he said. "Say hello to Cheryl."

Tong gave the girl a cool look and shoved the bag across the table. "Everything's there. Count it if you like."

"I trust you, Jacob." He unzipped the bag and flipped randomly through the stacks of money. "Looks fine to me."

"Give me the name."

"You want something to eat?"

"The name," Tong repeated.

"Not in a friendly mood, huh?"

"The name."

"Okay. Jesus, I thought we could talk a little first, reminisce about old times, but any way you want it." He looked around like someone might be listening, hamming it up a little for the girl. "It was a woman who went in with Haid. Her name's Rachel Starr. She's an undercover detective and I think she's here in town."

"What does she look like?" Tong said.

"Good-looking. Tall. Nice build. And she has red hair."

He saw the muscles tighten around the other man's eyes and mouth. Saw the skin go white. Enough to let Towers know Detective Starr was here and had made some move on the Asian.

He looked at Cheryl. She was listening, impressed, her lower lip sticking out a little, waiting to be bit. Maybe afterward after all . . .

Tong got up quickly, scraping his chair across the stone floor.

"Hey, you're not running off?" Towers said.

The other man swore softly, pivoted smoothly, and stalked out.

Towers shrugged. "Bad news, I guess."

"I didn't like him."

"I know what you mean."

He told her to order anything she wanted, and to wait for him while he took care of some business. Then he went upstairs, watching to see if someone was following, packed his clothes in a plastic bag, and came back down. Before he walked into the restaurant, he gave the lobby a careful once-over. No one seemed interested in what he was doing.

Feeling a good buzz from the money in his bag, he went to get Cheryl.

They took a cab to the Hilton a couple of blocks away. Towers asked for the best suite and ordered champagne. He paid cash.

They passed a sundries shop, and he gave Cheryl two hundred-dollar bills and told her to buy some things to eat, whatever she liked, and meet him by the elevator. He watched her, ass swinging, as she walked off. Then he found a phone.

The reservations clerk told him the next plane to Miami left at five minutes after midnight. He booked a seat, using the name John Martin, and asked the clerk to make arrangements for him to fly from Miami to Rio. He'd read somewhere that something like a zillion people lived in Rio de Janeiro. One American cop could get lost in a crowd likc that.

Cheryl was waiting by the elevator, fanning herself with a magazine.

"You hot?" Towers said.

"Uh-huh."

The way she said it, the look she gave him at the same time, he knew things were going to be good between them.

She handed him his change.

"You keep it," he said, folding the bills into her hand.

"Really? Thank you." She kissed his cheek, pressing her breasts against his arm. "What's your name? Don't you think I should know your name?"

"Johnny," he said, figuring now was as good a time as any to try out his new identity.

"Johnny. My favorite name." She hit the elevator button, careful not to break her bright red nail. "I think we're going to be good friends, Johnny."

At six, Rachel picked up their messages. There was a call from Tong, which Snow returned. He spoke less than a minute, then hung up.

"What's going on?" she said.

"He set the time. We go in tonight."

They spent four hours together, and when they were finished Towers wondered if he'd ever walk again.

Cheryl was eighteen and she'd taught him moves he'd never imagined, that made him think he'd never really had sex, that everything before this girl was bullshit, that this was the way it was supposed to be.

Lying in bed with the girl beside him, he thought of asking her to leave with him. Thought of it, knowing the idea was dumb; he had enough on his mind getting himself out without taking an eighteen-year-old along. But he kept kicking it around.

In the end he stayed in bed and watched her dress, stepping into pink panties, easing the mini over her legs, turning a little to let him zip her up.

When he took his hands away, she bent down and kissed him, her mouth like pillows, her tongue hot. He kissed her back, shoving his hands into her hair, pulling her to him, feeling suddenly young again, like he was starting out, like he could do anything.

He said, "Tell me how I can call you directly. Not going through Sean."

She gave him her private number.

"Ever been to Rio, Cheryl?"

She shook her head.

"Want to go?"

"With you?"

"Yeah, with me."

She kissed him again. "Yes, Johnny."

"I'm leaving tonight. In a couple of days, I'll call you. We'll work it out."

He opened the blue bag he'd stuck under the bed and gave her five banded stacks of money. Five thousand dollars. For tickets and clothes, he told her, wondering at the same time if he was being an idiot. This was a young and beautiful girl with everything going for her. What chance was there she'd actually use the money to meet him in Rio?

Except the way they'd been together made him think maybe she might come. If she was faking the last four hours, she was the best he'd ever seen. You don't fake what she'd done to him, what she'd let him do to her.

After she left, he stayed in bed. He thought of Cilla and his wife. He thought of the house in Westwood, the pool in the backyard, the barbecue, the elm trees lining the drive, giving the place some class. He thought of his job, realized he'd miss it, then realized he'd left it years before when he'd taken the first bribe. Just a small one. A few bucks under the table to keep him quiet about something, he couldn't remember what it was anymore.

That was when he'd turned his back on the kid from New York who was going to be the best there was.

That was the beginning.

This was the end.

He got up and started packing.

SIXTEEN

AT 10:15 TOWERS LET THE front desk know he was checking out and asked the clerk to call him a cab. By 10:30 he was outside waiting, dressed in his suit again, his casual clothes packed in the overnight bag he'd bought in the Hilton's men's shop. He had his overcoat draped across his left arm, the arm carrying the blue canvas bag.

At 10:40 the cab pulled up, an immaculate white Chrysler that for some reason made him think of tanned women and South American villages.

Towers put on his coat, got in, and said, "Airport," then caught one last look at the ocean, pitch black except where the moonlight hit the breakers. A couple of hours ago he and Cheryl had stood on the balcony of his room looking down on it.

The cabbie was a skinny Puerto Rican wearing a patchwork vest and a red cowboy bandana around his neck. After a few blocks, when the driver didn't start a conversation, Towers said, "You from around here?"

"No, man."

"It's a nice place."

The driver gave him a take-it-or-leave-it shrug. "It's okay."

"The weather's good. I like it warm like this."
"Too hot sometimes. Anyway, I seen better."
"Where are you from?"
"The city."
"Which one?"
"New York, man." Saying it like no other city existed.
"I'm from New York," Towers said. "Brooklyn. Avenue J. You know it?"
"Never went to Brooklyn." Saying this like he'd rather lose an arm than go.
"What part of the city you from?"
"Harlem, man."
Towers caught the kid's eyes in the mirror. Tough-guy eyes. "So why are you in Hawaii?"
Another shrug. "Why not? I got nothing else to do."
"You drive a cab in New York?"
"Yellow cab."
"I worked for the Yellow. Had the airport route. Made some good bucks."
"Yeah?"
"What's driving like over here?"
"Not bad. Good days you can clear a coupla hundred. Why? You thinking of reupping?"
Towers felt the blue bag under his coat. "Actually I just quit my job. I'm retiring. Going south."
"Sounds good to me."
He thought of Cheryl. "If things work out, it could be real good." He stopped talking then and watched the city go by, his mind on the girl. He saw them living in a fancy house overlooking the ocean in Rio. Big porches, sliding doors, everything open. He saw them holding hands, watching sunsets, walking the beaches under the stars, maybe dancing to Brazilian music. It was like a crazy high school fantasy, but he didn't care. It'd been a long time since he'd dreamed.
They were a mile out from the airport, on Nimitz, when the driver suddenly said, "Some shithead's on my butt."
As Towers spun around for a look, a black limo pulled along-

side them. A Chinese man was driving and there was another one in the backseat holding up a shotgun.

Towers slapped the cabbie on the shoulder and shouted, "Step on it."

"What's going on?" the driver demanded. "Shit, I don't want no trouble, man. I just bought these wheels."

"Then hit the fucking gas." Towers reached into his overnight bag and hunted for his gun. He should've known, he thought. Tong wouldn't let him go. Towers showed his gun and the limo slowed, then slid back. They were traveling in an open stretch, no other cars around. Towers figured if they moved up again, he could take out the driver.

In the front seat, the cabbie snatched a look in the mirror, caught the flash of the .45 in Towers's hand, and groaned. "I don't want no hassles. Leave me outta this."

"Just drive the goddamn car!"

Suddenly the limo pulled directly behind them and slammed into the cab's back end. The driver pitched sideways and lost the wheel. The Chrysler spun off the road and skidded back-end first into a vacant lot.

Instantly a bullet shattered the windshield.

The cabbie jumped into the space in front of the seat screaming, "Get the fuck outta my car, man! Get the fuck outta my car!"

A second bullet chopped up the tape deck.

A .45 with a silencer, Towers guessed, coming from his right. Grabbing the blue bag, he kicked open the door and scrambled out.

Through the space between the wheels he spotted two men about forty feet away running toward him. He leaned around the side of the car, shot twice, and fell back. A bullet zinged off the rear bumper, two off the roof. Towers dropped to his right and fired. That left him four shots. If he got lucky he could hold them off about ten more seconds.

Behind him the unlit lot stretched seventy yards. Then came a side street and the back of a used-car barn. In between were the decaying frames of abandoned cars. Towers locked his fingers around the bag, breathed deeply, and stood. He shot twice over the roof, saw the two Chinese split apart and roll. The squat one bounced up first and fired back.

Crouching, the bag hugged close to his chest, Towers zigzagged his way to the next car. One of the gunmen yelled something to the other. A bullet cracked the ground inches from Towers's foot.

The next car was fifteen feet away. He made a dash for it, lunged for cover behind the wheels, and got off another shot.

One goddamn bullet left.

He sat up and pressed his back into the fender, felt his heart banging, his breaths heaving out of him hard enough to hurt.

He let himself think of Cheryl. Let a picture of her fill his mind. The way she had felt, the way he had felt, like it was his first time. If he had to die, at least he'd had that.

A bullet spit up earth close to his knee. He jumped back, yanking the bag with him. He didn't want to die, but he could handle it if it happened. And if he did go, he planned to take one of those bastards with him.

He got ready to step out, was halfway there when the sirens dropped him to the ground. They were three or four blocks away, five or six vehicles coming fast.

He checked the Chinese, saw them frozen, listening, then moving back, screaming at each other over the noise.

Jesus, he loved the police.

He counted off five more seconds. Looked again. The hit men were back in their limo. Standing up in plain view he gave them the finger.

That's for your boss, you motherfuckers.

He was going to get Tong. Before he left the islands, he was going to get him, that was a promise. No one pulled shit like this on James Towers II.

The sirens whined down. Blue lights flashed across the lot.

He stuck the bag under his coat and ran.

Hunched low on the roof, Snow unhooked the rope and drew it carefully through the tree branches, at the same time winding it into a tight coil. He stuck the cord into the satchel, took out gloves, and checked the light striking the building.

The moon was close to the horizon and wouldn't be a problem. Palm trees blocked out half the streetlights. The west slope of the roof was in shadows.

Now was the time to do it.

Climbing up to where Rachel was sitting, Snow wondered how long she would last. The one small detail she'd failed to mention until they were thirty feet above the ground was her fear of heights. Had he known about it, Snow thought grimly, he'd never have let her come along. In his experience, it was always the one small detail that messed things up and got you caught. But they were on the roof now and on a schedule. He couldn't waste time getting her down.

He dropped the gloves onto her lap and said, "Put these on and let's go. We're on a schedule."

"Screw your schedule, Snow."

Though she tried to hide it, he could hear the shakiness in her voice. "Okay," he said, deciding the one way to get her to move was to rile her. "Stay here. Enjoy the night air. Maybe I'll see you later." He began sidling around her.

"Just hold on." Reluctantly she let go of the tiles and struggled with the gloves. Her hands were trembling and her skin was a shade of gray he'd never seen. Fighting the impulse to help her, he said impatiently, "Hurry up. Watch me. Do what I do."

"You're a real bastard," she muttered, but started pushing herself up.

"And you have a lousy disposition, which makes us even." He ignored the look she gave him and waved his hand. "C'mon, c'mon. We don't have all night."

She mumbled something he didn't catch and began inching her way down. When she was next to him, Snow looked at his watch. "We're forty-five seconds off our time. Try to pick it up, okay?"

"You're enjoying this, aren't you?"

"Enjoying what?"

"Me at a disadvantage."

"Actually, I am."

"Screw you, Snow."

He smiled and shook his head. "You've got the mouth of a Hong Kong whore, Detective."

"Yeah? Well, fuck you, too. I hate it up here."

"The sooner we move, the sooner we get to the ground."

He began working his way across the face of the roof, a yard below the pitch, checking each handhold and foothold for strength, making sure without making it obvious that Rachel grabbed the same tiles.

As they clambered over the middle building and reached the halfway point, he estimated they were ninety seconds off schedule. Unless they picked up their pace, they would lose another ninety getting to the drop site. It was time they would have to make up.

At twenty seconds past 11:52 they were balanced on the roof above the courtyard. Snow worked the hooked end of the rope into a crevice between the tiles, then into the wood under the terra cotta, yanking at it hard until he was satisfied it would hold.

He looked up at Rachel. Now that they'd stopped moving, she was thinking again about how scared she was. "Slide down to me," he called.

"I can't."

He could tell she hated admitting it. "Take it slowly. I'll catch you."

"I said I can't do it." She was shaking her head. "I can't."

"You'd better do it. If you don't move now, you can kiss Tong good-bye."

She glared at him and didn't answer. Then he saw one of her legs jerk forward. Then the other. When she got to where he was, she flung an arm desperately around his waist and gulped for air. "I feel like a real idiot," she said.

"You're doing fine."

"Like hell I am."

"You are. I mean it." He reached for her hand and wrapped

it around the rope. "Hold on and work your way down. I'll be right behind you."

"Big deal, Snow. All that means is you get to see me break my neck."

He wanted to laugh but didn't. "You won't break your neck. Now, move."

They worked their way to the edge and without giving her time to think, he swung her off the roof. "Take it hand under hand."

"Snow, I . . ."

"Go!"

He watched her hesitate, then loosen her grip. She lurched her way down and hit the grass with a thud. As soon as she was off, he slid smoothly after her, yanked the rope free, and stuffed it into a pocket as he ran for the office door.

They made up time getting into the galleries and down to the basement but were still a minute behind when they reached the hall leading to the safe.

Snow found the sensor panel on the first post and punched in the number Tong had given him. The faint hum of the instrument cut off. He flipped his wrist. Eleven fifty-nine. The relief guard was on his way back to the security desk.

They tugged on their masks and started for the door.

By the time they got there, Snow had the electric pick out. He guided it into the keylock and flipped it on. Rachel hung back to watch the corridor.

For fifteen seconds, the pick vibrated against the pins, working them up against the springs.

Nothing happened.

"What's wrong?" she whispered.

Snow didn't waste time answering. Keeping his movements unhurried, he turned the tool, thinking maybe what was needed was a change of angle. Another ten seconds and he felt the cylinder shift and the bolt spring back.

He turned the knob and the door opened.

It was now midnight.

Just inside the entrance, he located the sensor panel and hit the second code given to him by Tong.

The room was ten by ten and lit with low-watt lights. Paintings were stacked in bins along one side. A rectangular table sat in the center, and against the far wall was the four-foot safe.

He used the third combination to shut off its alarm, then took out the tools he'd need and lined them up on the ground.

On the long-shot chance that the box could be punched, he knocked off the combination dial, then placed the punch on the exposed spindle shaft, covered it with flannel to mute the sound, and hit it for about a minute before giving up and taking out the drill.

He was going to have to peel the box, which meant digging a hole deep enough to wedge in his chisel. Once he had the chisel in he could pry back the top layer of steel, then work the jimmy through the rivets holding the door on. He had about twenty minutes of hard work ahead of him, which made him wonder why Tong had come up with all the combinations but this one.

"Anyone coming?" he asked.

"No."

"It's going to get a little noisy," he warned and started the drill.

When it hit the metal with a grinding whine, Rachel whispered, "Jesus, they can hear that back in L.A.," but Snow was at work and didn't hear.

On Ward Avenue a black Porsche pulled across Beretania and continued up the block, taking a right into the narrow drive behind the museum.

Midway down the drive, the car stopped and the headlights cut off. Gregory Chee said, "It's twelve twenty-five, Mr. Tong."

Tong nodded, staring out the window with a vicious expression that, seen in the rearview mirror, gave even Chee the chills. "Captain Towers escaped. I don't want that to happen here. I don't like failure, Gregory."

"Yes, Mr. Tong."

"Wait three minutes, then move. We'll pick them up on Victoria Street."

* * *

At twenty-six minutes after midnight the drill broke through the locking bar and the safe door swung heavily back. Snow dragged the drill free, drew out the fourth tray from the top, and folded aside a satin covering. The Red Heart sat alone in the middle of the tray. Seen free of protective glass the stone pulsated with light.

They stared at it in stunned silence, then Snow reached in.

And froze.

Someone was walking in the room above them.

He brought out the map and shoved it at Rachel while he rummaged for the diamond pouch. "Which gallery is he in?"

"Eighteenth-century furniture. It's all wrong. He's supposed to do that last. From there he comes into the basement."

"Dammit." He dropped the pouch into a side pocket, swept his tools into a pile, and began jamming them into the bag. "What's the time?"

"Forty-five seconds past twelve twenty-seven." Her head lifted. "I can hear him on the stairs. Let's get out of here."

Snow caught her arm. "Not for fifteen seconds."

"Screw fifteen seconds."

His hold tightened. "We wait, Detective."

At 12:28 sharp the phone on the security desk rang. The guard reached around his coffee cup and picked it up, glad for something to do. He hated the midnight shift. Nothing happened except maybe once or twice a week he caught the sixty-five-year-old guard catnapping on the stairs. Other than that the place was so boring you could die.

He brought the receiver to his ear and heard a sultry voice say, "Are you the guy who wanted to have some fun?"

"Sorry, ma'am. This is the Honolulu Art—"

"Because," the girl interrupted, "I'd really like to show you a good time. We could start right now. On the phone. Would you like that?"

"Ma'am, I think you've reached the wrong number. This is the Honolulu Art—"

"You sound like the right number to me." There was a squeaking of bedsprings, then she said, "I mean your voice is fantastic. Has anyone ever told you that? I have this picture in my mind of what you look like just from the way you sound. You're big, aren't you? And you have these wonderful hands that do wonderful things. Can I tell you what I'd like them to do to me?"

"Ma'am . . ."

"Can I?"

The guard shut his eyes. What the fuck, he thought. He had a long, bullshit shift ahead of him. Why not start it off with some fun?

To the woman on the phone he said, "Yeah, sweetheart. Go ahead and tell me."

Snow opened the door an inch. The guard was walking in the opposite direction, away from the safe room. He waited until the man turned the corner leading to the library, then, with Rachel behind him, slipped down the camera-lined hall.

At the end of it they saw the delivery door thirty yards away. They ducked through storage racks, then circled a row of wooden bins and cut around head-high stacks of plastic sheets.

At the exit, Snow knocked out the alarm, then shoved back both bolts.

A minute and a half after slamming shut the safe, they were standing in the moonlight.

At 12:29 the Porsche rounded the corner into Victoria Street.

Snow saw the car turn, lights low, moving slowly enough to trouble him. Rachel was six strides ahead when all at once the Porsche picked up speed, jumped the curb, and hurtled along the sidewalk at her.

Rachel stopped and twisted around. "It's Tong," she shouted. "Get out of here, Snow."

The headlights dimmed. Snow spotted the Asian in the back calmly watching him. Looking to his left, Snow realized he stood a chance of getting away. All he had to do was get down the drive and back to the alley behind the museum. From there he could lose them in the maze of apartments.

And he had the Red Heart.

The driver's door opened. The stubby man who stepped out was just tall enough to see over the roof. He said grimly, "Don't make a move, Dr. Snow, if you want the cop to live."

SEVENTEEN

THEY DROVE OUT OF the city on the central freeway that cut west across the flatlands of Honolulu, wound past Pearl Harbor and over the Ewa plains. At the Wahiawa exit the driver pulled off and got onto a two-lane road that led up into the mountains.

The air cooled. Stands of pines clung to the hillsides, yellow houselights shining behind them. It became quiet enough to hear the wind in the grass bordering the road. A few minutes later the houses disappeared, and they were on an unlit highway threading through fields of sugar cane.

On both sides, cane stalks higher than the car and as thick as a wall rose up, making the darkness darker. Then the road inclined and Rachel saw that the fields stretched for miles toward a chain of rolling hills like a dark, rustling sea. The road swung down, then skirted a wide gulch and crossed over an empty stream bed on a single-lane wooden bridge. For another two hundred yards, the only light was from the headlights, strafing the red dirt road and the sugar cane.

Then Rachel saw a bright red triangle glowing at the foot of the mountains. As they moved toward it, streaks of orange and yellow leaped out surrounded by boiling smoke, and she realized it was a good-sized fire.

Tong tapped Chee's shoulder, then gestured at a smaller road branching off the one they were on. "Go that way," he said.

With a nod Chee made the turn, taking them straight into the cane. On either side, water washed by in shallow irrigation ditches. The fire was out of sight now, but the wind whipping down from the hills carried the smell of smoke.

Whatever Tong planned to do, Rachel thought, he would do it here.

She took a quick look at Snow, but his face was as neutral as a mask. She'd given him the chance to run, why hadn't he grabbed it? And how had Tong found out she was a cop? Who or what had broken her cover? And what was it going to cost?

Tong said, "Stop in that turnaround," and Chee brought the car around a small cul-de-sac and pulled to the side.

"Have you ever seen sugar cane before, Detective Starr?" the Asian asked pleasantly.

"No."

"It's quite beautiful, don't you think? Like tall, silky grass. Listen to the wind in it." He was silent a moment, then he said, "They're burning this field tonight. That's the fire we saw. They'll let it run until all the leaves are gone and only the stalks are left."

He took a cigarette out of his ivory case and tapped it against the back of his hand. "Do you remember the story I told you in my gallery? The one about my father's escape to Hong Kong?"

"Yes," Rachel said. The driver was looking out the window now, the gun in his hand braced loosely on the dashboard. Could she get to him before Tong reacted?

"There's more to the story," Tong said. "I want you to hear the rest of it so you will understand."

"Understand what?"

"Who I am. Why I do what I do." He crossed one leg over the knee of the other and folded his hands on his lap. "You see, my mother and I were with him on the journey. She was ill when we started out and grew worse along the way. Yet she was the one who never lost faith that we'd escape. Ironically, when we were less than two days from Hong Kong, she died. We buried her twenty miles from the bay she had longed to see."

He turned slightly and gazed past Rachel at the cane as though searching for a ghost. "In Hong Kong my father and I were very poor. Thousands of refugees had poured into the British Colony and there was nowhere to live, no work, little food. My father wouldn't touch the jewels. They were for me in case anything happened to him. And something, of course, did.

"The winter when I was eight there was a very bad flu epidemic. He died in it. I won't bore you with the way he died or where he died except to say that it was a terrible thing to see. But I had little time to grieve for him. It was very cold that year, and I had no money and was living in the streets.

"I took the painting with the jewels to a wealthy man who had a reputation as a buyer of gemstones. He lived in a mansion in the hills above Hong Kong. They made me wait for hours on the back stoop in a freezing sleet. When the wealthy man finally found time to see me, I was sick from the weather.

"I remember that they made me wash my feet. When they were clean and dry, I was taken into a beautiful room lined with books and paintings, and carpeted with a brilliantly colored Chinese rug. I had never seen such a perfect room. It was warm in there," he added softly.

"The wealthy man sat behind a desk of gleaming mahogany. He was a big Englishman, white-haired, with a curling mustache that he liked to fuss with. He seemed kind. He acted kind. He waited while I nervously took out my legacy, then glanced at the jewels and began to laugh, trying at the same time to stop himself because he realized he was upsetting me. Very gently he explained that they were fakes. Worthless fakes. But out of pity he gave me a few pounds for them and sent me on my way.

"Now, of course, I know that they were worth several hundreds of thousands of dollars. Since then many things have happened to me. But I have never been pitied and I have never been made a fool of again."

He turned to them and said without emotion, "You are going to die in the cane. This is regrettable, Nicholas, as I was almost fond of you. And you, Detective Starr. Too beautiful, really, for this kind of death. But you give me no choice."

Rachel said, "How did you find out who I was?"

"We share a mutual friend."

"Who?"

"Captain James Towers." He smiled as he watched her face, enjoying what he saw. "You look disappointed, Detective. Haven't you discovered yet that we are all corruptible?"

"How long?"

"Have we worked together? A few years. The relationship has been profitable for both of us." He flicked an ash out the open window. "I know you are the witness to the policeman's death. I assume that is why you are here. But why are you with her, Nicholas?"

"For Victor Chang," Snow said.

Tong thought a moment, then crushed the cigarette into the ashtray. "I see."

"Do you remember him?"

"A little. I remember his necklace better. All diamonds. Meticulously set. An exquisite piece. But why bother to avenge the death of a jewelry broker? There are so many others who might take his place."

"We were friends."

"Friends?" He gave a belittling laugh. "A foolish reason to risk your life, but that is the beauty of this country, isn't it? We are free to be foolish." He raised his hand. "I will take the diamond now, Professor."

Snow gave it to him.

"Thank you. Now I will ask you to get out of the car. Gregory, open his door."

Chee climbed out and stuck his free hand in to lift the lock. "C'mon, get out," he commanded.

Snow gave a nod and, before the Asian could read his intentions, bashed his shoulder into the door.

The man gave a yelp as he tripped backward and the .38 bounced out of his grip.

Shouting furiously in Chinese, Tong reached into his coat and had his hand on his gun when Rachel rammed her fist into his throat. For a second rage mottled his face, then he slumped forward, gagging.

Snow pulled her out of the car just as Chee found his weapon.

The first bullet cut into the ground inches from Rachel. Snow shoved her across the water ditch and into the cane. A barrage of gunfire followed them, slicing off leaves, flinging them into the air like confetti. Inside the cane, Rachel dropped to her knees and crawled, using her shoulder to batter her way through the tangled plants. The wind came in bursts and the smell of smoke turned stronger.

Behind them another shot rang out.

She heard Snow grunt and slowed long enough to spot him a few yards off to her left, clutching at branches. "Keep moving!" she shouted.

There was another shot, then Chee yelling and the roar of the engine starting. She heard the car reverse and careen down the road, parallel to them.

She yelled, "Cut this way!" and made a sharp turn into the thickest part of the cane.

The darkness she plowed into was different than any she'd known. A suffocating, clawing blackness that mixed you up. She could hear the fire, smell it, but couldn't tell where it was coming from. A dusty smoke swirled around her like a fog, biting into her eyes, clogging her lungs.

She knew it was the smoke that got you first. The fire came afterward.

That thought made her grab blindly for branches and drag herself forward.

The stalks cut into her legs. She felt blood on her arms, tasted it in her mouth. She knew she was hopelessly lost, then all at once the cane stopped and she was standing in a yard-wide water trench. She spun around to find Snow, suddenly terrified that she'd lost him.

Seconds later he stumbled out and clutched at a handful of stalks to hold himself up.

"Which way?" she shouted.

He pointed to his left.

They started running, sliding and falling through the water. After a hundred yards, the trench snaked westward and the air began to clear. Twenty more yards and the trench broke through the cane to a road.

In the open space Rachel fell to her knees and tried to catch her breath. Then a moan pulled her around and she saw Snow face down in the ravine. "Jesus Christ," she whispered and staggered back to him.

His arms were crushed between his body and the channel wall. She reached under them and slid her hand across his shoulder until she felt the hole. Blood pumped out of it and ran down his rib cage. "Goddammit, Snow." She found his wrist and searched frantically for a pulse. "Goddammit, don't die on me. Don't you . . ." Under her thumb she could feel the faintest heartbeat. "Christ." She squeezed his hand hard and realized she was crying.

She gave herself a moment, then caught him under his arms and pulled him out of the water to a place beside the cane. To her left the road seemed to dead-end into the vegetation. To her right was black smoke. She wondered how far she'd have to go before the road hit the highway, if it hit it at all. She wondered where the fire was, and where Tong and his goon were. She wondered if Snow would die.

When the headlights burst out of the dark, Rachel thought it was the Porsche coming back for them. Then she saw it was a truck, half rusted out, rattling noisily toward the next cane road.

She ran after it, waving wildly and screaming for help. Just as the truck made its turn, it stopped and the driver leaned out, looking startled.

"What's going on?" he yelled.

"A man's been shot. I think he's dying."

EIGHTEEN

"I'M VERY UNHAPPY, GREGORY," Tong said coldly. They were in his office, Chee standing with his head bowed. "First Captain Towers eludes us. Now the professor and the woman."

"Yes, Mr. Tong."

"What have you found out?"

"Nothing yet about the captain. A plantation worker picked up the professor and the woman in the cane fields."

"What's this worker's name?"

"We don't know yet."

"When will you know?"

"Soon."

Tong stood abruptly and Chee flinched as if expecting a blow. "Look at me, Gregory." Reluctantly the other man lifted his head. "I want you to find all three of them. I want them dead, understand?"

"Yes, Mr. Tong."

"And no stupid mistakes this time."

"He'll make it." Kapiolani Smith dried her hands and zipped shut the black case. "Someone else, losing this much blood, maybe not. But your friend is very strong. Very determined. He wasn't ready to die." She picked up the case and looked at Rachel. "You need to rest."

"When will he wake up?"

"In the next few hours. Come to the main house and sleep. I'll send Pono over."

"No."

"You'll be useless if you get sick."

"I'm not leaving."

The woman nodded. "He's that important to you?" she said. "Stay with him, then. I'll be back in the afternoon."

The room was small and cluttered with furniture—the bed he was in, a long dresser, bookshelves, a desk, two straight-back chairs. There were lace curtains on the windows, a square rug on the floor, papered walls. He thought of a room he'd once stayed in in Dublin. A bed-and-breakfast place above O'Connell Street not far from the river. Waking to the sounds of sheep in the road, the bells on their necks ringing as they walked to market. Was that where he was?

Then the pain started, shooting across his shoulder, and Snow remembered the cane fields and Tong.

Though it was dark outside, he could see trees through the curtains. He tried to sit, but gave up as a knifelike ache exploded across his chest. Lying back, he made himself breathe slowly while he pictured the still surface of the lily pond the way Victor had taught him.

When he awoke it was morning. Rachel was asleep in a chair beside the bed, her legs crossed at the ankles, a book in her lap. Her hair was loose and covered her shoulders. Her mouth looked soft. He had to fight down an urge to reach out and touch it.

In sleep her hard edges disappeared. Most of them were an act anyway, he'd caught on to that the first night in Freddie's bar. All you had to do was look in her eyes to know.

For an hour he watched her, wondering off and on why he'd stayed with her at the museum instead of running with the diamond.

Then she woke up, saw him, and started to smile.

And Snow knew why.

Falling for a cop. Very smart move, he told himself. Myles would like it.

"Hello, Professor," she said, and there was warmth in her eyes.

"Hello, Detective Starr."

"How are you feeling?"

"Not bad." He raised himself slightly to see out the window. "Where are we?"

"A place called Kahana Valley. On Pono's farm. Don't do that." She touched his unbandaged shoulder to keep him still. "You're supposed to rest."

"How long have we been here?"

"Almost two days."

"Two days?" He started to get up again.

"I said don't move."

"What's happening with Tong?"

"Forget Tong. He's not your problem anymore. All you have to do is get well."

"Like hell—" Pain knuckled him back to the mattress. He grimaced sharply, then lay grudgingly still.

"Like hell what?"

"Like hell he's not my problem," Snow rasped.

"You have a hole in your shoulder," she pointed out. "A couple of inches to the left and you'd have had a hole through your heart, so don't act like you also have one running through your head."

"Tong's mine," he insisted.

"Not anymore."

"Rachel . . ."

"Kapi will be by in about an hour to see how you are. Until then you should get more sleep."

"Who's Kapi?"

"Pono's mother. Kapiolani Smith. She saved your life." Rachel got out of the chair. "I'll be back to check on you."

Snow slid sideways and grabbed her hand. "Wait for me. I'm the one who can get him."

"Lee Chan is in town and Tong has the Red Heart diamond. Whatever's going to happen is going to happen soon."

"Wait for me."

"I can't." She slipped out of his hold. "Get some rest. I'll be back."

Cheryl's apartment was in a twelve-story condo on the beach at the foot of Diamond Head. One apartment to a floor, each with deep verandas and palm trees rustling nearby. A view of the curve of Waikiki and of the southern end of the island swinging out in the water toward the horizon. When Towers walked in, saw the expensive furniture, the chandeliers, the baby grand nestled in a corner, he wondered what an eighteen-year-old kid could do to pay for such a spread. Then he remembered.

"Two girls live with me," she said when he'd complimented her on the place. "They're out of town right now. Stews."

"Stewardesses?"

"Uh-huh. We split the rent. That's how I can afford this place, in case you're wondering."

"It's real nice."

She took him onto the veranda and they stood by the railing, watching the ocean roll in. "This is called the Gold Coast," she explained. "From where those hotels end until that lighthouse over there. Really expensive, but the view is great."

"Yeah, it is."

When he'd called, she wasn't surprised that he was still in town. In fact, Towers thought, by the way she looked when she'd opened the door, she was happy he'd stayed. He'd come in and put the bag under the bed, letting her watch him do it. He'd showered, shaved, put on the white pants and the shirt with the palm trees, then taken everything off again three minutes later at Cheryl's request.

Afterward, he'd told her everything. Why he'd come to Honolulu, how he'd been shot at, how he wanted to get even with Tong. She'd listened without asking questions or judging him. It was taking a chance telling her about the drug dealing and the money he'd made off Tong, but he wanted to be honest with her. He didn't want secrets between them.

That was yesterday morning.

Now they were in bed, Towers reading the paper, Cheryl painting her nails. There was a box of doughnuts on the sheets between them and some sliced fruit in a glass bowl. Both were drinking Cokes.

"Poor suck," Towers said and flipped the page over.

"Who?" Blowing gently on her thumbnail, Cheryl stroked her toes down his leg.

"Guy who picked me up. The cab driver. They hit him. Listen to this. He was twenty-seven years old, born and raised in Harlem. Some joke, huh? Makes it through Harlem, comes to paradise, and gets blown away."

"I'm glad it wasn't you."

"Yeah?" Towers grinned and she wiggled closer, holding her nails safely aloft. "Why?"

"You know why," she said.

"No, I don't. No idea. Tell me."

"You know."

"Are you blushing?" He tilted her chin. "Shit, you are. I don't believe it."

"Cut it out." She pushed his hand away.

"It's cute."

"Johnny."

"It is."

"You're messing up my nails."

"Oh yeah? I'll show you messed up." He flipped her onto her back and kissed her, playfully at first, then letting it change, giving in to wanting her again, feeling his skin heat and his pulse go crazy, wondering how long it was going to take to get enough of her.

Cheryl whispered, "I think I'm in love with you, Johnny."

"Oh yeah?" Trying to make it light, but feeling the rush.

He looked in her eyes. Powder blue and sweet. How long had it been since he'd been looked at by eyes like those? He touched her face, rubbed his thumb over her mouth, the dimple in her chin, asking himself how it had happened that all of a sudden, out of the blue, he'd gotten so lucky.

"You don't mind?" she said.

"No, baby. I don't mind."

In the afternoon they went downstairs for a swim. Cheryl brought along a six-pack of beer and they each drank three cans lying in the sun, the whole time holding hands.

On the way back to the apartment Towers bought a paper, thinking there might be more on what happened to the cab driver. He read it while Cheryl made dinner.

"Jesus, look at this," he said and spread the front page across the table.

"What?"

"This. 'Priceless Red Diamond Stolen.' "

"So what?" She leaned over his shoulder and looked at the article.

"It was stolen here, honey."

"So?"

"So I know who took it."

"Who?"

"The guy who tried to have me killed. Jacob Tong. That's the kind of piece he'd go for."

"Are you sure?

"You bet your ass I'm sure."

"What are you going to do?"

"What do you think? I'm going to take it away from him."

"How?"

He began tearing out the article, frowning as his brain started working. "I don't know yet."

"How long have you been watching me?" Rachel said. She'd fallen asleep in the chair and now it was dark outside.

"Not long. Can I have a cigarette?"

"No."

"C'mon, Detective. Light me a cigarette."

"No smoking. Orders from Kapi."

"One cigarette."

"Christ." She found the pack in the nightstand drawer and tapped one out. "Here." She struck the match.

"Thanks."

"It's your life."

Snow sucked in gratefully and blew the smoke out slowly, enjoying the feel of it moving through his lungs. He remembered how much Victor had despised the habit, called it a breach of discipline, but it was one Snow couldn't break and he'd given up trying. "You look tired, Detective."

"I'm fine."

"Are you?" You look like you could use some sleep."

"I've been sleeping."

"No you haven't. You've been taking care of me." He inched over and pushed aside the covers. "Get in."

"What?"

"You need to rest in a real bed, not that chair. So get in." He smiled as he considered her. "You looked shocked. I didn't think anything shocked a cop these days."

"Thanks for the offer," she said evenly, "but I'll pass." She picked her book off the floor, opened it, and caught Snow's eyes on her. "Now what?"

"All I'm offering you is a place to sleep, Detective. Nothing else is going to happen."

"I ever tell you I was second in my judo class at the police academy? I'm not worried about my virtue, Snow." When he laughed, she relaxed.

"Second?" he said.

"Second."

"Too bad." He closed his eyes, felt himself begin to drift. "Might have been interesting."

She took the cigarette from his hand and put it out. "You asleep?"

He didn't answer.

She tucked the blanket over him.

NINETEEN

AROUND MIDNIGHT IT STARTED raining again.

The drumming on the tin roof woke Rachel. Instantly she reached for her revolver before realizing nothing was wrong. It wasn't gunfire, only rain. She got up and put on her jacket.

From the window she could see the lawn stretching to the tall trees that blocked the main house from view. To the right was the road that ran from the highway past Pono's house and into the valley. If they came, it would be from that direction.

She walked back to the bed and pulled the chair closer to the light, tried to read, then gave up and let herself think about Snow. Why hadn't he run when he'd had the chance? And in the cane, when she thought he'd die, why had she cried? Getting up again, she went back to the window. What did it matter anyhow? It was the waiting that did this. Made her think about things it was pointless to think about.

"You all right?"

She turned. Snow was sitting up. "Yeah, I'm fine. Go back to sleep."

"Come over here. Talk to me."

She hesitated, then walked back and said, "What do you want to talk about?"

"You."

"Me? What about me?"

"Whatever you want to tell me."

She thought a moment, then said, "Want to know why I really became a cop?"

Snow nodded.

"When I was a kid . . ." She stopped, surprised at herself. She didn't talk about the past with anyone. Only Johnny Haid knew pieces of it, stuff that had slipped out over too many shots at Blackie's Bar over the years. But they'd been partners, so in a way that was okay. She could handle his knowing. But who the hell was Snow? "You don't want to hear this."

"Yes, I do."

"Look, it was no big deal," she said dismissingly. "No blinding desire to serve justice or do great good."

"What then?"

She could feel Snow waiting while she slumped back in the chair. Her eyes settled on the window on the other side of the bed. The rain was coming down heavily now, shaking the leaves of the ti plants, reminding her of other rainy nights, and all at once she was talking.

"My old man was a small-time hood," she said, her voice husky with memory. "He used to drag my mother and me up and down the East Coast, going from one small town to another, pulling scams in each one, splitting when it got too hot. He liked easy marks—old ladies who'd give him their savings, liquor stores late at night, drunks in pool halls.

"When he wasn't stealing, he gambled. And drank. When he drank, he liked to slap my mother around. She died when I was twelve. The doctor called it pneumonia, but I called it escape.

"After she was gone he tried to come after me, only I wouldn't let him. So he'd tear up the places we were staying in. One night he was really going at it, and the woman who ran the motel where we were staying called the cops. A policewoman took me away, then went to the courts and got me placed in a foster home.

For the first time since she'd started talking, Rachel looked over at Snow. "I was fourteen and it was like my world suddenly had hope in it. Like I finally stood a chance for the first time in my life. After I got out of college, I wanted to give it back, maybe do for somebody what was done for me. So I became a cop."

"Sounds like a big deal to me," Snow said gently.

"Yeah?" She shrugged. "Well, it wasn't."

"Is he still alive?"

"My old man? He's in prison. For assault committed during an armed robbery. He'll probably die there." She brought a bottle of scotch out from under the nightstand. "Want some of this?"

Snow nodded.

"My father's name was Ian Bain."

"Ian Bain the banker?" Rachel said.

"Yes."

"He's a very wealthy man."

"Yes."

"Why the different names?"

"Victor gave me the name Snow."

"Why?"

"Because snow is silent."

"I don't understand."

"That's my talent, Detective. Silence."

"Renoir is too lush. Lush and cloying."

"I agree," Snow said. "Pour me another one, too." He held out his glass.

"What about the contemporaries?"

"Who specifically?"

"The New York hotshots."

"I despise their work."

"Why?"

"Their paintings rely on explanations, on language, to circumvent their ugliness."

"Now you sound like an art professor."

"I am an art professor."

She smiled wryly. "You are, aren't you? Sometimes I forget."

"Detective novels."

"I thought cops hated detective novels."

"I find them interesting."

"What else do you find interesting?"

"Old movies, good scotch, museums."

"What about travel?"

"Don't do much of it."

"Why not?"

"Guess I moved around too much when I was young."

"What about Europe? Ever been there?"

"No." She laughed. "You look appalled."

"I am appalled."

"I planned a trip once, one of those art tours that take you to twenty countries in fifteen days. Then a case broke and I had to cancel."

"I'll take you."

"What?"

"To Europe. We'll go together. I know which museums to see, which art galleries. I know the best hotels to stay in and the only restaurants worth patronizing. I know all the quaint villages, the finest pubs—"

"I don't think so," she interrupted.

"Why not?"

"I just don't think so," she repeated softly.

"So. Never married. What about love?"

"You mean have I ever been in love?"

He nodded, watching her carefully.

"I date now and then. Had my share of lovers. But in love? No. What about you?"

"No."

"Funny, I would've thought . . ."

"Thought what?"

"Someone like you. I'd have thought there'd be a lot of women."

"Not a lot."
"Oh," she said, and looked away.

"My father opened the Hong Kong branch when I was ten."
"What was it like growing up there?"
"Lonely at first. Then Ian hired Victor as my tutor."
"Tell me about him."
"Victor taught me art, mathematics, history, literature, Latin. He also taught me how to pick locks and crack safes and hold my breath for four minutes under water."
"Interesting mix of subject matter."
"He was an interesting man."
"How does a teacher come to sell stolen jewelry?"
"We were in business together. The money from the jewelry was used as working capital."
"What kind of business?"
"You asked me that before."
"You didn't tell me before, Snow."
"I still can't."

"I ran," Rachel said. "Saw the shotgun and took off like a goddamn coward." Avoiding Snow's eyes, she gazed out the front window. The sun was coming up, shooting a thin gray light through the clouds. "So Johnny Haid died. My fault."
"What could you have done?"
"Yelled out. Tried to take one of them down. Something."
"Could you have taken one of them?"
"I don't know. Maybe. Maybe not. You see, that's it, Snow. I'll never know."
"The chances are you couldn't have."
"But I should have tried. He was my friend. I owed him." She felt tears start and said quickly, "God, I could tell you stories. What he taught me. The stuff we went through. The stakeouts, the drug busts, the homicides. He was smart. Smartest cop I ever ran into. Taught me how to think like a crook, and that's the key. The number-one trick. Think like they do and you can one-step them, be where they're going before they've even figured out where that is."

"You miss him."
She nodded, then said, "The rain's stopped."
"For a while anyway."
"You must be tired. You should sleep."
"You should, too." He folded back the blanket. "What do you think?"
"The truth? It's been three nights in a chair. I'd kill for a bed."
"Climb in."
"No funny stuff?"
He smiled. "No funny stuff."
"Because I *was* second in that judo class." She drew the covers over them.
"I remember."
Her leg brushed his, then pulled away. "Sorry."
"Go to sleep."
After a moment, "Snow?"
"What?"
"You're okay."
"Yeah?"
"Yeah."

The phone in the Porsche rang and Tong answered it with a harsh "Yes?"
"The man who picked them up is named Gonzales."
"Have you talked to him?"
"Not yet. He didn't come to work."
"Find out where he lives."
"I asked. They don't give out that information."
"Ask again. And, Gregory. Don't leave until you have an answer.

TWENTY

IN THE MIDDLE OF the night he remembered the name Pono Smith. Towers turned on the lamp, waking Cheryl. "Where's your phone book?"

"Shit, Johnny, it's two in the morning." She rolled away from him and stuck her head under the pillow.

He patted her bottom. "C'mon, where is it?"

"On the TV stand, on the TV stand."

"Thanks." Kissing her between the shoulder blades, he climbed over her and said, "We're gonna be very rich, baby."

Cheryl moaned.

In the morning Towers explained his plan. "You know what R & D is?" he said.

"Uh-uh."

"It means research and development. Big companies put a lot of time and money into R & D. That's how they develop new products or figure out ways to save cash."

"What's that got to do with us?"

"This lady cop—the one who's here, whose partner got killed, remember?—she's been doing R & D on Tong for us. I figure

I follow her, see what she's up to, what she's got in mind for him, then jump in at an opportune time."

"And then what?"

"Take the Red Heart, number one. Number two, make it real hard for Tong to ever walk again, and, number three, split for Rio. I was thinking we could buy a place on the beach, some place with a hot tub, maybe, and a volleyball court, whatever you want. Maybe even pick up a sailboat. How does that sound?"

"I love it."

"Me too. All we gotta do is get that stone."

Sean was cruising Kalakaua in his cab, looking at the girls strolling the sidewalks. A lot of them were in bikinis, a lot of them looking very good, tanned, nicely built, with no worry on their faces, just looking for fun.

He was twenty-two, he liked his job, and in general had no complaints about life. Financially he was doing well. He had what he told himself was a real knack for business, wheeling and dealing, bringing the right people together under the right circumstances and setting it up so he made a nice percentage.

Now Cheryl was telling him she was on to something big. How big? he asked. Really big, she said, but when he probed for details she told him she couldn't talk, she'd call him back, and hung up.

He was a little excited about the possibilities, although it could be nothing in the long run, but on the other hand, it could be something very interesting.

Cheryl was a smart girl. Her smartest trick was playing dumb. Gives you the advantage, she'd say. People tell you things they wouldn't trust with someone else. Things you could use, could make pay off.

She also told people—men particularly—she was eighteen, which was a crock of shit, though she looked good enough to pass. Actually she was two years older than he was—twenty-four. He knew this because when he was goofing off in the tenth grade, she was cutting classes in the twelfth to go on "dates" with tourists in Waikiki.

They were a lot alike, him and Cheryl. Like him, she had plans. Neither of them intended to live half-assed lives. Both wanted the good things, as good as possible, and as much of it as possible.

She had a clear idea of how to get where they wanted to go. Real estate, Seanny, she'd tell him. That's where it's at. She was reading books all the time. *How to Make a Million in Real Estate. No Down Payment. Buying and Selling Condominiums.* Crap that bored the shit out of him and pissed him off sometimes when he felt like having fun and all she wanted to do was read.

Still the businessman in him respected her. He thought they made a good team, balanced each other well. She liked the research angle. He liked rolling the dice. She was methodical. He was flashy. Together they'd go far, who knew how far? Like Cheryl always said, whatever they could dream up they could do.

He really wanted to know what was going on with her, what the Big Deal was all about. But he could be patient, he guessed. Cruise around some more, check out the women—Christ, look at that one—until Cheryl called back.

Not a tough life at all.

It was Franklin Gonzales's day off and he was watching television and drinking beer when the two Chinese men knocked on his screen door. He set his beer on the coffee table, remembering to slide a magazine under it to keep the wife happy, picked up his crutches, and went to see what they wanted, though his gut told him it had something to do with the couple he'd helped in the cane field.

The taller of the two did the speaking. "Mr. Gonzales?"

"Yes?"

A flash of an I.D. card, too quick for him to read. "We're with the D.E.A. We understand you assisted a man and a woman the other night near Ewa."

"What about it?" Since his years in Vietnam, he'd disliked the government.

"We're investigating a case in which they're involved. We need your help locating them."

"That was three days ago. I don't know where they are now."
"But you remember where you took them, don't you?"
"Yeah, I do."
"Where did you take them, Mr. Gonzales?" the man asked, beginning to looked annoyed.
"Pearl City," Gonzales lied, thinking why the hell should he help the government. "That's where they told me they lived."
"Where in Pearl City?"
"I dropped them at the Pearl Tower."
"Is that an apartment building?"
"Yeah."
"Did you see them go inside?"
"Well, it was late. I let them out and drove off. But I'm pretty sure they went in."
"Was anything wrong with either of them?"
"What do you mean?"
"Was either wounded or hurt?"
Gonzales shrugged. "The lady looked tired, but that's about it."
"Okay." The questioner looked back expectantly at his partner.
Gonzales said, "Is that it?" then saw sunlight shimmer off the barrel of a gun. His first impulse was to hit the ground like in Nam, but he knew the crutches would trip him. He took one step back. The blue of the sky seemed to pour toward him and the wind stilled. He thought of his wife, was thinking of how he would miss her, when the gun went off.

"She's there," Towers said, getting into Cheryl's Cadillac.
They were parked on the side of a two-lane highway running between the ocean and the pastureland on the north coast of the island. They were a hundred yards past the road leading to Smith's farm.
"You saw her?" Cheryl said.
"Yep." He took a sip of her beer. "Going into a cottage."
"What do we do now?"
"We wait."

"How long?"

"Until she drives out."

She took back her drink and slumped down, resting both knees against the dashboard. "This could get boring, Johnny."

"Think about the diamond, honey. Think about what it will let us do."

Cheryl closed her eyes and made her face dreamy to look like she was thinking. She could feel the man watching her, almost anxious the way high school guys got with their first girl. She knew he was crazy about her and she kind of liked the feeling. It was different from her usual dates, different from Sean.

Seanny liked her when she was around, but if she wasn't around, she didn't think it would break his heart. With this guy it might, and that made her feel special.

Old guys like Johnny were a trip. Easy to please, walking around thrilled all the time because you were letting them do it to you.

The funny thing was, with Johnny she liked doing it back. That was new and she hadn't quite worked out yet what it meant. In the meantime she reached for his hand and said, "I like what I'm seeing, Johnny. I like it a lot."

Rachel hung up the phone and, feeling someone behind her, eased around. Pono Smith was in the doorway with a look on his face that told her he'd heard part of the conversation.

"What's going on?" he said suspiciously.

"I could ask the same thing. You checking up on me?"

"This is where I live, Rachel. I'm just hanging out." He stepped into the room. "So, who were you talking to?"

"Cooper Kincaid."

"Kincaid? What for?"

"I'm making a deal."

"Tell me if I'm wrong," Smith said, "but the way I understood it, Kincaid and Tong are pals. What are you doing talking to him?"

"Kincaid and Tong aren't pals. They do business together, that's all. And people doing business don't mind doing it with whoever offers them the greatest profit." She settled back against the sink, holding the edge with her hands. "I'm offering Kincaid the greatest profit."

"Which is?"

"In exchange for his cooperation, I put in a good word for him when he's arrested."

"How does he know he'll be arrested?"

"I told him about the videotape we have of him talking to Tong about taking care of the shipping clerk."

"You what?" He shook his head with disbelief. "And for this good word of yours, what does Kincaid do for you?"

"Tells me the time and place where Tong is giving Tiger Lee Chan the Red Heart. Once I know that, I can bring in the local police department. Tong's payment to Lee Chan is witnessed, the department makes the arrest, and we've got him."

"When's Kincaid giving you this information?"

"In an hour at his warehouse."

"His warehouse? Jesus." Smith expelled an exasperated breath. "Forget it. I don't like it. It feels like a trap. Tell him to tell you over the phone."

"He wants to see the videotape. I'm taking him a copy."

"Right. So you go to his warehouse and who do you find?" Smith said sourly. "Tong and his gunmen."

"Maybe. Maybe not. Kincaid's scared. Scared enough, I think, to make this deal. Scared enough to finger Tong and help us bring him in."

"Maybe he's fingering you," Smith pointed out tersely. "I'm telling you, Rachel, you're making a mistake. Bring in H.P.D. now. Let them take it from here."

"We've had this conversation before."

"The problem is you didn't listen before. Maybe you should've."

"What's that mean?" she challenged.

"It means Snow almost got killed."

"He's not in this anymore. I'm solo from here on out."

"That's your best answer? Jesus." He hit the top of the counter. "You're still doing it your way, aren't you, Rachel? Doesn't matter who gets hurt."

She made herself look at him for a long moment, then she said, "It matters."

"Then turn the case over now."

"Not until I talk to Kincaid. Not until I have an airtight case against Tong. Then I'll give it up."

"That's it? You won't change your mind?"

"No."

"Then I'm going with you."

"No. I promised Kincaid I'd come alone."

"Jesus." He started to hit the counter again, stopped and sighed deeply. "You'd think after all these years I'd know better than to try to change your mind."

"Yeah, you'd think so."

"Do me a favor, okay?"

"What?

"Be careful. L.A.P.D. can't afford to lose a pigheaded lady cop."

Rachel waited a moment, then grinned. "Yeah, I love you, too, Smith."

Towers sat up straighter. A white station wagon was pulling out of the valley, making a right onto the highway. "There she is," he said, and started the engine. A tour bus rumbled past, followed by a break in traffic. He steered the car onto the asphalt, hanging far enough back from the wagon to put a half-dozen car lengths between them.

"This is just like the movies," Cheryl said.

"You having fun?"

"Uh-huh." She slid over and snuggled into him. "I'm having tons of fun."

TWENTY-ONE

THE SUN WAS HALFWAY under the horizon when Rachel reached the pier. She parked in a small lot at the top of the wharf and got out. Except for Kincaid's silver Cadillac sitting beside a wire fence, the lot was empty. She crossed to the fence, unhooked and pushed open a wire gate, rehooking it when it swung shut. Four low warehouses hugged the curving pier, already in shadows. The last one out, Kincaid had told her, was his.

The first three warehouses were locked, but as she neared Kincaid's, Rachel saw that a corrugated steel door was a fourth of the way up, leaving a three-foot opening. A pinkish light spread out from the right side; the rest of the interior was dark. She checked behind her, took out her gun, then ducked under the door where it was darkest.

Inside, she eased cautiously forward, checked the aisles between the stacks of wooden containers that filled the floor area, then circled a half-dozen fork lifts that looked strangely alive in the hazy light. Beyond them, a steep stairwell climbed the side of the wall, leading to a glassed-in office. The pinkish light was coming from this room. While she was looking up, she saw Kincaid walk into, then out of, view. She listened for a moment, but the only sound was the ocean slapping against the pilings. Keeping the gun out, she started quietly up the metal stairs.

Kincaid was pouring a drink when she entered the room. He spun around fast enough to almost lose his balance, fear skimming his eyes before he recognized her. Forcing a self-concious smile, he raised the glass in greeting. "I told myself I wouldn't drink, but it seems I need one. What about you?"

"No, thanks."

He walked around his desk but didn't sit. "Do you have the videotape?"

"Let's talk about Tong first. And the drugs. And Tiger Lee Chan."

He seemed about to argue, then nodded and sat down wearily. "I'd like to ask one question."

"Go ahead."

"What happens to me when Jacob finds out what I've done? I mean, how am I protected?"

"I can talk to the Honolulu police. Request that they give you protection."

Kincaid made a bleak sound and shook his head miserably. "That's not enough. You don't know Jacob. You don't know how powerful he is."

"Help us and we'll help you."

"Will you? I hope to God you can. I'm very scared."

"Tell me what you know about Tong."

"I know I should never have gotten involved with him. From the beginning I knew it was wrong. But I needed the money. Not for myself, you understand. For the company. I couldn't lose the company. It was my grandfather's and my father's and—"

"Talk about Tong," she cut in.

"He killed my clerk. Gave one order and Andrew Solomon showed up dead. I never meant for that to happen, I swear. Now I think he plans to kill me." Slowly, in disbelief, his eyes widened and he dropped the glass. "Oh my God," he whispered, terror pulling at his face. "Oh my God."

From behind her Rachel heard the level voice of Jacob Tong. "Move an inch, Detective Starr, and I will shoot you."

* * *

When Rachel turned off at the pier, Towers slowed and pulled the Cadillac onto the grassy shoulder of the highway. He was getting out when Cheryl said, "I want to go with you."

"You stay put. There might be trouble."

"If there's trouble, I want to be with you."

He leaned in and put his palm to her cheek. "I ever tell you how sweet you are?" Her hair was soft around his hand, lit up from a streetlight.

"I want to be with you, Johnny." She kissed his hand, then held on to it. "I don't want you to go alone."

"And I want you to be safe. So stay here, lock the doors, and wait for me. When I come back, maybe I'll have the diamond."

"Kiss me."

"Cheryl, Cheryl." He kissed her lightly, then said, "You wait for me. I'm going to take care of things. I'm going to make you happy. As happy as I can make you. Because I love you, baby. I really do." Tears filled her eyes and he brushed gently at them. "Hey, don't do that."

"I love you, too, Johnny."

"I gotta go." He started drawing back, then couldn't help himself and kissed her again. "I'm going to lose the lady if I don't move."

Towers hurried along the road, made a right onto the pier, and noted the two cars parked in the lot. He cut past them, opened the gate, and was starting toward the buildings when a black car swung through the driveway into the lot. Before its headlights found him, Towers darted behind a head-high metal container. He watched the car circle twice before moving slowly toward the outer edge of the platform.

As it passed, he crushed himself into the box, then peered quickly out, catching a glimpse of the passengers. Two men up front. Jacob Tong alone in the back. He darted to the nearest building and, staying in the shadows, made his way to the third warehouse, keeping the car in sight. Beside the fourth building, the car halted and the three men climbed out.

The stocky one who'd been driving stayed by the car while Tong and the other man slipped under the warehouse's steel door. The stocky man strolled to the edge of the pier and, resting his stomach against the wooden railing, looked across the water, then up at the sky.

He didn't hear Towers walk up behind him. Only in the last second did a twitch of his shoulder tell Towers that he was finally aware. By then it was too late for the guy because the butt of the gun was already coming down fast and hard. The man groaned and, with a helping shove from Towers, pitched over the railing, plunging face first into the sea.

Towers waited until the man bobbed to the surface and rolled against the piling. He looked like blubber in his tight gray suit. Blood was dripping from his scalp into his eyes, but he was alive. Towers weighed pulling him out, then figured the guy wouldn't do the same for him and thought, Fuck it, let him drown. Sticking his gun back in his belt, he headed for the building.

He stooped to get under the door and heard footsteps shuffling against metal. Very quietly he stepped behind a row of containers, was still a moment, then leaned a few inches forward. Rachel and a blond man were coming down the staircase, hands over their heads, while Tong and a tall Chinese man encouraged them with guns.

The blond man looked scared shitless, but Detective Starr was dishing out the brave-cop act. Head up, moving without hesitation, not giving Tong the pleasure of her fear. For a second, Towers envied her . . . saw something in her he'd once imagined in himself. Then he pushed away the feeling. What was there to respect? She was a dumb cop, sticking her neck out for assholes. For what? To pull in twenty-nine, thirty grand a year? To live in some dump while the criminals lived in the Hollywood Hills? To get the bastard who killed some drunken cop who'd once been her partner? Who cared? Haid was fertilizer now and she was a fool to put her life on the line for him.

Rachel was ten yards from the stairs when Tong told her to stop and turn around. The light here was faint, and she could barely see his face. "All right," he said. "Now we talk. Where is Dr. Snow?"

"I don't know." She kept her eyes on him but at the same time scanned the distance to the door. Too goddamn far.

"But I believe you do, Detective Starr."

"Believe what you want. I still don't know."

"Don't lie to me," Tong suddenly shouted. "Where is he?"

"I told you. I don't know. Back in Los Angeles maybe. After what happened, he wanted to get out of here."

"I don't think so. I feel him, you see. I sense him. He's still here. And close."

"Have it your way." She gave a bored shrug and glanced at the fork lifts to her right. Some protection if she ran in that direction, but not much and not for long.

"You think you are being amusing, Detective Starr, but let me assure you that you are not. In fact"—he slipped both hands into the pockets of his white jacket—"I find your attitude somewhat trying. So, let me be clear. In the next few minutes you are going to die. You can die instantly or you can die slowly. The choice is yours. Give me Snow, and I will make sure the bullet is quick and clean. Play amusing games with me and I will let Gregory"—he nodded at the man beside him—"have you. Gregory enjoys putting bullets in places that don't kill—at least not right away."

Rachel said, "It's not much of a choice," then tensed slightly, thinking she heard something behind her.

"You are in no position to bargain."

"She has a videotape of us," Kincaid anxiously broke in. "You and me talking about taking care of Solomon because he found out we were bringing in the drugs."

For the first time Tong seemed to see the blond man. "Where is this tape?"

"I don't know, Jacob. She was supposed to give it to me. That's why I'm here, why I met her. I was trying to find out and—"

"Shut up, Cooper. I know why you're here."

"You can't know—"

"Check your phone," Tong snapped, tired of listening to the man's lies. "You'll find a small microphone in the mouthpiece.

I've heard all your calls. I know all about the deal you made with Detective Starr."

Terrified, Kincaid shook his head. "It's not what you think. It's not, I swear. I was conning her. I was going to get the tape and give it to you. That's the truth."

"Lee Chan and I have arranged other means of bringing in future shipments of his drugs. We no longer need to smuggle it in with your sugar. Which means you are now extraneous." He took a moment to enjoy the stricken look on Kincaid's face, then, with a calculating expression, turned back to Rachel. "It seems you have two things that I want . . . a professor and a videotape."

"It seems that way." Another brushing sound, in back of her, to the left. Unmistakable this time. "Maybe we'll bargain a little after all."

"I think not, Detective Starr. With Professor Snow and the videotape, I will take my chances. With you, I won't."

"Other people know what you're involved in."

"Do they? Then where are they?" he asked, motioning dramatically at the cavernous room. "Why are you alone?"

"They're coming," she bluffed, staring straight at him, knowing the moment she saw Tong's cool smirk that he hadn't bought it.

"Ah, yes, of course they are." He shook his head as though disappointed with the feeble tactic. "You have one last chance. Where is Professor Snow?"

"Go to hell, Jacob."

Tong's mouth curled at the insult. Snapping his fingers at Gregory Chee he hissed, "She's yours. Make it hurt."

"Yes, Mr. Tong." Chee pointed his gun at her stomach. "Walk that way."

Rachel took a few steps back, moving out of the dim light into the dark. All at once, someone grabbed her shoulder and hauled her backward as a gunshot blasted out. Chee gave a shrill wail that stopped abruptly as he hit the floor.

"C'mon, let's go." Before she could see him, the man holding her swung Rachel around and pushed her quickly into the darkness of the aisle. On both sides, containers loomed up around them, blocking out all light. She wondered who the man was. Too short to be Smith or his cousin, but maybe someone they'd sent.

Twenty feet in, the cement floor gave way to a tricky latticework of wooden grates. They slowed to keep from falling. Suddenly a bullet ripped into a container ahead of them, sending them to the floor. The man beside her fired off two shots and waited, breaths panting out of him like steamblasts, heat pouring off his body. Whoever he is, he's as scared as I am, Rachel thought, then ducked as another bullet smashed past. When its sound died, the man caught her arm and hauled her up. "C'mon," he growled.

Hugging the sides of the containers and moving cautiously, they worked their way to the end of the aisle. Between the last container and the warehouse wall they found an eighteen-inch space, squeezed through it, and edged past two more aisles. "Hold it," the man wheezed, and Rachel heard him sink against a crate and try to catch his breath. "I'm not cut out for this shit anymore." Then he added, "But you're doing fine, Detective Starr."

Her heart slid and she could feel sweat coat her hands. "Captain Towers?" she whispered.

"Yeah. It's me." She could hear the irony in his voice but still couldn't make out his face in the dark. "Don't worry. I'm not going to hurt you."

"No? Last I heard, you and Tong were pals."

"Not anymore. He tried to have me killed last night. Now all I want to do—" He stopped as a beam of light raked over the warehouse's back wall. "Move it," Towers hissed. "Tong's got a flashlight."

They scrambled into the nearest aisle. For a couple of seconds the beam bobbed around the wall, then steadily brightened. "He's coming this way," Towers whispered. "Stay here." He stepped out and slid back around the container. Counting to three, he flung himself sideways, fired, and stayed in the open long enough to spot Tong stumbling backward. The light died, and Towers grinned. He didn't think the Asian would chance turning it on again and making himself a well-lit target. He slipped back to where Rachel was.

After a moment Tong shouted, "That is you, isn't it, Captain? I was wondering what happened to you."

"You shouldn't have sent your hit men after me, Jacob," Towers shouted back. "I was happy with the money. I was on my way out of town. Now I want more."

"What is it you want?"

Rachel whispered, "He's about halfway down the row."

"Yeah. Sounds that way."

She heard him open his gun and shove bullets into the chambers.

"I'll make a deal with you, Captain," Tong called. "Are you interested?"

"Depends on the deal."

"More money for you. A lot more."

"I get money," Towers yelled back, closing the gun and muffling the click with his palm. "And you get what?"

"Detective Starr."

Towers's laugh was dry. "What'd you do to him? The guy really hates you."

"You taking his offer?" Rachel asked.

"I don't think so. Not this time."

She felt his fingers find her arm, then work their way down to her hand. A second later, cold metal touched her palm and she pulled back. "What are you doing?"

"Giving you the gun. Go around and get him from the back. I'll keep him talking."

"Captain—"

"Do it, Detective. Now, before I change my mind." He gave her a push, waited a beat, then yelled, "Why do you want her, Jacob?"

"She knows too much."

"The same goes for me. That's why you tried to take me out. I didn't appreciate that." Now he could hear Tong scuffle forward and stop.

"I have a diamond, Captain."

"What kind of a diamond?" Towers began working his way down the row.

"A red diamond worth millions. I'll cut you in for part of the profit."

"How much would that be?"

"A hundred thousand dollars."

Towers snorted and kept creeping forward. "You get millions and I get a lousy hundred grand? What're you playing me for?" He felt between two stacks of boxes. A few inches wider and he could shove through and come out in the next row, surprising Tong from behind. The only problem with the surprise was he didn't have his gun.

"Two hundred thousand, then," Tong offered.

"Five hundred thousand," Towers countered. Something in Tong's row fell and rolled noisily over the grated flooring. "What happened, Jacob? I shock you? You have a heart attack?" He took a few more careful steps and felt between the next set of containers. Too tight to get through. He let out a frustrated breath.

"Be reasonable, Captain," Tong called.

"Okay. I'll be reasonable. We'll talk it over. Negotiate. How does that sound?"

"I'm willing to negotiate. You put down your gun. I put down mine. And we go outside."

Sure you'll put it down, Towers thought.

Suddenly, a blinding light flashed through the space between the crates, followed instantly by three shots. Towers lunged awkwardly sideways, caught his foot in a grate, and tumbled over. Pain splintered around his right knee, then rushed up his thigh. Swallowing a moan, he pushed himself to his feet. Behind him, he could hear Tong scurrying to the end of his aisle. Any second the Asian would come around the corner, and when he did, Towers thought, Captain James Towers II was a dead man.

He took a step, winced, and wondered why the hell he hadn't gotten on the plane to Miami, and why the hell he'd ever thought Rachel Starr would come back to save his butt. He took one more step, then stopped cold and spun around. The beam of the Asian's flashlight strafed over him. Towers rolled to his right, spotted a wide enough space in the stacks of containers, and hauled himself into it with a heavy grunt. Just as Tong's gun went off, Towers dragged himself through the opening and into the adjoining aisle.

He heard Tong curse and fire wildly, heard him trip, curse, and fire again. May the bastard shoot off his own balls, Towers thought. All at once there was a deafening whine and he twisted in its direction. The warehouse door was rumbling upward. Overhead, fluorescent lights burst on in a yellow-green glare, bathing the room in a sickly glow. Footsteps thudded in, four or five people, he guessed. He ducked back between the containers and heard Rachel Starr shout, "Drop it!" then two shots, the clank of a gun hitting the wooden floor, then three or four others running down the row where Tong was.

This was his chance, he knew. Right now while they were grabbing Tong. Taking a quick, steadying breath, he slid out and limped forward as quietly and quickly as he could until he reached the last container before the exit. He stuck his head forward carefully. He couldn't see anyone, but he could hear them shoving Tong up against a box and cuffing him. Outside on the wharf, blue police lights swept over the nearby buildings and off the water. The blond man he'd first seen coming down the stairs with Rachel was crumpled against a blue-and-white. Beside him, his back to the warehouse, a uniformed cop was talking into the car radio.

Now he could hear the officers pushing Tong forward. Rachel Starr shouted, "There's another man in the building. Fan out and find him!" Towers thought of Cheryl, her sweet eyes and sweet mouth, and how he wanted his chance with her. He stepped out and waited tensely for someone to spot him. When no one did, he kept walking out of the warehouse and around its side. Then, ignoring the agonizing ache in his knee, he broke into a run.

TWENTY-TWO

LT. HARRY DECOSTA RUBBED a thumb over his wide mustache while he measured her, then sat back heavily and said, "Look, I'm not the one figuring out the game plan and neither are you. When you called H.P.D. to the warehouse, you let go of the case. And we never really had it. The D.E.A. people are running the show now. They're the ones working a deal with Tong, not us. We're providing manpower. That's all."

"What's the deal?"

"Like I told you," he replied with worn-down patience, "you gotta talk to Donahoe. He's the government guy in charge. I'm not supposed to give out any info. I'm not even supposed to be talking to you, you wanna know the truth." He tipped his chair and began idly rocking it. He had nothing more to say.

"Lieutenant, this is my case," Rachel started off quietly to put him off-guard. "I set it up. I executed it. If you think," she went on, raising her voice, "that I'm going to sit around twiddling my goddamn thumbs while the D.E.A. goes to bed with Tong, then you better think again. The way I see it, you can tell me now or you can tell me in the morning because I'm not leaving until I find out what's going on."

DeCosta waited a moment, then lowered the chair with a bang. He hunched forward, narrowed his eyes, and studied her hard. "I made some calls, Detective. You live up to your reputation. You're about as bullheaded as your L.A. pals said you'd be. But I'll tell you something," he continued, his tone easing up, "in your place, I'd probably feel about the same. So, okay. Between you and me, this is what's happening. Your friend Tong is going to finger Lee Chan as a major drug supplier. The D.E.A. has been after Chan for a long time but could never dig up enough proof to bring him in on illegal drug trafficking charges. Tong's willing to give them that proof. In return he gets immunity.

"You mean he walks away?"

DeCosta nodded brusquely. "I mean he walks away."

"What about the videotapes I brought in? The ones of him and Kincaid? They implicate Tong in a murder case."

The lieutenant sighed. "You got a court order saying you could make these tapes? Uh-uh. It's not proper evidence, so how can we use the stuff? We can't. Listen to me," he added placatingly. "I know how you feel . . . your case being grabbed away from you. On the other hand, you knew the score when you came to town. You weren't playing by the book, so now the book won't stand by you." He sighed again and gave a file on his desk a shove. "Look at it this way. We actually lucked out getting Tong's cooperation."

"Lucked out?" she shot back. "Letting a killer go free?" She made herself take a breath. "What about Kincaid? We had him. He was ready to turn Tong in."

"Maybe you had him before, but for the past three hours he's been very quiet. Got himself an expensive lawyer who's been doing all the jabbering, most of it about lawsuits and slander. Take it from me, for right now at least, we're getting nothing from Cooper Kincaid."

"Which still leaves Towers," Rachel came back. "Your people pick him up yet?"

"Not yet, but we got A.P.B.'s out and people at the airports. Don't worry. It's a small island. We'll find him. In the meantime, take my advice, Detective. Be happy you helped catch a big-shot drug dealer. It'll go on your record. If you're lucky, you'll get a nice letter from the Federals you can stick in your file."

"I know where I'd like to stick it," she snapped.

The man snorted and for the first time looked almost sympathetic. "Yeah, I know what you mean. They're a bunch of bastards."

Rachel had walked over to the glass partition separating DeCosta's office from the rest of the C.I.D. unit. Now she moved back to his desk and said, "Tong killed the best police officer I ever knew, Lieutenant. What file do I put that in?"

"The one called being a cop. All right, all right." He pointed at a torn vinyl chair. "Sit down a minute."

"What for?"

"So we can talk."

She sat. "Okay. Talk."

He placed his hands flat on the desk. They were tight little hands, deadly looking, the knuckles of the right beaten into a single ridge crossed with scars. "I know how you feel, and I'm not just saying that. I've had cases pulled away from me, cases that mattered. And I've known good cops who got killed. So, okay, they've taken Tong away from you, I can't do much about that. But this is what I can do. I can keep you informed. That'll make the D.E.A. unhappy."

"I'd appreciate it," Rachel said.

He rolled sideways to a scratched-up filing cabinet, found a folder in the middle drawer, and tossed it on the desk. "Okay, this is what we've got so far. According to Tong, Lee Chan picked up the dope yesterday from Kincaid's warehouse."

"Why?"

"Part of the deal they made. Chan comes to town, claims his property, then arranges for a meeting with Tong to make the exchange. His drugs for Tong's red diamond."

Rachel looked puzzled. "What I don't figure is why Tong didn't walk off with the dope before this if it's been sitting around Kincaid's place."

"I asked that question, too. The way I understand it, this is the first drug deal Tong and Lee Chan have worked together. Tong wanted it to be the start of a long-term business relationship. He didn't want to screw that up by getting greedy. It makes good business sense."

"What's the drug?"

"Heroin."

"How much are we talking about?"

"About a million dollars wholesale." DeCosta pulled out the lowest drawer and propped his foot on it. "That's what Tong would pay if he was paying cash and not trading that red diamond. When he goes to sell the dope, he should clear five million easily."

"When's the exchange taking place between Lee Chan and Tong?"

"Hasn't been set. Tong's calling the old man later today to find out."

"What about Chan? Where is he?"

"In a suite at the Hyatt. We got men watching him around the clock."

"What happens next?"

"Once Tong finds out where and when the meet is, we put in cameras and bugs, if possible. If not, we go with wiring Tong. Also we see how we can situate our people. The second Chan hands over the heroin, we want to pick him up."

"And Tong?"

DeCosta frowned and closed the drawer with his foot. "I guess he goes home."

"Where's the diamond?"

"Tong has it. Where, we don't know. We sent people over to search his apartment, but they turned up nothing. His lawyer says Tong won't turn over the stone until the exchange takes place. Calls it his client's insurance."

"And the D.E.A.'s going along with that?" she said incredulously.

"Yeah. They've worked it out so Tong picks up the stone from wherever he's got it stashed about an hour before the trade takes place."

"I want to watch."

"Watch what? The trade?" He started rubbing his mustache again, using a fingernail to comb it down. "I don't know. The

Feds want you gone. They won't like having you in the middle of the deal."

"No, they won't. It'll probably upset them, which I guess you wouldn't want to do."

He flipped the folder over and grinned. "L.A. warned me you were pushy. Okay, Detective, you want to be there, why don't you be there. As a guest observer, something like that? At my request. I'll take any heat that comes down."

"I appreciate your help, Lieutenant."

He found a small pad and scribbled on it. "We got you booked into a Waikiki hotel. There's a blue-and-white out front to take you there. Everything's set, all you gotta do is pick up the key at the front desk. Also, we sent a squad car to get the luggage you mentioned leaving at the Royal Hawaiian. The guys should've moved it by now." He tore off the sheet and handed it to her. "I'll call you later and let you know what's happening."

"Good." She stood and stuck out her hand. "I owe you a favor, Lieutenant. I won't forget."

The blue-and-white dropped Rachel at a low-rise hotel on a side street off Kalakaua. She got the key from the sleepy desk clerk, then took a sour-smelling elevator to the tenth floor. The room she stepped into was cramped and grim, but what else did she expect, she asked herself, on a night when things were going so well? There was a sagging double bed covered with an orange spread, a TV on top of a dresser, a stained lime-green club chair in front of it.

The suitcases H.P.D. had brought over from the Royal Hawaiian were side by side near the veranda doors. She looked at them and wondered what Snow was doing, then told herself it didn't matter, he was out of it now, why think about him?

She went to the sliding doors and looked out. At the end of the street she could see a piece of the canal, then hundreds of lights reaching up the mountains like fingers. While she stood there, it began to rain—a soft, drifting patter that turned quickly into an onslaught. The last time it had rained she was in bed with Snow.

The image of him pushed into her mind. Briefly she struggled to keep it out, then gave in. She could see him against the pillows, brown hair pushed straight back showing the somber planes of his face, his steady eyes. The first time she'd walked into his lecture she'd thought: a homely man. Only she was wrong. Not homely but pure. A face and a man she would never forget.

Her own reflection was a haze in the glass, shifting and changing in the sheeting rain. For a long while she stared at it, thinking of Snow.

It was still dark when Rachel woke up. Without looking, she knew someone was in the room. Keeping her arm beneath the blanket, she dropped it to the floor and slowly felt around under the bed until she touched the revolver. One beat and she rolled over, swinging the gun forward.

Snow was sitting in the chair.

She swore and lowered the .38. "One of these days, Professor, I'm going to blow your brains out."

"Nice to see you, too, Detective."

"What the hell are you doing here? And how the hell did you get in?"

"Came to see how you were. Used a credit card."

He smiled and Rachel felt a jolt like someone had kicked the wind out of her. It was a new feeling—a man's smile getting to her—and because it troubled her, she dumped the .38 roughly on the lamp table and made her face hard.

"Didn't they tell you? You got shot. You're supposed to be taking it easy at Pono's. How'd you get past Smith anyway? I told him to sit on you if he had to to keep you there."

"Don't blame him. He fell asleep and I walked out. I even stole his car."

"Why?"

"I heard about what happened at the warehouse."

"How?"

"Moses talked to Pono. Pono talked to me."

"And said what?"

"That you were there when they picked up Tong. That you could've been hurt but weren't. I wanted to see for myself."

"I'm okay. Towers showed and helped me out."

"The captain from L.A.P.D.?" Snow said. "The one who's in it with Tong?"

"Seems he and Jacob aren't buddies anymore. Problem is, he split before we could stop him. H.P.D.'s looking for him now and L.A.P.D.'s going to want to talk to him as well." She was quiet a moment, then asked, "Did Moses mention the deal?"

Frowning, he shook his head. "What deal?"

"Arrangements have been made between the D.E.A. and Tong."

"What kind of arrangements?"

"The D.E.A. wants Lee Chan. Tong fingers him for them and goes clean." She waited for a reaction, but there was none.

"When does this fingering take place?"

"Tong'll find out today when and where he and Chan will make the exchange. H.P.D. will let me know."

"Where's Tong now?"

"Police custody until morning. Then they'll release him but keep him under guard."

"What happened to the Red Heart?"

"Tong still has it."

Snow straightened slightly. "The police didn't take it?"

"They couldn't. They don't know where it is. Tong's keeping it until the deal takes place. A little coverage for his back."

"Where's the old man?" Snow asked.

"A suite at the Hyatt. Under twenty-four-hour surveillance."

"I see. Then it sounds like we've lost Tong."

"Sounds like?" The anger she'd been holding in all night exploded. "Is that it? I tell you Tong's going free and you act like you heard the weather report?"

"How do you want me to act?" he asked calmly.

"How the hell should I know? Try normal, maybe. Or human. We lost some friends, remember? We almost got killed. And they're letting Tong go. Doesn't that make you a little angry?" She twisted the blanket in her hand. "I feel like bashing something in or pounding down the goddamn walls! Don't you ever feel like that?" Suddenly drained, she sat back and, shaking her head, let out a ragged breath. "No, I guess you don't."

"You're wrong, Detective."

"Am I?" she asked. "Then what do you do, Snow, when you feel too much? How do you stop it?"

He stared a moment at the floor, then looked up. When he did, his eyes were different. Harder, clearer, not letting her look away.

She wondered why her hands were shaking, why her heart knotted the second he got up. He said her name, and she knew what was going to happen, even knew she wanted it, had wanted it from the beginning, but still she shook her head. "Don't—"

He didn't let her finish. In one motion, he drew back the covers and pulled her into his arms.

She lifted her hands, made one attempt to push him back, aware it was all a sham the second her fingers caught his shoulders, the second her mouth opened under his, the second she fell back into the pillows, bringing him with her.

Long after she fell asleep, Snow was awake. At 4:00 A.M., he got up, dressed carefully because his shoulder was hurting him again, and went downstairs. The streets were empty. A drizzling rain rolling off the palm trees added to the early-morning loneliness. As Snow started for Kalakaua, he thought of Rachel—her warmth, her beauty, her lovely intensity. What he felt for her was much more than he had bargained for. She was an unexpected complication, that one small detail in the plan not taken into account. Last night, he admitted, his life had shifted off its course. Something strong and new had entered it, something he didn't want to lose.

But first he had to get the Red Heart. Detective Starr wasn't going to like it when she found out, but there was nothing he could do. The money was needed; the work had to go on.

He hailed a cab, got in, and asked the driver to take him to 100 Bishop Street.

Jacob Tong's address.

TWENTY-THREE

AT 9:00 A.M., WITH the radio in his Buick blasting, Sean pulled out of Ena Road, hung a wide right onto Kalakaua, and almost sideswiped a white VW van in the second lane.

"Christ!" Cheryl clutched the seat and jammed her feet into the floorboard. "Will you watch it!"

Sean gave a sideways glance, caught her spoiled-kid grimace, and laughed. "Don't be so tense, Cherry. Everything's cool."

"You drive like a jerk."

She snapped off the radio and he reached over and pinched her cheek. "Hey," he said. "I drive like a genius. This is my business."

She brushed his hand away. "Sometimes, Seanny."

"Sometimes what?"

"I wonder if you'll ever grow up."

"No kidding?" He whistled at a blonde swaying along the sidewalk in a high-cut iridescent-blue swimsuit. "Well, don't worry about it, Cheryl. I'm doing fine." Watching the blonde in the rearview mirror he said, "So, where are we going?"

"That drugstore on Kuhio. The one by your place."

"Okay." The blonde out of view, he turned back to her and

picked up that she was still angry. He figured he'd give it a shot anyway. "You wanna tell me the plan now?"

She stared out the window, her shoulders tight, her arms crossed defensively over her chest, and ignored him.

"The plan, Cherry? What's it about?"

She still didn't answer.

Sean rolled his eyes and thought, Okay, here we go again, Cheryl in one of her moods. Part of him wanted to let her sulk, forever if she wanted to. Who cared? Only if he did, he'd have to wait to find out about the next step in the Big Deal, and he'd never been good at waiting. "All right . . . okay, Cherry. What's the matter?"

"I hate it when you ogle other women. You know I hate it, but you do it anyway, don't you?"

"Sorry. I forgot."

"You're such an idiot."

"Look, I said I was sorry. What do you want me to do?"

"It really drives me crazy."

"I want to explain something," he said. "I look at other women 'cause they're there. Where else am I supposed to look? But it doesn't mean shit. You know that. You're the only one."

"Sure."

"Don't pull this stuff on me. If anybody's got a complaint, I do. You've been getting it on the side for years."

"That's different. That's business."

"Yeah, sure it is."

He honked the horn and flung the car into a small lot beside the ABC Drugstore. He didn't look at her because if he did he might take a whack at her. She'd been acting up all the time lately. Being moody. Sarcastic. Making digs at him like that shit about growing up. He was getting sick of it. "You get what you need. I'll wait."

"Fine," she said.

"Fine."

He swore when she slammed the door.

Five minutes later she came out carrying a paper bag. Sean watched her cross the lot, her hips lush, her legs stretched out and shapely above the red high heels, and figured what was the point of staying mad at her. Actually, he liked her a lot, even if she was a bitch now and then. Maybe he even loved her. Who knew? "What'd you buy?" he said and could tell she hadn't decided yet whether to talk to him or not.

But when she got in, she said, "Hair dye, cotton balls, some reading glasses."

He waited a moment, then said, "You still mad?"

"I guess not. Are you?"

"Nah." He reached for her. "Come here, honey."

She slid into his arms and let him kiss her. Let him slip his hands under her halter top and rub her breasts. "We're going to be rich, Cherry," he whispered, licking her ear. "You and me and four hundred grand. We're gonna have fun. Lotsa fun. Right?"

"Yeah," she said, but it was funny, she was thinking of Johnny. He was an old man, really. Almost twenty-five years older than she was. Good-looking. Kept himself in shape. But, still, pretty old.

She liked him, though. He was so sweet and, Jesus, did he like doing it with her. Made her feel special, like she was a princess or something.

He kept making all these crazy promises about how he was going to take care of her, and there were times she almost believed him, even if she'd given up counting on a man taking care of her when she was eight years old and her father split. And Johnny was different. He had a soft heart, not like Sean. And sometimes, after they did it together, he'd hold her tightly and cry and tell her how much she meant to him. It scared her a little, but she kind of liked it. No man had ever bothered to cry over her before.

She was going to feel bad taking his money.

Sean sat back, grinning. "Now I remember why I like it when we're friends."

"Me too." She straightened her top. "You wanna hear about the plan?"

He nodded.

"Buy me breakfast and I'll tell you."

* * *

He took her to the Ilikai and got a table in the outdoor restaurant near the pool. He made sure to keep his eyes on her and not on the girls in the water, but it was hard.

Cheryl ordered, watched the waitress walk away, then said, "Johnny's got tickets for Florida. We're supposed to leave tonight."

"So we gotta get the money today."

"Just listen. He's in trouble. He has to get out of town. That's what the dye and stuff is for. To disguise him. He says they'll be watching the airports."

"Who is this guy anyway? What's his story?"

"He's a cop from L.A."

"You're shitting me!"

"Be quiet." She glanced around to see if anyone was listening. "He's mixed up in something crooked, so he's gotta leave town and get out of the country. I mean, he can't go back to L.A., and they'll be looking for him everywhere in the States. He's talking about South America. He thinks I'm going with him."

"How do we get the cash?"

"I'm getting to that." The waitress returned with their food, poured more coffee and asked how everything was.

"Everything's peachy," Sean said and waved her off. "Go on," he said to Cheryl.

"The money's being split in four parts. One-fourth's going through on him. One-fourth's going through on me. And half's hidden inside a blue canvas carry-on that I'm putting all my makeup and things in."

"I think we should get the money now."

"Will you listen? If we get the money now, he's still around and still a problem. My plan, we don't get all the money—"

"Hold it. How much do we get?"

"Three-fourths."

"I was counting on four hundred thousand."

"I know, but my way, we don't have to worry about him coming after us."

"But losing a hundred grand . . ."

She let out an exasperated breath. "You want to hear this or not?"

"Okay, okay. Tell me."

"This is what happens. Johnny and I get through the gates, get on the plane, and get in our seats. Once he's on, he's safe, so he won't want to get off, right? Now, about five minutes before the plane takes off, I tell him I gotta take care of some business in the bathroom. I take the blue bag with me, 'cause the stuff I need is in it. I head for the john and go in to cover myself in case he's watching. I wait ten seconds and check him. If he's not looking, I walk out and head for the exit."

"What if he's looking?"

"He won't be."

"But what if . . . ?"

"I still walk out. He can't come after me. He's gotta stay on the plane and get out of town. You see why we're doing it this way? It's perfect. We can't lose. We get the money and there's nothing he can do about it." She smiled at the look on Sean's face. "What are you thinking?"

"That you're a genius." He leaned over and kissed her hard. "A goddamn genius!"

"Uh-huh." She was really smiling now. "I think so, too."

At twelve noon the phone in Rachel's hotel room rang.

"Detective Starr? It's DeCosta, H.P.D. Okay, we got word from Tong. The meeting's on for tonight. Eleven o'clock on an abandoned Chinese junk near the harbor. But, as usual, there's a hitch."

"What's the problem?" Rachel said, sitting on the edge of the bed.

"We sent some plainclothes people to check the boat. They reported back that Lee Chan's got three guards stationed on board. One's planted on the ship's only gangplank; the other two regularly circle the first deck."

"So how are you working it?"

"Tong gets to take along two bodyguards. They'll be our people and we'll have them wired. The boat's docked at the east end of Honolulu Harbor next to a parking lot. We'll have personnel in cars in the lot and concealed in the park. The rest of our backup will be standing by a few blocks away. Once Chan and Tong are on board, we can get our people on in minutes."

"Where are you putting me?"

"In Alpha Van. It'll be stationed about fifty yards from the boat."

"When should I be there?"

"The van will pick you up at five P.M. There'll be a rowboat on its roof. Once you get to the harbor, two of the cops in the vehicle will take the boat and go fishing. That'll give the van a cover in case Chan's men are watching. You and two other cops will remain inside the vehicle until the exchange goes down. When that happens, they're part of the team that goes on the boat."

"What about me?"

"You'll stay with the van."

"No way, Lieutenant." She heard DeCosta's familiar sigh.

"Any point arguing with you, Detective?"

"None at all."

"All right. Go on board with the cops, but stay out of the way. Understood?"

"Yeah. One other thing, Lieutenant. I'm bringing a friend with me."

"What? Who?"

"His name's Snow. He's been working the case with me."

"First I heard of it," DeCosta said.

"He's been essential to its success. I want him there."

"We already got enough people involved. We don't have room for more." He waited for her response and when he got nothing, sighed gruffly. "Okay, all right. Bring him along. But that's it. Nobody else. This isn't a party."

"Thank you, Lieutenant." She hung up and looked at Snow. "Okay, you're on. But I still think you should stay here."

"Could you?"
"I'm not the one who's been shot."
"Could you?" he repeated.
"No."
"Neither can I."

TWENTY-FOUR

AT 5:30, THE VAN swung into the harbor parking lot and wound slowly around its perimeter before pulling into a stall that faced the Chinese junk fifty yards away. Through the tinted rear window, Rachel spotted the boat, tethered fore and aft to stone pilings, heaving restlessly in the brisk wind as though trying to break free.

The vessel, she saw, had once been beautiful—a gaudy, floating Chinese palace layered with ornament and flamboyant colors, decaying now from neglect. The blood-red dragons twisting around fluted columns had faded to muddy orange. Wind and rain had flecked half the gold off the sloping roof and bleached the jade-green walls and the white filligree railings. Doors were boarded up, vandals had smashed the lower windows, and the sea was steadily rotting away the metal hull.

"What happened to her?" Rachel asked.

The smaller of the two cops in back with her said, "The boat used to be a restaurant, but about ten years ago it went bankrupt. It's been sitting like that ever since."

From the front seat the driver asked, "Can you see Chan's guard?"

The same cop checked the window. "Yeah, he's right by the gangplank, looking our way."

"Okay." The driver opened his door. "Time to go fishing."

The same cop she'd asked about the boat took out a deck of cards and asked if she wanted to play. Rachel nodded, thinking of all the stakeouts poker had gotten her through. Then she glanced at Snow. He was resting against the seat-back, one leg stretched out, the other bent with his arm draped over the knee, watching her. When their eyes met, when she remembered how it had been between them, she felt a yearning so strong she felt crushed by it. Then she remembered the rest of it. Who he was. Who she was. The gulf between them as wide as the distance from black to white. The impossibility of crossing it. With a dull ache, Rachel turned away.

By seven o'clock, gusting southerlies had blown rainclouds inland from the sea. The air turned humid and briny-smelling. Around eight o'clock, the winds suddenly stopped. There were a few moments of eerie silence, then as though someone had slit the clouds open with one sharp stroke, the rain poured down. Within seconds the wind returned, stronger than before, skating in off the ocean and whipping the rain into a thick, blurry froth. Along the lot, palm fronds beat the air like rotaries, and in the distance, the boat yanked fitfully at its moorings.

The cops who'd taken the rowboat out came dragging back with it. For a few minutes, they struggled to swing it onto the roof while the wind lashed wildly. Finally, they gave up and wedged the boat between the van's wheels, then clambered into the vehicle's front cab.

An hour later, the rains eased and, by ten o'clock, turned intermittent. In the eastern sky, a nearly full moon wandered in and out of a cloudbank. At 10:50 the van's radio crackled and Lieutenant DeCosta came on. "Tong's here with our guys and they're heading for the boat. Everybody stay alert."

While the other two men strapped on their guns, Snow joined Rachel at the rear window. A minute later, Tong came into view, flanked on either side by an H.P.D. cop dressed in a black business suit. One of them carried a briefcase. They passed for Tong's guards, Rachel thought, and Chan's man seemed comfortable as he moved to meet them and as he led them back to the boat. The cop with the briefcase crossed the narrow plank first, holding on to the railing as the boat swayed. Chan's man followed, then the second cop. Tong was last. He stepped onto the gangplank, then stopped and turned, holding on to the railing to keep his balance on the rocking boat, and looked over the lot until his eyes settled on the van.

"Can he see us?" Rachel asked.

The cop nearest to her shook his head. "It's too dark in here."

She leaned forward for a better look. Tong was holding a cigarette. She could see its tip glowing in the dark. He watched the van a moment longer, then gave a lazy nod and flipped the cigarette into the water.

"He can see us," she said.

Beside her, Snow nodded.

At 11:00 P.M. a white limousine made its way over the curving bridge leading into the lot and came to a silent stop alongside the boat. The front door swung open and two men got out. The taller one waited while the other reached into the backseat and carefully helped Lee Chan out. For a moment the old man stood by the car, the wind stirring his white coat around his legs as he stared at the boat. Then he flicked a hand toward the limousine trunk. The taller guard hurried over, unlocked it, and brought out a large suitcase and a briefcase. Chan gave them a brief glance, then impatiently flicked the same hand. The other guard placed a gold cane in the old man's stiff fingers and offered him his arm. Clutching it, Chan began walking slowly, stopping every two or three steps as if to gather his strength.

The cop beside Rachel sat back on his heels and sighed. "Figure another hour before the son of a bitch makes it to the boat."

A few minutes later, the radio crackled and DeCosta came on again. "Tong's in place on the second-level foredeck waiting for Chan. As soon as the old man gets there, all personnel take their first position. If the guards Chan already has on board keep their positions, Beta team will take them out. Once those guards are out, all teams move to second position and stay there until the exchange between Chan and Tong takes place. Once that happens, everyone moves in and we pick up Chan."

Rachel heard a rustling sound, then DeCosta said, "All right, this is it. Chan is on board and making his way to deck two." The rustling sound came on again as if he'd covered the microphone with his hand. "Okay. Lookout one reports Chan's guards are maintaining their positions. Beta team is moving in. Everyone else take position one."

The smaller cop slid open the van's side door and jumped out. The second cop followed, then Rachel, then Snow. They swiftly crossed the outer, unlit border of the lot, then cut along a path parallel to the boat and stopped behind a clump of trees twenty yards from the gangplank, waiting for DeCosta to give the next go-ahead. From where she stood, Rachel saw another team of cops moving down the bridge, approaching the boat from the back, while a third team pulled their van in front of the gangplank. A fourth team made up of D.E.A. agents was coming in from the park.

The walkie-talkie the smaller cop was carrying buzzed. Over it DeCosta said, "Chan's guards are picked up. All teams move in."

They darted across the last twenty yards, climbed the gangplank, hanging on tightly as the winds began gusting, and slipped through an arched doorway into a dimly lit foyer. Gilt stairs lined with tasseled lamps rose to a second level. Gold brocade fabric rotted on the walls and a damp, murky smell seeped up from the wooden floor. The cop with the walkie-talkie shone a flashlight on the stairs. There was a flurry of scurrying noises, a flash of something soft and white, then dozens of small, wormy creatures crawling out of the light.

The skin on the back of Rachel's neck broke out in gooseflesh.

The cop holding the light gave the lowest step a hard kick—scaring away whatever else lurked there—then drew his gun and led the way, testing each step before he put his weight on it. Halfway to the top, he stopped and pointed the light five feet ahead of him. The steps sagged noticeably to the left and the bannister had fallen off, leaving a gaping hole and a fifteen-foot drop. All four sidled nervously to the right and moved faster.

At the top was a smaller foyer with dark halls leading off it, fore and aft. The lead cop motioned to the left and they turned down the hall, winding forward. An inch of water soaked the floor, slopping noisily with each pitch of the boat, and Rachel could feel a damp slime oozing into her shoes. She wondered grimly what was down there, mixed in with the water, then forgot about it as the flashlight glinted off an overhead canopy of cobwebs, dotted with black, skittering spiders. "Jesus," she whispered, yanking her collar high around her throat and ducking low.

The hall passed between shadowy rooms stacked with overturned tables and chairs, then ran into a stateroom, at the same time branching left and right around it, to take visitors to the outside passageways.

"We watch the exchange from up here," the smaller cop said and turned into the stateroom.

The room was crescent-shaped, with waist-to-ceiling windows around the curve. There was no furniture except for a few broken tables shoved to one side. Rachel and Snow trailed the cops to the window.

Below them, Tong stood in the middle of the deck holding the railing to steady himself. He had lit another cigarette. She could see it burning bright orange against the choppy black of the water.

A moment later, the old man, thin and balding and clinging to the arm of his assistant, hobbled into view. "There's Lee Chan," Snow said.

The taller cop took out his camera and began snapping pictures.

A few feet from Tong, Chan stopped and brushed away the assistant. Standing alone, shoulders hunched forward, his cane stabbing the deck for balance, Chan accepted Tong's deep bow. Then the old man said something and stuck out a gnarled hand, palm up. It trembled with age and the impatience of someone used to having his own way. Tong quickly reached into his jacket, brought out an envelope and placed it in Chan's hand, then bowed again and stepped back.

Chan passed the envelope to his assistant, who lifted the flap and drew out and opened a blue paper packet. The other assistant came forward with the briefcase, unlatched it, and pressed a button. A blue light flashed on. Chan waved irritably to hurry the first assistant over. The blue packet was unfolded, then laid in the case. The old man bent over the fluorescent glow.

"What's he doing?" Rachel asked.

"Making sure it's the Martinos Red Heart diamond," Snow said. He lifted his hand to the glass to cut the glare. "Chan always was a careful man."

The old man stooped closer to the light, his fingers poking hungrily at the gemstone. Suddenly his head snapped up. He said something and the color drained from Tong's face. As Tong tried to answer, the old man turned contemptuously away and reached into the briefcase. With a guttural sound, he picked up the diamond and flung it across the deck, then spat at the floor near Tong's feet.

Both cops pressed closer to the window. "We got some kind of a problem," the taller one said. "Let's get down there." He shoved the camera into its bag and slung it over his shoulder. "You and your friend stay put, Detective Starr."

Rachel gave a nod and shot Snow a look. Like hell they were staying. A high-pitched cry from below caught their attention. With surprising strength, one of Chan's arthritic hands was holding Tong still while the other slashed again and again at the younger man's face. Twisting, Tong broke free, staggered back, caught himself on the railing, and lunged at the old man. One of Chan's bodyguards jumped between them; the other rushed forward to block the men who'd come with Tong.

In the parking lot, three police cars skidded to a stop, sirens wailing. Over that sound came a sudden crack of thunder followed instantly by a slanting downpour and battering winds. The boat heaved fiercely, throwing the old man and his assistant off balance and to the deck. Ducking to his right, Tong scooped up the diamond, then spun in a half circle, kicking the first cop across the chest, the second in the head. Snatching the second officer's gun, he hurtled up the stairs.

"Stay here," Rachel commanded, but Snow was already heading for the door. She ran after him as he veered right and ran down a musty passage, hunting for the exit.

"Up ahead," Snow yelled, pointing at a square of light hitting the wall twenty feet in front of them.

Outside the deck was slick and slippery. From overhead came the sound of quick steps. Gesturing at a stairwell, Rachel said, "Cut him off there," and as Snow plunged on, she climbed onto the railing, clutching at a column to keep from falling, and reached overhead for the railing of the top deck. Heart pulsing, telling herself not to look down, she pulled herself up until she could swing a foot onto the edge of the next deck. Then she hauled herself over.

Tong was thirty feet away, scrambling up a staircase leading to the roof. Rachel sprinted after him, then slowed as she neared the top stair and tried to see through the rain. On either side of a long, glassed-in room stood pagodalike towers with narrow stairwells circling them, leading to balconies. In front of her, Rachel caught a movement that quickly disappeared behind the left tower. Tightening her grip on her gun, she made her way to the tower's front, then braced herself against its elaborately carved door.

The rain was getting heavier—she could barely see through it now—and with each pitch, the boat gave out a complaining groan while the ocean smashed against the hull. Clinging to the building to keep herself upright, Rachel inched to her left. She could feel the blood sliding through her, as thick and hot as lava, could hear the air being sucked into her lungs, then exploding outward. She tried to calm down but couldn't. Circling around, she came out on the starboard side and squinted into the wind. Ahead she could make out a watery shape darting into the low building. She started after him, then slammed to her knees as the boat tilted roughly. She slid and rolled ten feet before she grabbed on to a round pin sticking out of the deck. She struggled up, then covered the rest of the deck in a half-crouching run. The building's door was ajar. Slipping through it, she shouldered it shut and was engulfed by a dark, fluid silence.

She waited a moment to let her eyes adjust. Barrels and crates were piled across the room, higher than her head in some places. On one side, a bar curved along the wall, fronted by five or six round tables and twice as many chairs. Just as she started toward the bar, a bullet exploded, shattering the glass behind her. Rain washed in and the wind howled as it rushed through the hole. Rachel pitched to the floor, then hurled herself forward, landing in the dampness behind the bar as another bullet winged past.

The sound of the second gunshot told her Tong was at the far end of the room, behind a mountain of barrels. She fired at him twice, then waited, then scuttled back as he got off a round and the corner of the wooden bar burst into splinters. Hearing fast, light footsteps, she took a quick look over the bartop and saw Tong running straight at her. He shot twice. In the second before she dropped, she felt both bullets heat the air near her head. One beat later, she came up, braced her arm, and pulled the trigger as fast as she could. Tong dodged sideways. He fired again and the bullet plowed through the bar-top, then smashed into the counter behind Rachel as she threw herself flat on the floor. Before she could shove herself to her knees, she heard the wind grow suddenly louder. By the time she looked around the side of the bar, Tong was out the door and running across the roof. She dragged herself up and followed.

The rain beat at her face. It was hard to breathe, hard to stay on her feet, the boat was rolling so violently. She scanned ahead of her, then a nagging sixth sense made her look up. Tong was clambering over the stairs of the right tower, his black coat snapping like a flag in the wind. She reloaded her gun and thought: Got you, you bastard.

The stairwell was two feet across, the steps shorter than normal steps. She covered them three at a time, hanging on desperately to the slippery railing, not letting herself look down. Above her, she could see Tong struggling to keep his footing, looking back to keep her in view. She forced herself to move faster and reached the last curve of stairs just as Tong leaped onto the balcony. He wrenched around and through the rain their eyes met. With a cold smile, he hoisted his gun and fired. Rachel dove sideways, lost her grip on the railing, and slid down a half-dozen steps. When she looked up, Tong's gun was aimed over the railing at her head. She could feel her muscles tightening in anticipation. Then the boat lurched and Tong fell back, arms flailing wildly to get a hold on the railing. Like a shark lunging out of water, she came up after him.

By the time she reached the balcony, Tong had vanished around the curve of the tower. Slowing down and staying low, she worked her way after him until she pulled even with an open doorway. Taking a quick glance in, she saw Tong half running, half falling down a staircase that circled the inner wall of the building. She stepped inside, locked her elbows to take aim, and squeezed the trigger. Tong's shoulder jerked back, the motion throwing him into the wall, then tumbling him down a dozen steps before he caught himself.

He took a wild shot at her that exploded into the ceiling and sprayed a thick, powdery, blinding dust. Coughing, Rachel scrubbed at her eyes, then hunted for Tong and saw him scurry off the stairs, at the same time turning toward her and raising his gun. She checked the distance to the floor—ten feet, she guessed—and, holding her breath, swung over the railing and jumped to the ground, letting herself roll as she landed. Keeping down, she maneuvered her way to the wall.

"Give it up," she called. "It's over. The boat's full of cops. There's no way out."

There was a long silence, and just as Rachel gave up on Tong's answering her, he shouted, "There's always a way out, Detective Starr. One must simply look for it. That's something I've learned."

"You were stupid to run, Jacob. It was a big mistake."

"My big mistake was being fooled by you and your professor. But we are all human, aren't we? We all err. The Red Heart blinded me. I wanted it too much and I became careless."

"Your deal with the D.E.A. is off now. You go to jail. How does twenty years in a prison cell sound to you?"

"They have to catch me to put me in prison."

Suddenly a bullet tore into the floor a yard to her left. She dove to her right and fired blindly.

"Wrong direction, Detective Starr. I'm over here." His voice was unexpectedly closer and on her left.

She spun sideways to find him but saw nothing.

"This time I'm going to kill you. That way I'll make sure you're dead." He started laughing. "You're afraid, aren't you? I can always smell fear. I have a talent for it."

A chill ran down her spine and she fired angrily at the sound.

Tong's laughter rose and floated through the room. Off to her right a chair crashed into the wall. She twisted toward it, then jumped as another chair struck the opposite wall.

"I have powers," Tong called. "You think I am here, and I am somewhere else. Like this. And this. And this."

His voice came from the left, the right, then behind her. Her heart lurched as though squeezed by a cold, hard fist.

A gun was digging into her throat.

"It will be my pleasure to watch you die," he hissed close to her ear. "Now drop your gun."

She dropped it.

He dragged her to her feet, then shoved her against the wall and pressed the revolver to the back of her head. "Are you afraid now?" He gave her a shake. "Are you?"

Rachel nodded.

"Good." He drove the gun barrel into her scalp, and she swallowed the fear that rushed up sickeningly from her stomach. "Everything has changed because of you, Detective Starr. I can no longer stay in this country. Do you know what that means? Do you know what you've taken from me?" He pushed the gun in harder. "I want to know where it is," he growled.

"Where what is?"

"Don't play games with me. Where is the Red Heart?"

"You have it."

Tong lifted her from the wall and smashed her back into it. "Don't lie to me! I know you have it. I want the diamond! Give it to me or I'll—" Suddenly he stiffened.

"Let her go," Snow said quietly. "Now."

The gun slid off her head and hovered near her ear.

"Drop it!" Snow said and the Asian opened his hand. The weapon hit the floor with a dull thud. As Snow dragged the man away from her, Rachel saw the thin wire he had wrapped around Tong's throat. "This is for Victor," Snow whispered and yanked at the wire.

The Asian's eyes rolled back. There was a stunned, disbelieving expression on his face as his thin fingers clawed furiously at the wire.

Let him die, Rachel thought. Let Snow kill him. She thought of Johnny Haid's last moments, his toppling back into Danny Tai's safe, then falling, falling—it seemed to go on forever—into his own blood. She looked up at Snow and knew he would kill the Asian. All she had to do was let him. She grabbed his arm. "Don't do it. He's not worth it, Snow. Let him go."

"I made a vow."

"I know. But it's over now. We've got him. Let him go."

For a long moment Snow didn't move or speak, then with a nod, he pulled the wire free and flung Tong away like a piece of garbage.

The Asian crumpled to the floor.

Snow turned back to Rachel. "Are you all right?"

"Yeah." She touched her lip, took a breath, and started trembling. Thinking she was going to throw up, she sank back into the wall and slid down it until she was almost sitting. She tried to make her hands stay still, but they kept shaking in her lap.

Outside cops were coming up the stairs and running across the roof.

Great timing, Rachel thought. Just fucking great.

"I gotta go to the bathroom." Cheryl stood. "I gotta go now." She put her purse on her shoulder and picked up the blue bag.

"What's wrong?"

"Female stuff. You know." She made herself look embarrassed. "Be right back."

"You'll be okay?"

"Sure." She ran her thumb down his cheek. "I'll be fine. Wait for me, huh?"

"My whole life I was waiting for you."

As she walked down the aisle, she felt tears in her eyes.

At the entrance to the lavatory, she looked back. Johnny was watching. She gave a small wave and went in.

She hated the mirrors in airplanes. They made you look like you'd died. Gray skin. Bleary eyes. She opened her purse. Might as well fix the lipstick while she had the chance. And the eyeliner. And freshen up the perfume.

When she was done, she checked her watch. About three minutes had passed. That should be about right. The purse went back on her shoulder, then the bag. She opened the door, stuck her head out.

Johnny was still watching.

Damn.

She took a breath and blew it out, making her bangs flutter. She had to do it. And the faster she did it, the faster it would be over. Anyway, she guessed she'd earned the money. All that time she'd spent with him, letting him stay at her place, helping him with the disguise. If it wasn't for her he might not have gotten this far, so really he was paying her three hundred grand for saving his life, which she figured he'd figure was worth it. By this time tomorrow he'd be in Rio, checking out the women, forgetting about her.

She stepped out, stared at him, knowing her face looked different, saw him catch her looking at the exit, saw his expression change, the smile fading into curiosity, then confusion, then bewilderment.

She gave another small wave. He lifted himself a few inches off the seat, like suddenly he knew what was going on and was coming after her. Then he sank back, giving up, his eyes looking soft and wounded.

Cheryl turned and walked out fast.

At the boarding entrance the clerk asked her what was wrong.

"Something came up. I'm taking a later flight." She hurried into the waiting area.

Sean was on the pay phone. Seeing Cheryl, he gave a thumbs-up sign, hung up quickly, and started for her just as a leggy blonde passed. He couldn't help himself from staring and whistling softly.

Cheryl stopped cold. She was such a fool, she thought.

"What's wrong?" Sean said, taking her arm. "You look funny."

"Come here." Catching the front of his shirt, she dragged him to an empty corner, reaching into her coat at the same time. "This is for you."

He looked at the stack of money she'd crammed into his hands, then looked at her, dumbfounded. "What are you doing?"

"I'm going with him."

A few stunned seconds passed while he absorbed what she was telling him, then he said, "You're completely nuts!" and gave her a hard shake.

"That's fifty thousand dollars. You can do a lot with fifty grand."

"This is crazy." He let her go and started stepping tensely back and forth, slapping his thighs with his palms. "You're bullshitting me, right? That's what this is about, right? A big game, right?"

She shook her head. "It's not a game. He loves me, Seanny. He really does."

"Hey, what about me, huh? What about me?" He reached for her shoulders desperately. "We had plans! What about our plans? The places we were going to buy. All the things we were going to do. What about all that?"

"You'll be okay, Seanny. Listen to me." She put her hand on his cheek and made him look at her. "He loves me. I never had that before, you know? Somebody who really loves me. And I love him. I know it sounds corny, but I do, and I don't want to lose that." Across the room the boarding clerk began closing the gate. "I gotta go."

"Don't." He was almost crying now and that made him mad.

"I have to. Tell me you understand. Tell me that." She waited until she couldn't wait any longer. "I gotta go."

When she was almost to the gate he shouted her name.

Cheryl hesitated, then walked back halfway to meet him.

"I could make it hard for you," Sean said. "I could tell that guard over there there's this guy on the plane the police want."

"I hope you don't."

"Why shouldn't I?" he demanded bitterly.

"Because we're friends. Because we had some good times. Because I want to be with him. I hope you understand. Tell me you do." She riffled his hair as though he were a kid. "Tell me, Seanny," she coaxed.

"Jesus, cut it out." He knocked her wrist away.

"Tell me."

"Okay, okay. I understand." He gave her a sullen glare. "You happy now?"

"Yeah." She blew him a kiss. "Be good, baby."

"I'm always good."

"Yeah. You always were."

"You're gonna miss me, Cherry."

She thought about that and said, "Maybe I will."

"Hey!"

She turned. "What?"

"Tell the fucker I said he's a lucky guy." He held up the bag of money. "And tell him thanks."

TWENTY-FIVE

BY THE TIME THEY reached the hotel, the rain was coming down hard again.

"I need a drink," Rachel said.

There was a bar in the hotel with fake palm trees stuck in the corners, lit up with yellow bulbs. They took the last booth in the back, one with a shell-shaped window that looked out on the parking garage of the next hotel.

"What do you want?"

"Scotch and water. Easy on the water."

She watched him walk off, then sank back and closed her eyes. Two hours had passed, but she could still feel Tong's gun digging into her skull.

Snow returned and handed her the drink.

Rachel took it and gazed out the window. A small pool was forming in the driveway, water shooting up from it each time a car drove through. "DeCosta's going for murder one against Tong in the Andrew Solomon killing. He thinks Cooper Kincaid will turn state's evidence. Lin-Cho will be charged as an accessory."

"What happened to the deal the D.E.A. made?"

"All off the second Tong ran. They're also unhappy the diamond he brought along was a fake. That wasn't part of the agreement."

"They have any idea where the real one is?"

"No."

"Tong's not talking?"

"Oh, he's talking. Long and loudly." She spun her glass around a couple of times, then said, "Remember the painting his father carried out of China?"

"Yes."

"He claims he hid the diamond he took from you in its frame. Swears the diamond he gave Chan was the same stone."

"The police believe him?"

"Two officers watched him open the frame. Both saw what they thought was the Red Heart."

"What do they think happened?"

"That he pulled a con. Salted the frame with the fake. Put the real stone somewhere else."

"Sounds possible."

"You think so?" She sipped her drink. "I don't."

"Why not?"

"Because when he had the gun on my head he didn't know where the Red Heart was. It wasn't an act. He was as surprised as the rest of us that it wasn't real. What I think happened is somebody else did the switching."

"Really? Who?"

"You." She was looking straight at him. For a second his face didn't change. Then he grinned. "The question is," she went on, "how did you do it? And when?"

"I don't have the diamond."

"Yeah, you do. I can feel it. I want to know where the stone is, Snow."

"I don't know."

"Where?" When he didn't answer, she sat back angrily. "Okay, play it your way. But keep this in mind. I know who you are. I know what you do. In twenty years I was the only one who caught you. I can do it again. Be careful when you try to unload the diamond. I'll be waiting."

"I'll keep it in mind."
"That's almost a confession."
"Not in a court of law." He waited until the group from the next booth passed their table, then said, "José Martinos has many gemstones, Detective Starr. More than he can possibly use. He doesn't need the Red Heart."
"And you do?"
"Friends of mine need it."
"What friends?"
"Old ones." The way he said it, she knew it was all he was going to say.
"You want another drink?" she said.
"Yes."
Walking to the bar, Rachel tried to understand what she was doing. She could still change her mind. One call to DeCosta and they'd pick up Snow and hold him until L.A. pulled him in. Three big collars in two weeks. She might even get a promotion. Only she knew she wasn't going to call the lieutenant.
"Here." She slid the refilled glass back to him.
"What happens now?" he said.
"I go back to L.A., prove Tong killed Haid, find out what he and Danny Tai and Captain Towers were mixed up in.
"I mean what happens between us?"
Rachel waited a moment, waited until her pulse settled and nothing showed on her face. "What could happen, Snow? We go out on dates? You meet my police friends, I meet your criminal friends? I spend my days catching thieves? You spend your nights being one? We talk about it Sunday mornings? It's two worlds. It won't work."
"It might."
"No."
"What if I told you . . ."
"Told me what?"
"That I . . ."
"What?"
As though he'd almost made a big mistake, Snow shook his head. "Nothing."
"See what I mean?" she said quietly. "We can't even talk."

Feeling tears start, she reached for her bag and coat and the papers DeCosta had given her. "I'm booked out on an early flight. If I don't see you in the morning, thanks now for your help."

"You're welcome."

She got out of the booth, and because he was watching her closely, she made herself face him. "What I said before about being careful? I meant it. Our deal was a one-shot arrangement. Next time I put you in jail."

"I'll be careful." He pushed back the money she was handing him. "This one's on me."

"Okay." She stuffed the bills into a pocket, looked at him a moment longer, then said, "See you around, Snow."

TWENTY-SIX

IT WAS 7:00 P.M. Easter Sunday and the detective division was deserted except for the two unmarried detectives who'd volunteered for duty. At her desk on the other side of the large room, Rachel could hear bits of their conversation punctuated by loud laughter. The sounds were beginning to get on her nerves. She pulled the paper from her aging Royal, stuck it in a folder, and shoved the folder into the filing cabinet, letting the drawer slam shut. Then she stared at the cases piled on the top right corner of her desk. The plan when she came in this morning was to clear the stack. Ten hours later she'd barely made a dent. She rubbed her shoulders, then her neck, and looked at the files again. Enough, she thought, and pulled a sweater from the bottom drawer.

She started for the elevators, but then decided to see if Molly was still around. She took a left, crossed the hall linking the detective division to vice, passed the clerical section, and went down the back stairs.

A single light was on in records. Molly was slouched in her chair, staring at the computer screen.

"Feel like getting something to eat?" Rachel said.

"Can't. Got a date." She hit a few keys, checked the screen, then swung lazily around. "Don't tell me you don't. That makes it—what?—the twentieth weekend in a row? Are you going for some sort of record?"

"I didn't know you were keeping track," Rachel said and idly picked a ball-point pen out of a jar Molly kept on her desk.

"It's Easter," Molly pointed out impatiently. "You can't spend Easter alone. It's sacrilegious. Look, why don't you come with us? Bert's taking me to dinner—pizza probably, the cheap son of a gun—then a movie."

"Thanks, but I think I'll get a hamburger and come back here. I got a desk piled with folders."

"Forget the paperwork. Easter's a holiday, did anybody remember to tell you? We're supposed to relax on holidays. So go home. Get some rest. And you know what? Don't come back for a few days. People are beginning to think you live here."

"Yeah?"

"Rumor is you didn't pay your rent—can't imagine why with the salaries we get—and the landlord kicked you out."

Rachel dropped the pen back in the jar. "Just putting in some extra time, that's all."

"Every day for the last four months?" Molly shook her head. "Go home, Starr."

"Right." She slid off the edge of the desk and started putting on her sweater.

"And go out on a date now and then. The other rumor is you joined a convent."

"Anything else?"

Molly hesitated a moment. "As a matter of fact, yes." From her center drawer she drew out a thick envelope. "This is for you."

Rachel turned it over, found it sealed, and looked puzzled. "What's in it?"

Molly said evenly, "A deep trace on Nicholas Snow," and returned nonchalantly to the keyboard.

"What's it for?"

"For you. Wait a minute," she said quickly as Rachel tossed

the envelope back at her. "I know you didn't ask, but I figured . . ."

"You figured what?"

Molly took a deep breath, then took the plunge. "I figured he's the reason you've been acting the way you've been acting since you got back from Honolulu."

"And what way is that?"

"Moody as hell."

"I'm not interested in a trace on the man," Rachel said.

"I think you are."

"Well, you're wrong. See you in the morning, Stowkowski."

"Hold on."

She stopped and made an exasperated gesture. "What?"

"I called in a lot of favors to get this info. It was pure luck I stumbled on to someone who was willing to talk. At least you owe me a reading."

"Who talked, Molly?"

"I can't say."

"Who?"

"Will you read it?"

"Christ!" She snatched the envelope out of the other woman's hand. "All right. Who's the source?"

Looking satisfied, Molly smiled. "A very nice old guy named Myles McDonnell. A real oddball. Eccentric as hell, but very charming. Seemed to know all about you, by the way. When he found out this was for Detective Rachel Starr, he was more than happy to talk. Seems he was hoping you and the professor might get together. So why don't you read it? You might find it interesting."

"When I have time."

"Make time soon," Molly countered. "McDonnell says they're leaving for Europe."

"If I can. Good night, Stokowski."

When Rachel reached the stairs, Molly called out, "You're going to thank me, you know."

Snow closed the double doors behind him and held his breath until they locked silently. Then he looked over the clipped lawn, the pruned hedges, the phosphorescent swimming pool, all gleaming under a full moon, all silent and serene, exactly the way he preferred.

Out of habit, he patted his inside pocket. The tools were there and, under them, the Cartier bracelet. A delicate strip of flawless diamonds encrusted in platinum, surrounding a Kashmir sapphire of hypnotizing blue. A partial payment, he thought, on the new wing.

He used a row of stately white palms as cover while he made his way to the high stone wall. Checking the grounds one last time and seeing no one, he hoisted himself up and jumped lightly down onto a grassy bank at the end of a cul-de-sac. From there he could see his blue compact waiting under a tree.

Walking at an easy pace—a man out for fresh air, a smoke, and a gaze at the stars—he headed for the car. When he reached it he took a last pull on the cigarette and flung it against the curb. Then he stuck the key in the lock.

"Good evening, Dr. Snow."

His heart skidded and every muscle tightened. His first impulse was to take a chance and run. She was fast, Snow remembered, but he was faster. He could lose her in the maze of rambling estates. Instead he let go of the keys and looked casually over the roof of the car. She was standing in the shadows of the tree, wearing something dark and loose over jeans.

In that instant, Snow decided that seeing her again was easily worth going to jail for.

"Good evening, Detective Starr. Out for some fresh air?"

She started walking slowly toward him. "Among other things. What about you?"

"Taking my evening stroll."

She stopped on the other side of the compact and gave him a measuring look. "You make a habit of strolling in neighborhoods other than your own?"

"Sometimes. Is it a crime?"

"Sometimes. Depends on what you do besides stroll."

"Occasionally I study the stars."

"And occasionally you steal Cartier bracelets."

His smile came gradually and contained a grudging respect. "You have a vivid imagination, Detective."

"Do I? What if I asked you to empty your pockets?"

"What do you expect to find?"

"A signed Cartier sapphire bracelet taken from that estate." She nodded at the mansion from which he'd come. "Why don't you empty your pockets, Dr. Snow?"

He relaxed against the car. "If I remember correctly, a search requires probable cause."

"I have probable cause. You were informed on by a reliable source."

"No one knows . . ." He stopped and smiled again. "You always did bluff well, Detective."

"Does the name Myles McDonnell sound like a bluff? A few days ago, he and I had a nice talk. All about you."

"He didn't mention it."

"No? We spoke in his studio. That rather large building on your estate?"

"I know the place," Snow said.

"Nice estate, by the way."

"Thank you. Did he give you the full tour?"

"Of course. He said you wouldn't mind. You have a lovely collection of paintings. All quite authentic-looking."

"Myles has a knack for forgeries."

"He mentioned the knack isn't limited to paintings. He copies sculptures, too, I understand. And gemstones." She waited for some change in his expression, but he kept smiling pleasantly. "He showed me some of his work," she went on. "Quite amazing."

"I'll let him know you liked it."

"He also told me some rather interesting things about you."

"Did he? I should probably tell you that McDonnell is a con man and a liar. You can't believe a word he says."

"Too bad, because everything he said was nice."

"Really? Like what?"

"Well, for one thing, he claims you're a kind of modern-day Robin Hood. That you steal from wealthy criminals and use the money to build hospitals for the poor in Southeast Asia. That you do this because your father and his banking partners made a lot of money selling illegal arms in the area. You have a need, McDonnell says, to right your father's wrongs."

Snow gave a disbelieving laugh. "Myles is also mildly touched. Has a tendency toward delusions."

"I thought he might, so I did some checking on my own. What I learned was quite interesting. It seems every painting you stole, every piece of jewelry you took that I know about, was taken from a known or suspected criminal. For example, the man who owns the bracelet in your pocket runs a bank that's under investigation for laundering drug money."

"He does more than clean money," Snow said. "He arranges the drug deals."

She looked at him levelly. "If you know that, then maybe the D.A. needs to talk to you."

"I'm not interested in talking to the D.A."

"Maybe you should talk to him anyway."

"Are you arresting me?"

"I haven't decided." She walked around the car, then leaned against it a yard away from him and stared at the winding drive beyond the intricate wrought-iron fence. "I'm going to ask you a question, Snow, and I want the truth. The Red Heart. How'd you switch it?" She glanced sideways. "It's been bugging the hell out of me for months."

He took out his cigarettes, lit one, and flicked the match away. The smoke curled toward the streetlamp. "You really want to know?"

"Yeah, I really do."

"All right. You let me go in Honolulu, the least I can do is tell you. Actually it was quite simple. Myles made the fake and sent it to me along with the special tools I asked for."

"How did he make the fake? He'd never seen the Red Heart, had he?"

"He worked from a photograph and from a gemological report on the stone obtained for him by a friend. He knew all the dimensions, so it wasn't too difficult to make the duplicate."

"When did you switch the diamonds? In the museum?"

Snow shook his head. "I didn't have time. I was keeping it in my shoe, in a hollow heel. I figured I could make the exchange before I saw Tong in the morning, only he showed up early and I had to give him the real stone. But that was all right," he added. "I knew where he'd put the Heart."

"How?"

"It was something he'd do, a gesture he'd make, putting it in the same frame that had held his father's gems."

"How'd you get it?"

"I went into his place the morning the police had him under arrest."

She looked over sharply. "Where was I?"

"Asleep."

She looked away, remembering. "You're a bastard, Snow."

"I needed the Martinos diamond. Things had happened. We needed funds."

"What had happened?"

He dropped the cigarette, crushed it, and kicked it away. "A hospital was blown up in Cambodia near the Vietnamese border. We had to rebuild it. The Red Heart would give us the cash we needed."

"So McDonnell was telling the truth."

"Since Victor died, McDonnell runs the show."

"I see."

They both stared straight ahead into the silence of the hills and night. Finally Snow said, "It wasn't the only reason I made love with you, Rachel. The first time you walked into my lecture, I thought about it."

She pushed off the car and faced him. "When Myles told me about you, I guess in my gut I knew it was true. But the question is: Does what you do with the money make the stealing all right? I don't know the answer. And I don't know why I'm doing this, Snow—maybe I'm crazy—but I'm going to let you go. And by my calculations, that means you now owe me. One day I'll collect."

"Anytime." He squinted into the cold wind.

"Then I guess that's it. See you around, Snow."

"Need a ride?"

"What?" she asked, turning back to him.

"I don't see your car."

"I took a cab."

"I could give you a lift. It's tough getting a cab in L.A. Especially at night."

"I'm all the way down in Venice."

"I know where you live." He opened the door and waited.

"How do you know that? I'm not listed."

"Connections." He waited until she got in, then he walked around the front of the car and slid behind the wheel.

"Why?" Rachel said.

He started the engine. "Why what?"

"Why do you know where I live?"

"So I'd know where to pick you up." He pulled into the street and started up the hill.

"Pick me up when?"

"When I got around to asking you out."

"I see. And what the hell made you think I'd say yes?"

"Would you have?"

"I don't know." She studied the wide, shadowy lawns flowing by. "Maybe. If I didn't have anything else to do."

"Do you have anything else to do tomorrow night?"

She looked over at him. "You asking me out, Snow?"

"I am."

She let a few more lawns roll past. "I guess we could try it. See how it goes."

"I'll pick you up at eight."

"Make it seven. I'm pulling second watch. I get up early."

"I'll come by at seven."

The car pulled under a stone archway, and off to her right Rachel could see the lights of the city spreading endlessly outward. "You know," she pointed out, "this dating business between you and me will probably go nowhere."

"Probably not."

"I mean, where could it go?"

He shifted into second as they started down a steep hill. "I was thinking of Europe. There's a small town in the south of

France I think you'd like. Great restaurants. Pleasant scenery. A charming museum."

"Really? And what's in this charming museum?"

"The usual. Paintings. Sculptures. Furniture." He waited a second before adding, "And one perfect Grecian urn. We'll spend a day looking at everything."

"That's all you have in mind, Snow? Just looking?" He kept his eyes on the road, but she could see him start to smile.

He said, "Of course, Detective Starr. What else?"